WITCHES & WOLVES

Book 13 of
THE WARDEN

FELICIA JEDLICKA

To those who can't forgive,
because they can't forgive themselves.

SISTER WITCHES
THE DEVIL'S SHADOW
THE DEVIL'S SOUL

DESTINY REJECTED
DESTINY RECLAIMED
DESTINY RAZED
DESTINY RESTORED

DÉJÀ VU

SAVE THE HUMANS

THE NECROMANCER'S CHILD

THE NEBRASKA APOCALYPSE NOVELS
CORN COWS AND THE APOCALYPSE
COW TIPPING AFTER THE APOCALYPSE
CORN HUSKING AFTER THE APOCALYPSE

THE WARDEN SERIES
SUCCESSORS
RIVALS
LOVERS AND LIARS
BAD BLOOD
TENANTS AND TYRANTS
THE RING BEARER
GODS AND MONSTERS
BEASTS AND BURDENS
MAGIC AND MAYHEM
FORK IN THE ROAD
DETAILS AND DEADLINES
*CURSES AND SACRIFICES**
*WITCHES AND WOLVES**
*SAINTS AND SERPENTS**
*ENEMIES AND ALLIES**

MARRIED TO DEATH*

WITCHES & WOLVES

FELICIA JEDLICKA

1

HEATON NEARLY PULLED HIS gun when he saw the mess of paperwork in Sophie's office. The clutter looked as if someone had ransacked the place. Fortunately, she was the only one doing the rummaging. She popped up from behind the desk, hair disheveled and yesterday's makeup on overtime. She gasped when she saw Callin, but relaxed when she noticed Heaton standing next to him.

"Heaton," she breathed his name like a sigh. "I've been trying to call you."

"I've been off the grid since I got to the prison."

"Do you..." Sophie looked at Callin again. "Who's this?"

"Callin Caldwell." Callin extended his hand to her.

"He's a werewolf," Heaton added, in case she suspected Heaton had just brought just any man off the street to see her.

"Oh, right." She gazed at him a long moment before turning back to Heaton. "I..." She lifted a piece of paper in her right hand, her eyes tearing slightly as she spoke. "I wanted to find the beginning."

"The beginning of what?" Heaton asked.

"When the money started disappearing."

Heaton reached out for the paper. She handed it to him reluctantly—like she was afraid to let go of it now that she had found it. He pulled it from her grasp and examined the bank statement. The numbers meant virtually nothing to him, but something in Sophie's accounting experience had made this mixture of numbers a smoking gun. He looked at her, hoping for some explanation.

"It started after Nevia was recruited. I told you they stopped hiring after her. I didn't realize it was nearly to the minute that they started reducing the allowance." Sophie pressed her hands to a stack of papers on her desk. "These are the quarterly reports for the entire *company*." Sophie air-quoted company. "The money isn't drying up. It's being diverted."

Heaton grabbed a statement from the top of the pile and looked over yet another list of numbers. Since the prison and the collaboration that ran it was nameless, each department was just as vague in its description. It was clear enough that containment number three was the facility losing the most money. Shortly after was the EU aggregation team. Though all the locations in the U.S. were significantly better financed, one particular operation seemed to take the lion's share of the money. "Research and development?" Heaton verified. "I thought the military was done playing God."

"Not the military. They paid us for our facilities and the use of our... subjects. This operation is internal... and it appeared overnight." Sophie leaned her hands on the desk. "I've done the math. Every dime that was subtracted from our facilities and teams was put into that project. Assuming it is a project." She slumped down into her massive chair. "I didn't even get paid last week."

"Sophie," Heaton said softly.

"How do they expect me to—"

"Daniel's dead."

Sophie froze, eyes stricken with disbelief. He expected a litany of questions, but as her shock turned somber, she stood back up and hugged him. He wrapped an arm around her, consoling her as best he could while shutting down his own emotions on the topic.

"How?" she asked, leaning back to look at him.

"Transmorphs," he answered. She shook her head as if it were inconceivable. Surely the most dangerous man in existence couldn't be brought down by parasites. "The woman we brought back to the prison. She was apparently a hybrid—part transmorph, part human."

Sophie pushed away from him. Anger flared in her eyes. "No. No," she whispered. "No fucking way!" Heaton stiffened, prepared to defend himself. "As if there aren't enough monsters in this world, they are building new ones!"

"There's more. Given what you've told me, I strongly suspect they've infiltrated the board. That transmorph hybrid was handed to us on a platter. She was an assassin. She was sent to kill Daniel."

Sophie took a moment to absorb that information—as if matching the numbers to his words. When at long last she had reconciled the facts, she picked up one of her paper piles and threw it into the air. Then she cleared her entire desk with one swipe, scattering paper, pens, and her personal decor everywhere. She stared at the wood top of her mammoth desk. The self-declared symbol of her importance was completely empty.

"Shit," she muttered as her hand flew to her mouth. "Shit, shit, shit."

Sophie dropped to the floor and dug through the papers she had just tossed away. Heaton glanced at Callin, but the werewolf was not nearly as uncomfortable as he expected. In fact, he seemed to be concerned for the poor woman. As if he couldn't stand it anymore, he kneeled down and began searching the floor with her.

"Did I miss something?" Heaton asked them.

"A pink paper," Sophie answered. "Find it."

Heaton saw a sea of white, yellow, and light blue, but there was only one pink paper. It was lying on Sophie's chair, having made a very short trip up and then right back down. He picked it up and waved it at her. "Is this it?"

She looked up and practically leaped at him to get it. She pulled it from his hand and looked it over. She sat back down at her desk and pulled a laptop out of her drawer. She went through a series of dummy websites before she reached the final screen that looked like a DOS interface.

"I don't even look them up anymore. What's the point? The less I know, the better." She poised her finger on the long number code on the top of the paper and carefully typed it onto the screen with one hand. "I just sign the paper and authorize the payment."

Heaton shifted to look at the screen as Sophie slammed her finger into the enter key. After a moment, a new, slightly more sophisticated page opened, revealing an image of Sophie. The photo was nearly a decade old, but the written description was accurate, give or take a few pounds and a dye job.

Sophie let out a barking laugh before settling into a rather mirthful giggle. She looked up at him, her eyes tracing his face before locking eyes with him. "I just signed and delivered payment on my own execution."

Heaton frowned. "What?" He looked at the pink paper, but despite his ample knowledge of double-talk and hidden language, he couldn't understand what it said. As near as he could tell, it was just an offer of payment in exchange for services rendered. He checked the submission date. "You sent this yesterday?" he asked.

"Yes," Sophie said somberly.

Heaton looked at Callin. "They'll send a cleaner."

"Which kind?" Callin asked, already dreading the idea of what was to come.

"I'm only human. They'll send a hunter to do it," Sophie answered.

"What?" Heaton shook his head. "What kind of hunter is sent to execute a human?"

"One with far less morality than you."

Heaton stepped back. "Wait. You know who they're sending, don't you? How many of these pink slips have been coming in?"

Sophie's jaw twisted as she stood. "The EU's high turnover is not just because of on-the-job accidents." Heaton glared at her. "Not everyone can keep secrets, Heaton. Not everyone really reads the nondisclosure agreements either."

"That's your excuse for murder?"

"Please don't lecture me on murder, soldier."

Heaton nearly slapped her right then and there, but Callin shifted forward to defend her. "I was doing the duty of my country."

"I thought I was representing a greater good too, Heaton. But the truth is, I don't know anymore. I don't know why any of us are doing this anymore. I lost track of who or what I was supposed to be protecting a long time ago." She swallowed hard and glanced between him and Callin. "You're going after them, aren't you? The transmorphs?"

"Nevia's gone AWOL. She's going after them. My priority is finding her, but if I kill a few of those bastards on the way, that's fine by me."

"I can help you." Sophie pulled open another drawer and dug through a mess of Post-it notes and paperclips to find a little black book. She handed it to Heaton. "I can't guarantee all the addresses are up to date, but that should at least get you started."

Heaton flipped through the book of names that he assumed belonged to key characters running the board. He noticed a familiar name in the M section and flipped back to it. "Come on. We'll get you out of here." Heaton slipped the book into his back pocket. "Do you have somewhere you can lie low for a few—"

"Years?" Sophie said sarcastically. "You know what pisses me off the most?" She pulled her oversized purse out from under the desk and looped it over her shoulder. "If they had consulted with me, I could have found a dozen ways to funnel money to this project without shutting down the entire operation."

As Sophie headed out, Heaton frowned at Callin. He wasn't sure if this was something Sophie should be proud of, but he had to wonder if she wasn't a little more resourceful than her position was allowing for.

"I mean, not that I condone transmorphs," Sophie continued as they walked down the hall to the elevator. "It's just that their reputation for being clever is extremely exaggerated." Despite the "out of order" sign, Sophie pushed the button for the lift and the doors opened. Heaton questioned the contraption, but Sophie waved them both in. "I think sometimes that's all it takes, you know?" She looked at Heaton, but he had lost track of her thinking process. "I just mean that we twist ourselves into a frenzy because of emotion or anger, but they don't have that issue." Sophie looked at Callin. "Is any of this making sense?"

"You think the transmorphs have gained a superiority over humans because they are indifferent creatures?" Callin summed up.

"Right, but more than that. Our weakness is what lures them in, which then becomes our strength." Sophie looked back at him, but as far as he was concerned, she was speaking gibberish. "I know it's too philosophical and hardly a battle strategy, but I just think it's something you should take into consideration." Sophie reached out and touched Heaton's chest. "I guess I'm just telling you to be careful."

"I will." Heaton patted her hand, acknowledging her display of concern.

The elevator dinged, and the doors opened. Sophie pulled her hand from beneath his and turned to exit the carriage. She stopped abruptly just outside the doors. Callin lunged forward to grab her just as shots fired.

Blood sprayed across Heaton's neck as he ducked back into the interior corner. Callin pulled Sophie down and shielded her body with his. She was bleeding from at least two places, but Heaton couldn't tell how urgent the wounds were.

"How many are out there?"

"Three!" Sophie shouted over further gunfire. "I think I'm flattered!"

Heaton tried to close the doors, but the moment they started to close, they opened back up again. Rather than play tug of war with the men outside, he shot blindly, hoping to scare them away from the call buttons.

A warbling whistle sounded from the front foyer. "Come on, Sophie. You know you're not getting out of here alive."

Heaton peeked out to confirm the voice that he was hearing. "Kendrick? Is that you?"

"Who's there? Heaton?"

"Yeah."

Kendrick laughed. "Well, I wasn't expecting to see you here. Do me a favor. Put another round in her, so we can go get sloshed."

"You know that's not gonna happen?" Heaton dared to peek out at his long-ago friend. His skin was deep black, his voice a soothing bass, and his eyes like diamonds. Though not technically supernatural, he claimed to have an ocean ancestor. A story that became a bigger fish tale every time Heaton had heard it repeated. Though he considered the man a friend, he also considered him to be full of shit. Never more so than in this moment. "Have you thought about what it means if you kill Sophie?"

"I'm not paid to think."

Heaton resisted the urge to tell him he wouldn't be any good at it, anyway. "There's more going on here than you realize."

"There always is."

"Just let me explain, and if you aren't convinced, then we can go back to the dueling dicks." Heaton shifted his hand to show he was directing his gun at the ground for the time being.

Kendrick seemed to consider this. "I'll make you a deal. I'll kill Sophie. Then you can negotiate for your life with whatever bullshit you think I would care about."

"Kendrick!" Sophie shouted from within Callin's supportive embrace. "How about you negotiate with this!" From somewhere deep inside her purse, Sophie pulled out an oblong green object and tossed it out into the foyer.

"Grenade!" someone yelled, and the men scattered. Sofia reached over and pushed the button for the basement level. The doors closed as everyone huddled down, waiting for the explosion.

The seconds ticked by and they arrived at the garage level. "Go, go, go!" Sophie shouted.

Callin assisted her out, and Heaton followed, watching the stairwell.

"Over there." Sophie pointed her key fob at a silver four-door BMW, which flashed and honked at them. Callin climbed into the backseat with Sophie, while Heaton took the liberty of the driver's seat.

"Must have been a dud," Heaton said as he pushed the start button and brought the beautiful machinery to life.

"It was a pencil sharpener," Sophie ground out as she shifted into a position that didn't make her wince.

Heaton laughed as he shifted the car into drive. "Leave it to Sophie Plum to save the day with office supplies." He glanced back at her in the rearview mirror and saw that she was smiling.

He stepped on the gas just as the three hunters poured out of the stairwell. Heaton offered no mercy as he came barreling at them at full speed. He swerved and side-swiped two of them before speeding toward the exit. Gunshots pelted the back of the car, making Heaton cringe.

What bastards could do that to such a sexy automobile?

Heaton barely looked as the car emerged from the parking garage into the sunlight. Several cars honked at his audacity to drive like a maniac, but he ignored them. He quickly calculated the closest hospitals and the likelihood of the hunters catching up with them before they could help Sophie. He decided that his best bet was the VA hospital. He knew more than a few doctors he could trust to keep her injuries under the radar.

"Heaton," Callin called from the back.

"Just a little further. I can't trust the private hospitals."

"Heaton," Callin said again.

"I'll have to dump the car after I drop you off."

Callin's hand slipped over the seat and clutched his shoulder. Heaton looked up in the rearview mirror and saw Callin's uneasy expression. "You can slow down now." Callin leaned back, and Sophie came into view. She was in a slumped position in the backseat. The blood from her shoulder and stomach had completely saturated her blouse and the seat beneath her. He could no longer see her face, but he recognized the pale color of her forehead and assumed that her eyes would be hollow.

Heaton had been in the presence of dead bodies nearly all of his life. And though the experiences had diminished his faith in God, they had ironically strengthened his belief in the human spirit. A man only needs to look into the eyes of the dead to see what's missing—what has gone—what was once given and now taken.

However, despite his ardent and further deepening belief in the human soul, it did not make the exchange of life for death any less painful. Heaton was once again back on the battlefield, with fallen comrades all around him. A debt of vengeance passed on through every empty face.

Enraged by his growing antipathy, Heaton gripped the steering wheel tight, making the leather creak. He pushed every bit of his pain into an elongated curse he hoped the heavens could hear.

When he was done, he slowed the car and changed direction. Callin waited a moment before asking. "Where are we going?"

"We'll need to get out of the country fast—before my credentials stop working. You and I are going to be targets now."

"I assumed we already were."

"There is still a chance you can get out of this."

"And you think I would take you up on that?"

"No, but I don't have the best track record with partners right now."

"If this is as bad as you believe it to be, we are going to need help."

"Yeah, and I know just where to go to find it." Heaton peered at Callin through the mirror. "How do werewolves feel about swamps?"

2

E FRAT SLIPPED OUT OF the truck and squeezed his hands tight, cracking his knuckles. His fists let off a few static snaps, but they were otherwise under control. Something had changed since Cleos had touched him. It wasn't clear at first, just a new level of clarity in his mind.

Earlier, he had blamed it on the stress of his recent battle with Danato. His instincts had set in hard when he was standing by Ethan's side, protecting his child. He was wielding his power as easily as he ever had. It wasn't until later that he realized his resting energy had diminished significantly.

Efrat still didn't fully understand what Cleos had done to him, but whatever it was, it was working. He had made it to Ireland without electrocuting Ethan or short-circuiting the plane and killing them both. That was progress, as far as he was concerned.

He looked over the small farm that was apparently Daniel McGrath's childhood home. It didn't seem to match the man he knew, and yet he wasn't sure that any other environment would have matched his personality better.

Efrat was certain the trailer park he had grown up in didn't match his character. Then again, a military base didn't seem to fit either. The truth was, he didn't know where he belonged anymore. He had fought long and hard to get his title, and now it meant nothing to him. He was at best a guard and at worst a prisoner.

The acreage was lush green despite winter threatening to drop snow at any moment. Efrat missed green. The summers at the prison brought color, but it was always dark greens and gray greens. Not the bright emerald colors Ireland boasted.

He hoped Ethan would want to stay in the country for another day or two before going back, but he wasn't sure what he had planned. In truth, they had barely spoken since they had left the prison. Not that Efrat could blame him. He wasn't a father, but he assumed losing a child had to be a singular heartache incomparable to other losses. Especially when that loss came at the hands of his wife.

Efrat still couldn't believe Cori had done it. That she had killed her own child.

And yet... what else could she do?

They had weighed the pros and cons over and over, but both sides were full of negatives. A shit bucket balanced by another shit bucket. The only difference was who would suffer for the choice.

In the end, Efrat knew Danato would choose to save the world. That was his job.

And Ethan had to save his son. That was *his* job.

Cori had followed Danato's lead and made the hard choice. The choice that is almost never made. The choice that everyone says they will make when the time comes, but won't because saving millions has no meaning when the one you know and love is at gunpoint.

As much as he hated to watch Ethan sinking deeper into his grief, he was thankful that they didn't have a living god to deal with. Everyone was secretly glad Cori did what she did.

Everyone except Ethan.

Efrat looked back at the truck and realized Ethan was lifting the long wooden box off the bed by himself. He knew the man could handle it just fine, but he still rushed over and took one end of the crate. Ethan glanced at his grip, no doubt making sure Efrat didn't light the coffin on fire.

They shuffled down the drive to the cottage-style house in the center of the property. They stopped at the front door and set the box down on the grass. Ethan stepped up to the front door and rang the bell. Less than a minute later, the door opened up and a hefty elderly woman peeked out. "I'm not interested." Her snippy tone rang with an Irish accent. She slammed the door even as Ethan began to explain. The woman hadn't noticed the box behind them.

"Mrs. McGrath," Ethan called to her through the door. "My name is Ethan Pierce. I used to work with your son, Daniel."

The door opened back up, and she peered out at him suspiciously. "So?"

Ethan's eyes flickered over her hardened features, and his mouth draped open soundlessly.

"Speak your piece, lad. I haven't got all day."

"There was an incident, ma'am," Efrat spoke up, "at the prison."

Mrs. McGrath turned her attention to Efrat, analyzing him with an unwavering frown. "What sort of incident?" Her eyes caught on the wooden box behind them, and her features softened.

"I'm sorry to inform you that your son has been killed." Efrat could hear the formal tone in his voice. The soldier inside him was reporting the necessary information.

Mrs. McGrath locked eyes with him. Her frown was now a scowl. He braced himself for the tears and yelling that would inevitably follow. He even expected that she might attack him, so he adjusted his hands so he wouldn't accidentally shock her.

"Is he in there?" she asked, pointing to the crate.

"Yes," Ethan said.

"All of him?" she asked.

Efrat exchanged a glance with Ethan. Neither of them seemed to glean her meaning.

"How did he die?" she asked, irritated by their stalled response. "Did he hurt himself?"

Efrat frowned at the thought of Daniel using his power on himself. He had honestly never considered it, but he was not immune to it. Just as Efrat was not immune to his own electricity. Although if he were a natural elemental, he would have been.

"He was stabbed to death," Ethan answered solemnly.

"Stabbed?" Mrs. McGrath scoffed.

"It was multiple stab wounds. I'm afraid he couldn't heal fast enough. He…" Ethan cleared his throat. "He bled out before we could get to him. I'm so sorry."

"Who stabbed my boy?" There was finally a waiver in her voice. She kept her eyes on the coffin, as if she hoped Daniel would pop out of it like a vampire come to life. They had all been hoping for that, but the body had stayed cold and lifeless. "Who murdered my son?"

"The—" Ethan tried to answer, but something about the question forced his throat to go hoarse. He had to clench his jaw and look away to control his reaction.

"It was transmorphs," Efrat answered.

Mrs. McGrath's gaze snapped to Efrat. "Those leeches!" Her face contorted with disgust and anger.

"I assure you, ma'am, they're dead." Efrat sounded a little more sinister than sympathetic now. "All of them."

Mrs. McGrath must have recognized his mutual loathing, because she nodded curtly with approval. "Good." She turned her attention to the coffin. "Leave him in the barn. I'll take care of it when I'm done with the dishes."

Ethan shook his head. "We can help with that. Just show us where you would like to lay him to rest."

"I don't need your help."

"I understand you want to grieve privately, but you shouldn't have to trouble yourself."

"Do you think I'm not capable of digging my own son's grave?" Mrs. McGrath stared blankly at him. "What are you even doing here? Where is Nevia? She should be... Oh, no, did she pass as well?"

"No, ma'am, she's... alive. I mean, I assume. She ran off after the incident. No one knows where she is? She took Daniel's death pretty hard."

"Well, that's at least a blessing." She stared out at her property. When she looked back, there were tears in her eyes. "I appreciate you bringing him back to me, Ethan. And I respect a man who wants to do right by his friend, but you see, I brought Daniel into this world, enduring the pain that all mothers do. And I'll be the one to give him back to God. Put the coffin in the barn. I'll bury him when the dishes are done."

Ethan nodded. "Yes, ma'am."

Mrs. McGrath went back into the house and shut the door behind her. Efrat turned to Ethan. "Well, she's... interesting."

"Everyone grieves differently," Ethan mumbled and moved to the crate. Efrat took the other end, and they carried it to the barn and laid it down on the hay-strewn floor. When they stood, Ethan stared down at the box.

"Do you want to take a minute?" Efrat asked.

Ethan looked up at him, eyes glistening with fresh tears. "Why do I feel like I'm abandoning him?"

Efrat shook his head. "You're not. You did right by him. You brought him home. You're giving him a proper burial."

Ethan nodded, but Efrat's words did nothing to ease his tears. "This shouldn't have happened. None of it should have happened."

Efrat nodded, understanding his true meaning. Daniel, Duke, and his boy...

It was too much.

Ethan's face hardened, and his eyes glazed over as if he had placed a mask back over his grief.

"Come on." Efrat raised his hand to rest on his shoulder, but thought better of it and let the camaraderie fall short. "Let's go find a pub to drink ourselves stupid in."

Ethan shook his head, but started heading out of the barn. "No, we have a plane to catch."

Efrat gritted his teeth and followed Ethan out. "Oh, come on. Have a heart. This is my first time out in the real world in frickin' forever. Just one drink before we go back to the prison."

"We aren't going back to the prison," Ethan said.

"What's that?" Efrat jogged up to his side.

"I have some other business to attend to before we can go back."

"Other business?"

Ethan stopped at the passenger side door of the truck and opened it for Efrat. He climbed in, and Ethan assisted him with his seat belt as well. Efrat despised being treated like an invalid, but he had made many concessions since becoming a human lightning rod—most of which were far more demeaning than vehicle safety devices. The fact that Ethan had voluntarily taken on those other duties for the sake of having company for this trip was a testament to the man's tolerance. In fact, Ethan was handling all of his personal duties with the discipline of a well-paid healthcare worker.

"Where are we going?" Efrat asked once Ethan had slipped into the driver's seat and started the truck.

Ethan held his grip on the gearshift, staring out the window at the barn. "How do you feel about Mardi Gras?"

3

"HAS SHE COME OUT yet?" Danato asked Chuck on the other end of the line. He was in his home office speaking on the red phone. The last few days had been a nightmare for him. He had never wanted to lose his grandchild, and he most definitely didn't want Cori to take the boy's life with her own hands. The travesty of it all was that he had done this to her. He had trained her to be a hardhearted killer.

It was all to protect the prison and save the world. That's what he told himself when Belus pulled the trigger. That's what he told himself when he shot Adrianna. He was certain that was what Cori had been thinking when she took her son's life.

The arguments for and against his death still swirled in his mind. He wanted the justification to make sense. He wanted the logic of preventing the immortalization of a cosmic power to stamp out his grief, but it wasn't working.

Try as he might to understand, he couldn't help being angry with her. Not perhaps for the act, but for taking on the role of the villain. That mantel was never meant to be hers. She was supposed to be the voice of reason in this chaotic place. She was supposed to be a beauty among beasts. Now she would descend into the murky depths of the moral gray area. A place where Danato lived every day of his life, balancing lives against the so-called greater good.

As if his anger toward Cori wasn't already eating him up, he also had Ethan on his mind. It was no surprise that his successor had fought to save his son. As a father, it was his right and his duty. But what Danato couldn't accept was his abandonment. What did he think Danato was preparing him for all these years? What lessons had he learned if not that this world did not offer leniency or second chances? How many times did he warn him—warn them—that this place was dangerous? Was Cori the only one listening?

"She came out for supplies a few hours ago," Chuck reported. "Mostly just food, I think."

"Well, at least she's feeding herself. That's something." Danato paused. "How did she look?"

Chuck hemmed and hawed on the line before answering. "She... She looked a little ragged, to be honest. Not hurt or anything, just tired, you know?"

"Yeah, I know." Danato rubbed his forehead. The feeling was mutual. "Has she spoken to you?"

"A bit," Chuck sounded nervous.

"What did she say to you?"

"Oh, you know, just... like when to pull her out and stuff."

"That's it?" Chuck dithered. "Tell me the truth, Chuck. I need to know."

"She kind of threatened to beat my ass if I pulled her out a minute before she had designated."

Danato groaned. "I'm sorry, Chuck. You know she doesn't mean it."

"I think she kind of did."

"What's the clock running right now?"

"It's still a bit wobbly, but it's averaging about two days per hour now."

Danato cringed. "Christ, that means she's been in there for nearly five months."

"Closer to six."

Danato clenched his fist and tapped it against his desk. He tried to remember how long it took him to get over Olivia's death. Considering that he hadn't fully recovered until Ethan and Cori came into his life, that wasn't the best example. However, he remembered burying himself in his work for at least six months before he came up for air and started taking part in his usual activities. "Okay," he breathed. "You just keep an eye on her for me. When you see her, tell her..." Danato sighed. "Tell her that I..."

"I'll tell her, sir," Chuck offered without the sentence being completed.

"Thanks, Chuck." Danato hung up the phone and headed over to the laundry room to put a load in to wash. Much like a college student, Cori was still stopping by to drop off her dirty clothes and pick up new, but she always came and went when Danato wasn't around. He knew she was avoiding him. He could only imagine how much she regretted her decision to kill her son. She probably hated him just as much for pushing her into that decision.

His first concern was that Cori might try to hurt herself. He couldn't remember how many times thoughts of suicide had crossed his mind after Olivia died. Grief was one thing, but combined with guilt, it was too much.

Danato reached into the basket to pull out the clothes he needed to wash. His hand hit something sharp, and he drew back with a hiss. He looked down at the puncture wound in his palm that stung like an acid burn. As he examined the wound, he saw the surrounding tissue blanch, and the discoloration spread across his skin like a frosty snowflake. Before it could reach his fingers, it relented. The white tissue slowly returned to normal, and a single drop of blood emerged. Danato wiped it away, but there was no injury beneath it.

He stared at the clothing in the basket, searching for the cause of his temporary pain. His heart pounded with dread as he reached in for the pants that he suspected were concealing the weapon. He carefully pulled them out and searched the pockets. From a leg pocket holster, he drew out a six-inch rod that to the untrained eye might have looked like an ill-designed ice pick or awl, but he already knew what it was before his eyes landed on the medallion at its head. Danato dropped the pants and backed out of the laundry room. He gripped the rod in his hand, feeling the glacial metal pressing into his skin. It was enough to burn him, but he didn't care. He had already been burned; he just hadn't realized it until that moment. His legs moved even before his mind reached a conclusive decision about his potential retaliation for this betrayal.

He left the house without a coat or any concern about his current state of dress. He wasn't sure what Belus thought when he stormed into the prison office five minutes later in his bathrobe, but the cross look on his face surely would have left no room for humor.

Belus looked up from his paperwork, saw his face, and frowned. "What now?"

Danato stepped forward and dropped the awl on the desk. Belus looked down at the object. "Did you know about this?"

Belus looked up at him. "What?" he asked, legitimately confused.

"Did you give her that?" Danato was yelling now. He couldn't explain his anger. His trust in Belus had always been implicit. For him to go behind his back in this way was unfathomable. And yet, how else would Cori have known about this device? They kept the details of the prop room objects very guarded.

"What are you talking about?" Belus picked up the tool and examined it as if he didn't recognize it. Perhaps he didn't, since Danato had been the one to stab it into his chest. "I didn't give Cori this."

"Did you tell her about it?" Danato asked. "Were you part of it?"

"Part of what, Danato?"

Danato ripped the pick from his hand and held up the gold medallion topper for him to see the Papa Legba design. "How did Cori know about the voodoo pin?"

Belus leaned back in the chair, realization hitting him like a slap in the face. He was already contemplating the many ways this discovery could be problematic. However, at the end of his internal contemplation, a small smile perched on his lips. "She must have seen it in my file."

"You showed her your file."

"Danato, Cori is a clever girl. Whether I showed her or she found it, there is nothing I can do to prevent her from using the knowledge available to her."

"Do you realize what this means?" Danato asked.

Belus lost his smile. For once, the stoic man looked fearful. He shook his head slowly. "Maybe it doesn't mean what you think it means."

"And in what world would that ever be true when Cori is involved?" Danato turned and left the office.

"Danato!" Belus shouted down the hall after him, but he didn't wait to listen to his reason. He was so sick of the lies. The danger Cori had put them in was unforgivable. He had never expected her to surrender her son without a fight, and apparently she hadn't. The question in his mind was how far she would go to protect a living god.

Danato caught sight of Belus approaching the elevator just as the doors closed. His second did not look happy with him. Perhaps Belus hadn't known about the plan after all, but if he didn't have Danato's back now, then he just needed to stay out of it.

When the doors opened on the den's level, he found Belus standing outside the elevator. He looked at him and the other elevator. "How did you..."

"Apparently, she's siding with me on this one."

"And which side is that?"

Belus didn't answer for a moment. He swallowed hard and shook his head. "I'm going in with you."

"Fine." Danato pushed past him and shoved open the heavy metal door leading onto the bubble's home floor. Chuck jumped and looked back at him. He pulled his hands from the shimmering orb.

"Oh, hey, I was just about to pull her out." Chuck checked his watch that was synced with Cori's on the other side. A complicated piece of tech that Chuck's programming skills had helped invent.

"Don't bother. We are going in."

"Oh." Chuck looked around as if he had forgotten something. "You know, she's pretty particular about her timeline. Maybe I should just pull her out and you—"

Danato clamped his hand over Chuck's mouth. "I appreciate your loyalty to Cori, especially now that Ethan is gone. I'm glad she can rely on you for help. But I think you know that there is more going on inside this bubble than she's telling any of us. What I don't appreciate is your helping her keep those secrets?"

Danato released Chuck's face, and the man straightened up tall. "With all due respect, Warden, I think you misunderstand the meaning of loyalty then."

Danato let the man walk away without correcting him. He really was just trying to help. He just didn't fully understand what he was helping with. His anger needed to be directed at Cori and her duplicitous nature. Danato and Belus stood side by side at the entry point that had been mapped out on the sphere since his visits many years ago. There was no need to hold hands since they would arrive at ground level.

He stepped inside, feeling the instantaneous pull on his body. Though very little of him was really moving, it still felt like a roller coaster drop. When he felt everything steady again, he opened his eyes.

Blank white walls and floor stared back at him. He looked to his right and saw Belus looking around with the same confusion on his face. They were back in the prison. No bubble. No Chuck. No monitoring station. Just a vast empty room and the doors behind them. "What is this? Please don't tell me the bubble grew again."

"If it had Chuck would still be here," Belus surmised.

They wandered out the door to the elevators. One of the carriages arrived promptly, announcing its arrival with a melodious high-pitched *ping* instead of the pathetic *ponk* sound his elevators made. Belus and he exchanged looks before stepping inside.

They didn't even make a selection before the doors reopened on the main level without so much as a single butterfly in his stomach to indicate they had gone down. Danato peeked out before exiting the carriage. Belus came out after him and nodded toward the gym.

Danato moved to the door that should have led to the gym. A painted skull and crossbones took the place of the official plastic gymnasium sign. He looked through the window in the door and saw a vortex. It was a slow blur of white and gray, as if someone was melting the gym. He looked at Belus, who was also viewing the odd spectacle.

Belus shook his head. "I'm sure this is just an interpretation of the Earth Barrier."

"A brick wall is an interpretation of a barrier. *That* is something else entirely."

"Come on, let's find Cori. I think I know where she'll be."

Danato followed Belus out the back exit. Night was already falling outside this pseudo-prison. In addition, the air was warm. Trees and extravagant gardens filled the courtyard. Unlike the outbuildings on his property, the bubble's collapse had not damaged the auxiliary structures in this place.

"Belus, what is this?" Danato asked, though he suspected he already knew the answer.

"This is what the entity has created for her." Belus looked at him. "A world of her very own." He nodded toward the house at the far corner of the property. His house. Or perhaps this one was Cori's house. An exact duplicate, right down to the roof tiles. "A place for her to hide in."

Danato tightened the belt on his robe and stood up straight. "I guess it's time that we found her."

Danato had walked the distance between the prison and his home a thousand times and then some, but this was the first time that his feet slowed to a stop at his front door. He even debated knocking, as if he might be intruding. Which was ridiculous, of course. This was his home—just an imaginary version of it.

"Perhaps only one of us should go in," Belus suggested, no doubt feeling the same hesitation to interrupt Cori's personal space.

"No." He shook his head. "This we do together," he insisted. For once, he wanted to stand united with Belus. Not a good guy, bad guy routine, just an immutable force.

He pushed open the door slowly and quietly. He stepped inside without difficulty and, to his surprise, so did Belus. Apparently, this house didn't hold a grudge against him.

Slanted rays from the sunset, coming through the windows, tinted the main floor of the house orange. Despite the fire crackling in the fireplace, the space was cooler than the outside. Cori was sitting on the couch with her back to them. Her head was downcast as if she were reading.

He circled around to confront her and found that she had indeed been reading. Right up until she had fallen asleep sitting up.

Before he could debate how to awaken her, Belus dropped the heavy voodoo pin on the coffee table. The clatter against the glass top startled Cori into consciousness. She looked up at Danato and her eyes widened. "Danato." She tossed aside her book and scooted forward to stand. She stopped at the edge of the couch when she saw the source of the noise that had awoken her. Her gaze drifted from the medallion-headed pick to Belus.

Danato watched the standoff between them. Belus never had the ability to intimidate Cori, but he had something that no one else did. He could dangle his approval and make her jump for it. Danato had never understood the connection between them and likely never would, but he was glad there was someone in this prison she dreaded disappointing—even if it wasn't him.

"Why don't you walk us through it, Cori," Danato said.

Cori picked up the voodoo pin. "I think it's pretty self-explanatory." She rubbed her finger over the emblem. "The genie needed a warm body, so I brought him a cold one."

"There were no guarantees that would work," Belus said. "It's not easy to pull one over on a cosmic being."

"I didn't need to pull one over on him… just you two." Cori's eyes landed on Danato, and he realized at that moment she had no expectations of tricking the genie—just him. After all, he was the most pressing threat at that moment. He was the one threatening to kill her child. The genie was only threatening to possess him.

"You risked the safety of the human race for one boy?" It wasn't a question so much as an accusation.

"Not just a boy. My son."

"If the genie had gotten to him—"

"He didn't," Cori snapped. "And neither did you. It was a risk, but it paid off."

"For now," Danato amended. "But what happens when he leaves the schism?"

Cori rolled her jaw. She had likely already contemplated that scenario. "He doesn't have to. As you can see, we have everything we need right here."

Danato scanned the room, now noticing the subtle differences between his home and Cori's. The modern stove and fridge were gone, replaced by antiquated devices. Quite literally a wood-burning stove and if he wasn't mistaken, the icebox standing in place of the fridge probably had a big block of ice in it. Electrical parts were always harder for the entity, so his appliances had to be brought in to ensure that they worked properly. The laundry room probably contained a hand-crank washer. Thus, the reason Cori was still bringing him dirty clothes.

"You've already been in here for six months." Cori's eyes danced over the floor as if calculating her time in. It no doubt felt like less to her—or perhaps it had felt like more. "You can't stay in here for the rest of your life." She looked up at him with an argument poised on her face. "I still need you." The objection died before it could pass her lips. "Ethan and Duke are gone; hell, I'd be happy to have Efrat back at this point. I need someone to help me run this place."

"You still have Riley."

Danato cringed at the thought of putting Riley back in charge of his men. He was not a born leader like Ethan. He was a born dictator. His response to every problem was to yell at it or beat the hell out of it. Not that Danato had a lot of room to talk on the yelling front, but at least he knew when to use his fists and when to use his words. "Riley's knowledge is outdated. His techniques are too domineering. I'm already getting complaints from the men. I need someone familiar to lead them."

"What do you expect me to do? Just leave my son to raise himself."

"Mommy," a little voice called out from upstairs, but Danato couldn't yet see the boy. He gravitated forward, wanting to see him.

Cori jumped up, blocking his path. She brandished the voodoo pin with wide, terrified eyes. "If you lay one finger on him..." Her rasping threat trailed off as tears poured from her eyes.

He hated being the bad guy. He always had, but part of him was still considering the worst-case scenario. What if the genie was just lying in wait? What if—

"Papa D!" the boy at the base of the stairs rejoiced at seeing him.

Danato barely recognized him. He had to be nearly three by now. His hair was a mop of wavy blond hair, like his mother's. His face was a mix of both his parents, but he mostly saw Ethan. The boy ran forward on sturdy, confident legs—unlike the wobbly sticks he had last seen him operating.

Cori tried to stop the boy, but he was hell-bent on reaching his grandpa. Instinctively, and perhaps stupidly, he leaned down and caught the boy up in his arms. The moment his head landed on his shoulder, Danato broke into tears. He held the boy against him, rubbing his back and trying in vain to pass his stuttered breaths off as rocking.

"Hey, little guy." He pushed a greeting past his trembling lips. He turned to Cori. She was also crying. She had lowered her brandished weapon... for now.

"Oliver," she said. "His name is Oliver."

The name hit Danato like a brick, dumping a backlog of buried memories into his mind. He remembered Cori asking him what he thought about paying tribute to his wife. He had been speechless—so much so that Cori had assumed she had offended him, but her consideration had honored him. He had hoped to be a part of the child's life, but to be included in such a personal choice had awed him.

Danato's legs faltered. He sat in his usual chair before he dropped the boy. Cori reached out as if to catch Oliver, but the boy clung to Danato like a spider monkey. He was a strong little boy.

"Where were you, Papa?" Oliver picked up his head and gave Danato a scolding look that melted every suspicious thought in his head.

"I was busy, but I missed you very much."

"I missed you too," he said before plopping his head back on Danato's shoulder. He stroked the boy's back rhythmically. He noticed he was wearing dinosaur PJs. Not something he had ordered, which meant that the entity must have provided it. A rarity since the entity didn't usually dabble in accessories.

Danato noticed Belus had lowered his face to look at the floor, as if he couldn't bear to watch this scene play out. Cori was still gripping the voodoo pin, but she had at least sat back down on the couch. For a long moment, everything stayed very tense.

He searched his mind for an answer to this conundrum—one that would satisfy all of them. "If the boy is named, then the danger of possession should be passed."

"Should is a very big word, Danato," Belus pointed out before sitting in the chair opposite him. "Our knowledge of his name could be due to the separation between this world and ours. What if when he leaves we forget it and with it will go his protection? This place could only be a temporary haven from the genie's jurisdiction."

"My son spent a year in the bubble, and no one remembered his name then."

"That we know of," Belus said. "Who's to say that we didn't remember, but then forgot again when it was lifted? The power of the cosmos is the same power that shifted the events of your life and put you into an alternate reality. That wasn't a dream or a mirage. Time and space were restitched to make that happen. We must assume that Oliver…" Belus glanced at the boy as if the use of his name had relegated him to the same impact of memories Danato had previously experienced. "We should assume he is still a potential host."

"So, he'll stay in here with me until we can prove otherwise."

Danato exchanged a worried look with Belus. "Cori, the timeline is starting to stabilize. We can expect two days for every hour now."

Cori shrugged. "I know. That's why I have been leaving when Ollie is asleep. I give myself ten minutes to get food and supplies."

Danato scoffed, thinking about Cori running around for ten minutes of every day—dropping off laundry, picking up food and necessities. "You can't keep doing this."

"Now that you know, you can help. Drop in the food."

"No, I won't let you do this."

"Mother trumps warden, remember? I have to stay with my son."

"And what about you?" Danato frowned. "Despite the longevity of the wizard's lives, they did not stay young. You will still age here."

"That doesn't matter."

"It does to me." Danato kept his voice low, so he didn't disrupt Oliver, but his free hand fisted on the arm of the chair.

"I won't abandon my son," Cori said firmly, also keeping her voice low.

"And I won't abandon you. I will not stand outside this bubble watching you age one month at a time." Cori stared back at him, her features hard and unrelenting. "Cori..." He trailed off and took in a calming breath before speaking. "I can't lose you too."

Cori's eyes glistened with tears, and she looked away. "I don't know what you want me to do. I won't leave him in here alone."

"Then we need to hire babysitters," Belus said.

Cori glared at him. "I'm not going to just pass this off to someone else, like a duty roster assignment. I want to raise my son."

"I wasn't suggesting that you surrender your duties. I was suggesting that you share your duties."

"With whom?"

"With me, for one," Danato said. "I think I can manage a few days with my grandson." A small smile tipped her lips, but then it fell.

"And me," Belus said. Cori looked at him somewhat surprised by his contribution.

"So, what? Are we just going to bounce in and out every ten minutes?"

"No," Belus said somberly. "In order to make this work, we are going to have to break this up further. We will need more than three people to rotate."

"Who else?"

"You tell me." Belus raised his hand to her. "Who do you trust to care for your child?"

Danato watched her eyes flicker as if she were mentally making a list of the nursing staff and the few guards that she knew well enough to share this responsibility with.

"We'll have to put pen to paper and get more reliable numbers from Chuck, but initially I'm certain Danato would allow you eight hours inside the bubble per day. That would effectively be your sleep cycle in normal time."

Cori nodded, but then frowned. "Wait, that means..." Her eyes flickered again as she calculated the new numbers the bubble was forcing them to juggle. "I'll be gone a month each time."

"You'll have about two weeks on and four weeks off."

"I can't—"

"You can," Belus insisted. "Let go of your preconceived ideas about motherhood, Cori. You should have thrown those out the minute you brought a child into this place." Cori narrowed her eyes at him. "Think about how many hours a day you spent with him before. On a good day, you would have had a few hours at the end of the day, most of which you spent getting him fed and ready for bed." Cori frowned. "You will have two weeks of uninterrupted time with him, followed by a long workday, and then he will be right back in your arms. I imagine it won't be nearly as disappointing to him as it will be to you."

Cori rubbed her face and looked at her son in Danato's arms. She was still struggling with the idea of leaving him behind. She had already lost a year of his life. Now she would miss another two-thirds of his development, but of course, Belus was right. In the real world, she would be lucky to have that much.

"Don't forget, sweetheart, he won't be alone. Papa D and Uncle Belly will be here while you are gone."

Belus glared at him for using Oliver's moniker for him. He wasn't sure the man could hate any name more than his given name, but it was a very close second.

"This isn't a trick, is it?" Cori asked.

"What do you mean?" Danato asked.

"I mean." Cori looked between them, her face scrunching, ready to shed tears again. "Can I trust you to be with my son?"

Danato frowned and glanced at the boy, who was fast asleep on his shoulder. He shifted to the edge of the chair and stood, lifting the boy with him. He turned to head upstairs but stopped at the couch. "You made the right choice, Cori." Her face went blank—she wasn't expecting his approval. "Thank you for saving him from me." He left her in stunned silence and took Oliver upstairs to the room that was obviously designated for him.

Danato sat on the edge of the bed, which was an adult bed, much like the ones in his spare bedrooms. However, Cori had outfitted it with blue camouflage sheets and piled it high with teddy bears. He looked around the room, noting the other toys littering the dinosaur floor rug. From action figures to monster trucks, Oliver was not lacking in childhood amenities. Once again, since he hadn't requisitioned the toys, he could only assume that the house had provided them. A feat that should be beyond her creativity level. Unless, of course, a toy catalog had slipped into the prison along with the mail. Regardless of how they had come to be there, Danato was glad that Oliver would have a semi-normal life.

Hopefully, a long life.

4

HEATON STARED OUT AT the soggy mess of land before him. He hadn't expected to be back here so soon. Certainly not to beg for Jack Macey's help again.

"What are we doing here?" Callin asked. The werewolf seemed uncomfortable in this surrounding. He wasn't sure if the climate or terrain bothered him particularly, or if he was just concerned about his expensive leather shoes sinking into the mud. Heaton could normally empathize with the desire to protect one's wardrobe investment, but at this point in his journey, he had no tolerance for frivolity. He had too much blood on his shoes to worry about the approaching mud.

"We're getting help." Before Callin could ask another question, Heaton yelled at the top of his lungs, "Mace!" Despite his volume, the trees seem to eat up the name—not allowing for an echo. He yelled again and listened for the sound of sludging footsteps or cracking branches. Something to confirm that his former partner was at least nearby. He yelled a third time, his voice nearly cracking from the effort he put into it.

"You don't gotta yell so damn loud," Mace's voice came from the trees ahead, but Heaton couldn't see him. "I heard ya'll coming from a mile back."

"Come on out. We need to talk."

"Who's your friend?" Mace asked.

"This is Callin."

"He a wolf?"

Callin looked at Heaton, questioning the observer's astuteness. "Why do you ask that?" Callin asked for himself.

Mace let out a soft snort. "Because you look like you're about ready to start panting. What's the matter, Wolf? Ain't you never been anywhere that feels like you're breathing under water?" Callin shifted and sniffed the air, searching for Mace's scent. "Don't bother. Can't smell nothing out here but mud, fish, and dead gators."

"Alright, Mace, you've got your jabs in. Now get out of here. I didn't bring him here for a fight."

A twig snapped in the distance, and the sound of boots squelching in the mud came nearer. After a few seconds, Heaton laid eyes on Mace as he trudged through the soft ground to meet them. The short, rugged man always had an angry look on his face. The only smile Heaton ever saw on his face was a lopsided smirk—which was usually at the expense of someone else.

Mace stopped and looked Callin over carefully. They couldn't have been more different. Mace was donning jeans and a plaid shirt with the sleeves cut off to show off his enormous biceps. Callin, by contrast, was in slim-fit gray slacks and a low-collar white polo shirt that accentuated his muscular chest. Callin had his brown waves combed back with a heavy dose of pomade; however, with the steamy air, it was releasing and curling at the ends. Mace, on the other hand, made no efforts to style his hair, which was overdue for a trim. The dirty blonde locks, that may as well have been called brown, sagged against his head, flattened by humidity, sweat, and God knows what. The tobacco that he was rolling around in his cheek only added to his hayseed portrayal.

After the measuring, it was clear neither man was impressed. Pompously disgusted with each other, they exchanged sneers. Heaton didn't care whether they liked each other. This visit wasn't about making friends. Quite the opposite.

"I figured Daniel would want his revenge for what I done to his girl."

"Daniel's dead." Heaton blurted out the statement like a comment on the weather. He didn't want to waste any effort on coddling Mace, since he wasn't likely to shed any tears for his former colleague.

Either because of his blunt announcement or legitimate shock at the news of Daniel's demise, Mace lost every ounce of his bravado. The angry mask he used to hold everyone at bay, friend or otherwise, fell away. For a moment, he looked like a human being with real feelings. He turned away and looked out into the swamp beyond. "Sorry to hear that." He spat something on the ground—no doubt the remainder of his *cud*. "How did it happen?" he asked, as if the story of his death might somehow honor the man. Better to die in battle than in bed.

"He was murdered—stabbed to death."

Mace swung around and stared at Heaton—an accusation in his eyes. "How the hell did that kill him?"

"He wasn't immortal. His body could fail just like the rest of us," Heaton said, unable to hide the sour tinge in his voice.

"I get that, but the man is a fucking priest."

"Don't call him that; he hated that."

"Nobody gets the drop on Danial McGrath!" Mace yelled at Heaton as if he might have simply made a mistake. It wasn't Daniel lying there dead in a body bag, white as a ghost, and peppered with dozens of knife wounds. It wasn't his blood smeared all over the prison walls—like the graffiti of a madman. No, surely Heaton had imagined it all.

"What do you want me to say, Mace! You want me to tell you that we all fucked up! Well, we did, alright? We fucked it all up. We missed something, and he suffered for it. It doesn't matter how powerful he was. It doesn't matter how clever he was. Daniel McGrath is dead!"

Mace winced at hearing the words a second time, but he stopped arguing. After a long, uncomfortable silence,

Mace shrugged. "You come all this way just to tell me that?"

"No. I came here because I need your help."

Mace shook his head. "I ain't cut out for huntin' anymore. Besides, I got plenty to do out here."

"I'm not offering you a job. I came here because I need your help to kill the motherfuckers responsible for Daniel's death."

Mace's brow furrowed—no doubt surprised that his name would be called for such an assignment. He nodded at Callin. "Looks like you already got your muscle. What do you need me for?"

Heaton moved in a little closer, getting in Mace's face as much as he could since he already towered over the man. Mace naturally puffed out his chest in response to his domineering position. "I need you to tell your daddy that you're finally interested in claiming your birthright."

Mace opened his mouth wide and let out a raucous laugh. He raised his head high, exaggerating his glee for the entire swamp to hear. When he finally looked back at Heaton, his face instantly sobered and his eyes went dead again. "That's got to be the stupidest thing I have ever heard you say. My daddy didn't claim me from day one. What makes you think he is going to listen to the requests of his little bastard now?"

"I just need you to get me close to him. After that, we can decide if there's room for a family reunion or not."

"What are you talking about? What do you need with my father?" Mace sounded a little defensive despite his hatred of the man.

"I told you already. I've come here to kill the men responsible for Daniel's death."

5

EFRAT SMILED AT A passing young woman with blue hair and angel wings on her back. Mardi Gras was in full swing, and there were plenty of interesting characters roaming the streets of the French Quarter. Especially after sunset.

Efrat turned his head to catch another glimpse of the attractive blonde. She also peeked over her shoulder, giving him a coquettish smile. He chuckled and looked forward again.

"What's that about?" Ethan asked, either about his laughter or the cockeyed smirk lingering on his face. Efrat found it unfortunate that Ethan was now the one wearing a perpetually grim expression, while he was more frequently the one with a contented expression. He thought Cori might be proud of how quickly he had regained his human nature. Since his hands were becoming increasingly more controlled was a major part of that transformation, but it was also being away from his confinement. Away from so many terrible memories.

"Nothing," Efrat said. "I was just thinking that Duke was a very smart man."

"Is." Ethan stopped in the middle of the sidewalk, forcing more than a few people to walk around the roadblock he caused. "Duke is still alive," he said firmly.

Efrat shifted clear of a gaggle of laughing women and faced Ethan. "Yeah," he agreed. "Present tense then. Duke is a very smart man. Except for the last bit where he put himself in that statue."

"He made a sacrifice. That's a noble thing."

"Yeah," Efrat said again. He tried to keep the bitterness from his voice, but he couldn't quite stifle his opinion. "I've heard it all before, Ethan. I've got the t-shirt and the coffee mug too, but if you don't mind, I'm gonna keep being mad at him. Just like you're gonna keep being mad at Cori." Efrat felt the grip on his throat before he registered the movement. The passersby did double-takes, monitoring the altercation unfolding before them.

"I told you we aren't going to talk about her." Ethan cautioned him.

Efrat could feel the tension dragging his inhalations down, but he could still breathe. "And what if I don't agree? What if I want to talk about her?" He lifted his hand and wrapped his fingers around Ethan's wrist. It was an intentionally gentle touch. Not a threat—just a reminder that he was never unarmed.

Ethan's eyes shifted to the touch. He retracted his throttling grip and pulled Efrat's hand open to look at it. He pressed his hand against his, palm to palm, and held it there. "It's gotten better. I can barely feel anything."

Efrat glanced around, noticing that this interaction was drawing almost as much attention as the hostility Ethan had been displaying. "Whatever Cleos did, it's working."

"But it's still there, right?" Ethan asked, sounding concerned.

Efrat rolled his eyes and sent out a shock that forced Ethan to release his hand. "Yes, it's still there. I haven't had a chance to let loose lately, but I'm pretty sure I haven't lost any potency."

Ethan nodded introspectively. "Good."

"What's the matter, Ethan? Afraid your personal battery charger might be broken?"

Ethan allowed him a small, fleeting smile. "Well, you have become pretty useful."

They continued walking, passing every potential stop for entertainment. Efrat gave the last bar a rueful look as they continued to walk into the neighborhood beyond the entertainment district. "So, I take it we aren't drinking tonight." Efrat pushed a breath of air past his lips. "Great. Another night of witch-hunting."

"Would you rather wait at the hotel?" Ethan asked.

"No. No. I thoroughly enjoy watching you freak the shit out of civilians. Especially when their children are in the next room watching."

"I told you before, I didn't see them."

"And I told you, that's a load of horseshit."

Ethan stopped to face him. "Do you really want to have this argument again?"

Efrat considered his options and nodded. "Yeah, actually, I do. You called that poor girl Cori."

"I told you we aren't talking about her."

"Oh right. The name that shall not be mentioned." Efrat threw his hands up and spun. "You know what? I was serious back there." He pointed vaguely back toward the sound of people having much more fun than him. "What if I want to talk about what happened?"

"It's got nothing to do with you." Ethan moved past him, but Efrat shoved him back—or at least tried to shove him back. Mostly, he just pushed himself ahead of him.

"Nothing to do with me?" Efrat ran his fingers through his hair. The slight static charge made his hair stand on end. "Alright, let me think about this." Efrat held up a finger and paced in front of Ethan.

"What are you doing?" Ethan asked.

"Shut up, I'm thinking."

"Thinking about what?"

"I'm thinking about how Duke would handle you in this situation. W.W.D.D. What would Duke do?" Efrat stopped and faced Ethan. "Yeah, you know what? I think I know exactly how Duke would handle this. He'd be polite and kiss your ass, all the while telling you off. I guess since I don't know how to do that, I'll just skip to the end." Efrat stepped closer to Ethan, using his height to lord over him.

"If your PTSD puts anymore innocent women in danger, I'll put you down, and I'll put you down hard. We clear?"

Efrat waited for Ethan to glare at him or return his threat, but he didn't. He stared him down for a moment before nodding. "We're clear."

Slightly disappointed in Ethan's talent for de-escalation, Efrat stepped back, and they continued to walk. "Who's the mark for tonight's hunt?"

"Mistress Safir." Ethan pulled a newspaper clipping from his pocket and handed it to Efrat. "She's apparently very sought after and difficult to get an appointment with."

"Can't be that difficult if she advertises in the Penny Saver?" Efrat unfolded the clipping and read the outrageous advertisement in a crotchety old woman's voice. "The mysterious Mistress Safir is here to open the doors to your past and part the veil between worlds. If you are done with psychics and so-called witches, come see a real voodoo priestess..." Efrat's amusement faded and he lost his impersonation. "...and witness the true power of necromancy."

Efrat crumpled up the article and tossed it back to Ethan. He wasn't ready to have this conversation with Ethan. The conversation where he had to explain that his son was dead and gone and not coming back. It wasn't as if anyone should have to have that talk. But of course, they both lived in a world that defied logic and physics on a daily basis. What was one more miracle? Never mind that necromancy was taboo even among the greatest occultists, and only spoken about in hushed tones in back rooms. "Promise me something, Ethan," Efrat said.

"What's that?"

"If this one turns out to be a hack like the rest, can we please get a beer?"

"I promise."

6

CORI RAN UP THE stairwell and burst through the door to the seducers level. There was no bleating alarm for this occasion, because no one cared about the death of an inmate. No one except her—at least for this inmate.

Cori rushed into the section and slipped on the wet floor. She landed hard against the sloppy mess beneath her. She stayed there a moment and stared at the ceiling—evaluating if her lungs were ever going to let her breathe again.

Her supine position on the floor caught the attention of a few guards who were trying to mop up the excess water. One of them rushed over and helped her up, apologizing for not keeping up with the defrosting cell.

She dismissed his apology as unnecessary and looked over at the gigantic ice block responsible for the puddle beneath her. "Is she still in there?" she asked. She approached the frozen cube that filled the entirety of the prison cell. It had even expanded beyond it, breaking the containment glass.

The guard pinched his lips and nodded. "I'm afraid so. We think maybe she tried to escape and—"

Cori pushed the glass remnants around with her shoe. "She wouldn't have tried to escape," Cori said, lost in thought. "Onna had accepted her punishment. Despite her crimes, she was a good woman."

"You're kidding, right?" The guard seemed shocked by her defensiveness. "You know what she did, don't you?"

Cori knew very well that from an outsider's perspective, Onna was fiendish, but as someone who had far too often skirted the lines of morality to preserve the status quo, she knew some crimes were just a matter of perspective. The devil is in the details—or perhaps for her it was the opposite. "Regardless of that, she was clearly unsuccessful. What would possess her to make such a mistake with her own power?"

"Maybe it wasn't a mistake," the guard suggested. Cori frowned at him, even more unhappy with the suggestion of suicide over ineptitude. "Well, you can never tell what's going on inside a person's head," the guard reasoned. Something about that irritated Cori. Perhaps she vainly assumed that the woman would have reached out to her instead of resorting to such measures. But also because the level of power required to make this much ice was superfluous.

"She wasn't suicidal. I brought this woman hot cocoa every month for years. We talked about everything. I knew her better than I know most of the staff."

The guard looked her over, his expression turning to disgust. "Yeah, that doesn't surprise me."

Cori didn't bother looking at him to rebuke his obvious insult at her less than chummy leadership style. "Dismissed."

"Yes, ma'am." He gave her a lazy, sarcastic salute, not unlike the ones she used to give to Belus when she thought he was overstepping his authority. Judging by how angry it was making her; it was a wonder that she had ever won him over.

"You have such a way with the men." Riley was leaning on a wall dividing two cells, watching her. When she turned her usual disinterested gaze to him, he took it as an invitation to join her.

"Don't start," she grumbled.

"You do have a reputation for snubbing the part-timers."

Cori turned to him. "And you have a reputation for being an asshole, so maybe... glass houses."

Riley shrugged. "Oh, please, that was the old Riley. I'm a changed man. Nine years inside the Medusa statue will do that to you."

"Is that so?"

"Sure, I'm straight-up Zen now."

Cori stared at him for a long moment. This was not the first time Riley had tried to strike up a playful conversation with her. She wondered if he was trying to flirt with her.

Or if he was honestly just lonely. For whatever reason, the guards didn't seem to like him either.

Cori offered him a noncommittal grunt of acknowledgment before sloshing to the nine by nine—and presumably—by nine ice block that was taking up the entire space Onna had lived in during her years at the prison. She brushed away a frosty film that had developed on the ice and gasped at Onna's beautiful elderly face staring back at her. She was encased—as if memorialized in resin. The last moments of her life were displayed for all to see.

Her expression was a picture of her last thoughts. Cori tried to decide whether the emotion was shock or fear. Either would be appropriate, she supposed, and yet, why? What could cause her power to malfunction in this way? Was it normal for a burst of energy to be released upon the death of a natural elemental? For a moment, Cori tried to access the memories of Dr. Jillian Frank, the surgeon responsible for the creation of their former resident elementals. She hoped that she might have more knowledge of the subject, but those memories were long gone—buried or dissolved or eaten, she presumed. All that remained was the memory of a memory. As if Cleos had left a bookmark in place of what he had taken from her. He had given her many placeholders over the years.

Cori examined her friend's hands—pressed flat against what would have been the containment glass of her cell. That was why everyone suspected she was trying to escape.

Her ice power could have been enough to break the glass. However, it always was. Her containment—much as with Cleos or Daniel—was as much about guilt as it was about the walls surrounding them.

Why would she try to break out now?

And why overload the cell with ice—effectively killing herself?

Surely she had more control than that.

Riley moved up beside her to examine the ice. He scraped his finger on the ice, shaving some of the frost away. "Wicked way to go." He shivered and recoiled either from the coldness of the ice or the creepiness of the woman inside of it.

Cori sighed and looked at him. "Seriously, Riley, this was a friend of mine. I'm actually really upset right now."

"You are?" Riley looked her over, inspecting the controlled grief that was coming across as fatigue. She imagined all of her emotions were presenting as fatigue these days. Trying to keep track of real time and the bubble time was taking its toll. "Why?"

Cori decided she was done with today's torments and moved to leave. Working with Riley hadn't been an excruciating experience on the whole, but he always seemed to have a nugget of wisdom to share with her. His condescension would drive her insane.

Riley rushed around her to block her path. "No, I'm serious, Cori. You have a history of teaming up with the bad guys. Efrat, Cleos, Onna?" Riley plucked at his fingers as he named off just a few of her odd partners.

"I'm aware of my history. What's your point?"

He scanned her face, mouth shifting several times before he spat out the words. "Are you a danger junkie or just attracted to bad boys?"

She wanted to slap him. She wanted to dig her nails into his stupid face. Naturally, he had reduced everything she had done to save herself and others to an addiction or turn-on. "Dismissed," she said in the same bitter tone as before.

To her annoyance and surprise, Riley's eyes flickered with delight. He glanced around at the men working on cleanup before shifting out of her path and standing stiffly at her side. All that was missing was a salute and projected, "Yes, sir."

Cori went back out the way she came, trying to consider how much time had gone by since she had left the bubble. She glanced at the watch Chuck had given her, but it was impossible to read sometimes. The hands moved so fast and in unpredictable patterns. It was no longer a question of the careful calculations of Father Time. She was now at the mercy of the entity's whim.

Before she could reach the next section, a pair of running footsteps clattered up behind her. She didn't bother turning to face Riley as he slowed to a stop and panted beside her. "Now, where were we?" he said between breaths.

Cori should have been glad that he hadn't outright rejected her dismissal in front of the other men. She was fairly certain Danato had given him the respect for authority speech long ago—assuming he remembered it. However, it didn't change the fact that he was like a leech when he wanted something. Riley wasn't the type of guy to take "no" for an answer. She imagined that if he was truly interested in pursuing her romantically that she would have long days of flowers, chocolates, and a serenade or two in her future.

"Belus told me you have trust issues, but I don't think it's that simple."

Cori stopped and turned to face him. "Belus told you that."

"Well, he said it more psychologically, but whatever. I think it's bullshit."

"Oh, you do?" Cori crossed her arms and prepared herself to be schooled.

"Yeah, I think you're just resourceful."

"You mean lucky?" she said snidely.

He frowned. "No, I mean... back to the wall; haven't got a shot in hell; so you just use what you got."

Cori felt flattered, but also suspicious. "What do you want, Riley?"

Her bluntness caught him off guard, and he stepped away from her. "I'm not... This isn't a come-on."

"Okay." She waited for him to answer.

"How did you know that you could trust Efrat? I mean that first time. What made you believe he would help you?"

No one had ever asked her this question before. She was certain there were plenty of "What were you thinking?" or "How could you do that?" type of questions. But no one had ever thought to ask her what had happened that day, or any of the days she had made the wrong choices for the right reasons. She started to answer, but stopped, concerned that he was goading her to reveal some personal detail he could use against her later.

Trust issues indeed.

"I didn't trust Efrat—not that day, anyway. I just convinced him that he could trust me. Once he knew I meant what I said—that I would do everything in my power to help him—he was more compliant."

"It must have taken a lot for you to reach out to the enemy. To a man who had hurt you in the past."

Cori didn't particularly like this line of questioning. She didn't want to talk about either the men who had left her so recently and so long ago. But she especially didn't want to talk about Efrat. She couldn't explain why that betrayal cut deeper than Ethan's. She understood why the father of her child would leave—run from his monstrous, murderous wife. But Efrat had traded his allegiance to her. Their long, complex, and contentious friendship was not enough to hold him to her during dark times. Although she pretended not to, she knew why. She had never given Efrat enough of herself to warrant his true devotion.

"I had no choice. I did what was necessary to help Belus. There was no one else who could help me."

"You were alone?" Riley stared at her in earnest, without a shred of amusement or pity on his face.

"Yes, Riley, I was alone. I think you'll find that most of my sorriest decisions were made when I felt I lacked a proper partner to back me up."

"I think that's why I was never good at this job. I tried to do it all myself. Of course, I did it out of ego and not desperation." Riley stepped back to her again. "I wonder what would have happened if I had had someone like you... to back me up. I made the wrong decisions back then and pissed people off. Maybe with your help, I can mend my ways."

"What are you saying? You want to team up?"

"Basically."

Cori's mouth turned up in a resistant smile. "Are you sure this isn't a come-on?"

Riley chuckled and lowered his eyes bashfully to the floor for a moment. "Um, actually, I'm still hung up on this other girl that I can't have." He smiled shyly at her. "But I'll let you know when I get over that."

"Okay." Cori moved to walk away, but Riley touched her shoulder, beckoning her to stay. She turned back and found him floundering to say what he wanted.

"I know something is going on in the bubble. Something Danato won't tell me about." Cori tensed. "It's obviously important if all of you are in there so much." Riley sighed. "I don't know how to say this, but... I want in."

"You want to go into the bubble?"

"No—I mean, yes. But I also want in... you—no, fuck!" Riley covered his eyes. "Why does this still sound like a come-on?"

Cori couldn't help but laugh, because for once he was trying to be straightforward with her.

"Okay. I'm going to try this again." Riley looked at her somberly, draining the amusement from the moment. "Since I came out of that statue, I have wanted nothing more than to just crawl right back into it." Cori's mouth hung open. She hadn't thought that he was that miserable. "The woman I love is gone, and it hurts so fucking much!" Riley balled his fists and bore his pain through clenched teeth. "I don't really have a purpose here anymore, Cori, but I would like to."

He moved up to her and grabbed her hand. "I know this is still going to sound like a come-on, but screw it. I want to be part of your life. I want to help. Danato doesn't trust me. I'm pretty sure half of this prison has considered throwing me back into that statue to save Duke." Cori averted her eyes since she was included in that half. "Just..." His words failed him. He looked down at her hand in his. His brow furrowed as he observed the one finger without a ring. He looked back up at her. "I know I'm not him—any of them—but... You can trust me. Whatever is going on... I can handle it and I can help."

Cori had never even considered bringing Riley into the bubble. But after hearing his petition—his earnest request for inclusion—she wondered if he could be useful to her. There were only a few people in the prison she would want to reveal that part of her life to. Since Riley was a permanent employee like herself, there was no harm in taking a few months or years off his life.

"Come with me," she said quietly and dragged her hand from his.

They walked together in silence to the elevators. And after a terribly slow descent to the den floor, they met with Chuck. He gave them an update on the bubble's readings even though Cori couldn't understand what he was saying. He had always impressed her with his ability to translate the ebb and flow of the sphere into numerical measurements, so she listened patiently while he made her feel like a simpleton.

As they stepped up to the edge of the bubble, Riley took her hand. She looked down at the contact and then at his tensed body. "We don't drop in anymore. Chuck has mapped the bubble, so we can pop in almost anywhere at ground level."

Riley looked at her, to Chuck, and then back at the bubble. "Oh," was all he said.

His hand tightened around hers, and she decided he wasn't worried about the separation as much as going into a foreign place with a skewed timeline. Another small smile tugged on her lips as she guided him forward through the spacial rift that Chuck had carved into the time fissure.

Light blinded her, and for a moment, there was nothing—no sound, no scent, no air—just pure, unadulterated light. Then the world righted itself, offering the scent of dewy grass, the sound of birds, and the warmth of a breeze from a forever spring.

Riley opened his eyes and looked around. His hand slipped from hers, and he frantically looked from the forest to the south, to the prison entrance at his back. The mountains to the west were seeing the last of a dissipating storm. Somewhere beyond the prison, there was a lake Cori still enjoyed swimming in, but Riley's eyes had caught on the house in the far corner of the courtyard. "Holy shit," he whispered.

She understood his confusion. From his perspective, they had just walked out the prison's backdoor. But the air was warm and sweet. There were trees standing on what should have been an Arctic desert.

"Come on," she said softly, touching his arm as she passed to urge him forward. "I'll make you some lunch." She glanced back and saw him following her, his legs moving on autopilot. There were a thousand questions on his lips as his eyes roamed over the landscape. When he finally caught her eye, his face went blank, and he frowned.

"Did you say lunch?"

7

HEATON WOULD'VE EXPECTED MACE to put up a bigger fight when he threatened to kill his father, but he presumed it was nothing he hadn't considered himself a time or two. Not to mention, Mace probably assumed that Heaton was exaggerating his desire to put cold-blooded murder on his resume.

"Why did I have to get all dressed up for this?" Mace asked as he tugged on his suit jacket. He had drawn the line at wearing a tie, which was for the best since his neck was a little thick for the accessory.

"To improve the smell," Callin contributed as he followed behind Heaton and Mace.

"I smell like hard work and accomplishment." Mace glanced back at him. "Doesn't matter how much of that perfume you put on. You still smell like a wet dog."

A low growl came from behind them, but Heaton ignored it. In another minute, it wouldn't matter what the three of them smelled like. Only what Matthew Montgomery smelled like.

As they arrived on the doorstep of the large house that could only be described as a mansion, the front door opened. The butler had already been informed of their arrival since they had to be buzzed through the front gate. The formally attired gentlemen bid them inside graciously.

"Mr. Montgomery is expecting you, Mr. Macy." The butler looked at Heaton and Callin. "You didn't mention you would be bringing guests."

"These two?" Mace vaguely motioned to them. "My driver and my bodyguard. You know how dangerous my work is. Got more and more marauders entering the territory. Guns just don't cut it. And when the muscles don't cut it either, we just gotta drive away."

The butler stared at Mace, barely understanding a word he said past his heavy southern drawl, let alone the description he was giving. He nodded and motioned for them to follow him.

As they walked down the wide corridor past tasteless and gaudy works of art, Heaton made a note of all the rooms they passed—plotting his exit strategy and making sure that there was no one else in the house.

As they came to a stop near the end of the hall, the butler motioned to a doorway that appeared to lead into a den. Mace headed inside, and Heaton followed.

"Could I trouble you to use your facilities?" Callin asked the butler. Heaton matched eyes with Callin as he left them behind.

Heaton should have felt bad about what he was about to do, but too many offenses filled his mind for him to think of anything other than defense. It didn't matter what form it came in. So long as it came.

"Hey there, Daddy," Mace said casually as he strolled across the room and picked up a random trinket on his father's desk to play with.

Matthew Montgomery spun in his chair, first seeing Mace and then Heaton. His eyes bloomed with annoyance, and his chest puffed, ready to bellow. However, the only thing that came out was a harsh whisper. "Don't call me that here. Who is this? You never said anyone else was coming. I don't understand why you had to come all this way, anyway."

"Well, I was just thinking about my obligations to my paternal lineage."

"What are you talking about?"

"You know what I'm talking about. The prison. My namesake. I'm like the last of the last of the last, right?"

"Who is this?"

"Don't worry about him. He's a hunter, European division. He's had a run of bad luck lately. His partner got killed."

"You can't be doing this, Jack. You can't just show up here talking about that place like it's a goddamn Applebee's." Matthew stood up and moved around the desk. He snatched the paperweight from Jack's hands and slammed it down on his desk. "Tell me what you're doing here?"

"I'm here because my friends want to find out who killed Daniel McGrath."

Matthew's eyes narrowed to slits as he tried to place the name. Heaton wasn't sure if anyone in the inner circle could be oblivious of Daniel's existence. There were so few—if any—of his kind, or at least that made their powers public. There was no way that a member of the board would not know him, at least by reputation.

"I have no idea who killed Daniel McGrath. I didn't even know he was dead." Matthew looked at Heaton. "He was your partner?" Heaton nodded. "I'm sorry. This is the first I've heard of it. I'm not as active on the board as I used to be."

"Thing is, Daddy, Heaton here has a theory, and I'm not sure you're gonna like it."

Matthew looked between Heaton and Mace. "And what's that?"

"He thinks that the people responsible for his death are on the prison board."

Matthew gaped at Mace for a moment and then let out a scoff. "That's the most ridiculous thing I have ever heard. Hunters die all the time. It has nothing to do with the board. They know the risks in their duties. We can't be held responsible for everything that happens in the field."

"He didn't die in the field," Heaton said. "He died inside the prison." Heaton moved in closer to Matthew, making his accusation more obvious. "In fact, he was murdered."

Matthew's eyes flickered over Heaton's, fear setting in as he realized he was alone in a room with two unsettling men. "Then Danato needs to conduct an investigation."

"We know who murdered him. The murderer is dead. She was a transmorph-human hybrid. You wouldn't happen to know anything about that, would you?"

Matthew's brow dipped slightly, and his eyes drifted to the left. Despite whatever memory he had just accessed, his head shook vehemently with denial. "That's not possible."

"And yet, my partner is dead."

"You don't understand. We tried to hybridize transmorphs decades ago, but we were unsuccessful. All of our introgression experiments failed."

Heaton momentarily lost focus as a thrum of anger surged through him.

Mace chuckled. "Well, ain't that just the sugar on the shit? Why in God's name would you try to crossbreed us with those parasites?"

"Because they are the greatest threat to our existence on earth," Matthew rationalized. "The deception they are capable of could upend the entire world. As everything stands now, it's nearly impossible to see through their lies."

"Just to be clear, we're still talking about the transmorphs, right?" Mace wandered over to the bookshelf behind his father's desk and picked up a framed picture of Matthew's socially approved family. His wife's augmented smile, breasts, and face were enough to win a beauty pageant. Even his two high-achieving sons looked like they had been plucked and tucked for the camera. "Near as I can tell, they're just playing monkey see, monkey do. Maybe they just learned how to be assholes from watching us."

Matthew's expression cooled as he looked at Mace. "You arrogant little shit. This isn't an issue of morality or questionable integrity. These things aren't devils or angels—they are walking, talking diseases. Fighting them is like fighting a virus. It's hopeless. The only way to survive is to develop a vaccine. That's why the board approved the experiments. Everything the board does is in anticipation of the threats that we will face in the future. The decisions we make are meant to save lives, even if the path is less than desirable."

"The problem though, as you say, is that transmorphs are liars." Heaton propped his hands on his hips. "Could have one standing right in front of me and never even know it."

Matthew scoffed. "Is that what this is about? You think I'm a transmorph."

"I think the board has been compromised. So, I'm going to find every last pest in your ranks and exterminate them."

Matthew shifted clear of Heaton, putting space between them again. "This is ridiculous. Your grief is clouding your judgment. Whatever information you have about the board is likely just an obfuscation."

"I trust my source. I don't trust you."

"This is absolute nonsense. I'll have no more of it. Frank!" Matthew headed for the door just as it opened. "Frank, show these men out."

Instead of the butler, Callin appeared from behind the door, blocking Matthew's path of escape. "I'm afraid that Frank is incapacitated at the moment."

"What's going on? Who the hell are you?"

"The house is clear," Callin reported to Heaton.

"Then let's get on with it." Heaton nodded to Mace, and they dragged his father back against his desk.

"Stop this!" Matthew struggled, but he was no match for either of them, let alone both of them. "Leave me alone! Help!"

Mace shoved aside the knickknacks on the desk and pushed Matthew down on top of it. He flailed on his back, kicking his feet but ultimately unable to get the purchase he needed to right himself.

Callin sauntered forward and looked down indifferently at the pinioned man. "Ready?"

"Have at him," Mace answered.

Callin moved forward and ripped the man's shirt open, casting buttons everywhere. Matthew stopped flailing and stared up at the werewolf, whose eyes now looked predatory. "No, no, no, no," Matthew whispered to himself.

Callin smiled at the man and dove forward into his exposed chest. Matthew screamed for dear life, no doubt expecting a very painful death.

Callin's fangs did not so much as Nick the man's skin. Instead, his nose trailed along the flesh, through his chest hair, to his underarm, and down toward his crotch. Matthew's screams stifled as he tucked his chin into his chest to watch the strange assault.

The werewolf popped back up; his mouth slightly ajar, like a cat tasting the air. He shook his head. "He's all human."

Mace made a clicking sound with his tongue and released his grip on the man. Heaton suspected this revelation was a little disappointing to him. Mace probably liked the idea of killing a man who looked like his father. It was the cleanest revenge one could ever hope for.

"Now what?" Callin asked.

Heaton gripped the tiny black book in his pocket. "One down, thirty more to go."

8

C ORI WAITED PATIENTLY AS Chuck unrung her ears with her designated tuning forks. Though the severity of the eardrum torture fluctuated from day to day, they had made few adjustments to her tonal cure. She blinked and pressed her hand to the side of her head as visions flashed before her.

"Are you okay?" Chuck asked when she could hear again.

She gave him a warm smile and nodded. There had been six or seven occurrences of this type since she had started spending her days in and out of the bubble. She presumed it was a side effect of Chuck's unnatural portal into the bubble. She hadn't even considered mentioning it since Danato was likely to overreact to any issue concerning the entity. She couldn't risk him restricting her time inside any more than her job already demanded.

So, she ignored the ghostly images of being shot by Efrat, seeing Sophie for the first time, or the hundreds of other memories that overlapped her reality for a split second following her arrival into this timeline.

Cori knew the bubble's ability to rearrange her mental chronology wasn't just a theoretical risk. If something similar were happening to her now, then she could find herself jumping forward in time—or possibly backward. It was that thought alone that prevented her from mentioning the visual abnormalities. If there were even the slightest chance that she could travel back in time and warn Ethan about what was about to happen... To prepare him...

Much as with every other terrible choice in her past—she would risk everything to make it happen.

Chuck handed her the roster that she had passed off to him just minutes earlier. To say that her days were endless was a sort of quandary in philosophical thought. To measure the passage of time required a constant—be that of the ticking of a clock or the age of a reflection. However, at the moment, she had only one thing to measure time, and that was how much of it was slipping through her fingers.

The clock over the door drew Cori's attention as it ticked loudly at her. It was calling to her, but she wasn't sure why. It was obviously trying to tell her something, but until the entity learned how to talk, she wouldn't get any answers.

"Danato wants to see you right away," Chuck reported, as if he were passing on the message under the warden's strictest command.

"Didn't I just see him?" She looked down at her roster, which not only held the to-do list for the day but also notes in the margins. Since it had been far more than a minute since she had left, she had taken to scribbling detailed entries about her day on the margins.

"He wants to see you again. Oh, and Cleos was looking for you again."

Cori grimaced at the thought of speaking to Cleos. He had been putting off the conversation he requested to have with her out of deference for her grieving, but now he was becoming more insistent. Since he seemed vehemently opposed to entering the bubble, it had been left up to her to go to him when she had time. Not surprisingly, she had found she was just too busy to meet with him.

"What does Danato want?" she asked.

"Don't know."

Cori couldn't place the emotion on Chuck's face. He was usually a pretty straightforward guy, but as she inspected him, he averted his eyes to the tuning forks he was packing up.

"He said it was important though," Chuck added and scurried away, preventing her from getting more information out of him.

Cori groaned and headed out for whatever lecture or disciplinary action was waiting for her. The elevator doors didn't open when she arrived, and she was forced to wait much as the other members of the staff had to. As excruciating as it was, she enjoyed the momentary alone time. Lonely as she was sometimes, it was still rare for her to have time for herself. There was always someone waiting for her.

When the elevator finally arrived, both carriages opened. She stepped into the closest one and pressed the button for the main floor. As the doors shut, a thick arm reached through, blocking them from closing. The retreating doors revealed Danato. He placed his body in their path to keep them open. "There you are," he said, as if he had been searching all over for her.

"I was just coming down to see you." Cori glanced at her watch. She was certain that she had left the bubble on time, but her watch now claimed that she was fifteen minutes late. She frowned, irritated by the device that was supposed to be her bridge to both timelines. She would never maintain a schedule if it broke. "What's wrong?" she asked.

Danato's mouth tipped up, and he chuckled. "Nothing's wrong. I have good news for a change."

Cori hugged her clipboard, preparing herself for bad news despite what Danato might consider it. "How so?"

"Do you remember the discussion we had the other day with Levi about magical connectivity? The difference between tension and retention effects on naturally resistant energies?"

Cori clenched her jaw and nodded. "Was that the one where he tried to compare Gypsy to a sponge? Or the one where I fell asleep and landed face first into a bowl of pudding?"

"It was the one where he devised an equation to anticipate the amount of earth magic required to break a dark magic curse constructed around one's own energy."

Cori hated this game. The one where she had to pretend to be smarter than she actually was. At one time, she would have presumed magic would be easy to understand. Just say a few words or flourish your hands and out pops a curse or a blessing. Of course, it had to be more complicated than that. If it weren't, then Efrat wouldn't be a bare wire, Gypsy wouldn't have gone crazy as a loon, and Daniel wouldn't be dead.

No, the world of magic was a complex set of energies, all working with and against each other. There was a mathematical balance and a scientific principle for each of them. Unfortunately, math and science were not Cori's strong suits.

"I take it they made some progress then," she said rather than admit she still had no idea what he was talking about.

Danato watched her intensely as his smile faded. He nodded slowly. "Yes, sweetheart, they made some progress," he said softly and shifted his body back so only his arm was blocking the doors from closing.

Cori looked out at the empty foyer space that led to the doors to the den. She was a little disappointed by the lack of a gift-wrapped box, until a prison-issue guard's boot stepped into view, followed by another. The tall, familiar frame in all black was not who she expected to see. Of all the missing men in her past, she had counted him among the dead in order to bear his absence.

Her mouth dropped open, and her hands went slack. The clipboard slipped away and clattered to the floor of the elevator. She stared at his slightly weathered face. His cheeks dimpled deeply as he gave her the sincerest smile she had seen in months.

"Well, hey there, darlin'," he drawled, bringing instant tears to her eyes.

Cori ran forward and barreled into him with a hug. He let out an "oof" as she nearly knocked him down and then chuckled softly, patting her back gently.

All at once, her anger surfaced, and she pulled back. Without thinking, she slapped the beautiful face. The impact startled him, and he scoffed as he recoiled slightly from her.

"Cori," Danato scolded, but Duke waved him off.

"Don't you ever do something like that again!" Cori screamed at him even as her eyes poured overdue tears. "That's an order!" Her voice was raw and shaking, but Duke nodded.

"Yes, ma'am," he whispered and took a step back to her, inviting her to finish her hello.

She wrapped her hands around his waist and pressed her face to his chest. She couldn't stop the weeping now even if she tried. There were too many reasons for her to rejoice in his return.

"It's alright," he repeated as he wrapped her up in his arms. "I'm back now." He kissed the back of her head and whispered, "I'm here."

Cori wasn't sure how long she stood there entwined with her friend, but when she surfaced, she was thoroughly embarrassed. She had just unloaded the tears she had been holding for four men onto Duke's shirt. She was a little mortified to find that she had left more than tears on him. "I'm sorry," she murmured as she backed away.

"It's all good. I've got other shirts."

Cori turned away to wipe her eyes and nose. She looked at Danato, who had remained to watch the reunion. Despite the happy moment, he looked at her sympathetically. Duke was perhaps not the first man she would have preferred to have back in her life, but at this point she would be thankful for any loved ones being returned to her.

Ever aware of the time expenditure, she moved to the elevator. She looked back at Duke and motioned behind her. "I have to go, but I... I want to catch up." She looked at Danato. "Can you tell him the basics?"

Danato nodded somberly. "Of course. Do you want me to take him into the bubble when you're done?"

Cori's heart wrenched as an exquisite, but torturous, excitement shuddered through her body. She nodded at Danato. "Yes, I'd like that."

Duke looked a little confused as he looked between the two of them. "You need help with anything?" he asked as she backed into the elevator.

She smiled at him—another rare and honest expression of joy. "A lot, actually, but speak to Danato first."

"Will do," he said and held her gaze until the doors to the elevator closed completely.

Cori took a breath and laughed. A world of stress seemed to drain from her as she slid down to the floor. She couldn't remove her smile. She couldn't even stop laughing. She hadn't felt this happy in a very long time, and she needed it.

Although she no longer needed to go to the main floor, the doors opened there. Outside the door were two guards waiting to go up. They looked at her strangely. "Ma'am?" one of them said, no doubt questioning her condition of arrival.

"I'm fine." Cori grabbed her clipboard off the floor and cleared out of the carriage so they could get in. They gave her a nod, and she waited for the doors to close and the dial to reach the second floor before she called the adjacent carriage.

Since it was a busy day for the elevators, she once again had to wait. The privilege that came with being on the entity's list of favorites had spoiled her. She turned her attention to her roster to see what she had left to accomplish before she stepped back into the bubble.

Her eyes immediately went down to the scratched scribbles across the ladder half of the page. These words had not been here earlier when she had taken it from Chuck. She considered that it might have been someone's idea of a joke, but the handwriting was hers. When had she written this? Could she have indeed jumped through her own time consciousness again?

If so, why was she leaving herself this message? This warning?

Cori stared down at the urgently scribbled words and the exclamation point that followed them. Although there was an unnecessary space between the o and b, the message clearly read: Trust nobody!

The clock high on the wall nearby resounded with every *tick, tick, tick*. Cori felt an instant headache take hold of her. She gave up on the elevators and headed toward the exit. She needed to get some fresh air. Some *real* fresh air.

9

E FRAT SAT DOWN AT the small round table covered in a black cloth. There was a white pentagon painted on it accompanied by several scorch marks, no doubt from mishandled incense punks. Apart from the noxious smell of frankincense in the air, Efrat detected an undertone of curry.

Decorative masks and paintings covered the walls—all themed after the Day of the Dead. Naturally, they were all for sale. As were the homemade rosary beads hanging beside the register at the front desk.

Efrat leaned back to look at the long line of people waiting to see Mistress Safir, much as they would for a pile of pancakes at an IHOP. He leaned over to speak to Ethan, who had taken the seat next to him. "Please, Ethan, I beg you. If I have to listen to one more bullshit psychic, I'm gonna—"

"Good evening. I am the Mistress of the Undead!" A large woman in an ornate robe seemed to appear out of nowhere in the back of the room, but Efrat was certain she had just come through a flap in the black curtain that hid the rest of the house from view.

"Too late," Efrat mumbled and leaned back in his chair.

"What has brought you to me tonight, gentlemen?" The mistress of the undead sat down across from them. Efrat noted that the smell of curry got stronger. Apparently, she had just finished supper.

Before Ethan could answer, Efrat spoke for them both. "My lover and I recently lost our most beloved Juniper." Efrat reached over and squeezed Ethan's leg—a level of physical humor he would not have been capable of a few weeks ago. "Isn't that right, love muffin?"

Ethan smirked as he rested his hand over Efrat's and gave it a squeeze. "That's right."

Efrat winced as his knuckles cracked. He smiled at Ethan and let a shimmer of static prickle his skin. Sensing the futile standoff, they each retracted their grips, but neither of them lost their expressions of humor.

"Is Juniper your pet?" the mistress asked.

"Forget about Juniper." Ethan leaned forward to speak conspiratorially. "I'm not really interested in talking to the dead. I'm more interested in exploring the power that allows such an interaction."

"Oh?" the mistress perked a brow. "I would be happy to tutor you, my dear." She reached across the table and touched Ethan's hand seductively. "But first!" She yelled and snapped her fingers, making both of them jump. "I must get a sense of your auras." The mistress reached over and touched Efrat's hand. "I must get a measure of your energy."

Efrat couldn't help releasing a slight shock as she touched him. It made the woman draw her hand back. She looked at him now, even more intrigued. He raised his eyebrow. "Enough energy for you?"

She tipped her head and narrowed her eyes at Efrat. "You are not what you seem, Mr..."

"Alston." Efrat supplied without hesitation.

A group of ladies appeared at the table and stood behind each of them. The one behind the mistress placed a heavy crown over her bouffant hair. As she did, the woman seemed to go into a trance. "Spirits of the nether world speak to me! Speak through me." The woman began to rock and sway.

The women behind them joined hands and chanted. The soft murmurs were nonsensical, but the background they provided was admittedly rather creepy. It wasn't until the lights flickered that Efrat rolled his eyes.

This place didn't house any real practitioners. They just had a better show. But of course, that's what the IHOP crowd wanted. And hell, who was Efrat to deny them that?

Efrat reached below the table and fed an additional current into the tiny salt lamp on the table. It glowed brightly before burning out entirely. The mistress took notice of this but continued to play along.

"The spirits are angry tonight. I must lull them before they will speak to me."

Efrat noticed Ethan shaking his head, but he really couldn't take any more of these hobby occultists. If they wanted to see real magic, then he would give it to them.

The air in the room became tangibly electric as he fed energy into his palms. Every movement in the room caused snaps left and right. He aimed a bolt at the nearest electrical socket, and the previously flickering lights went out. A nearby canvas, caught in the crossfire, burst into flames.

That was when the screaming began. At first, it was the women at their backs and then the groupies in the waiting area. The mistress cursed and jumped up from her seat, yelling for someone to get the fire extinguisher. Efrat had missed when the tablecloth had started on fire, but he and Ethan had to jump clear of it or risk setting their pants on fire.

Efrat noticed the Jamaican woman standing behind him had not yet moved to assist in the fire extinguishing efforts, as the others had. He snorted at the stony look she gave him. "How's my aura lookin' now?" he asked and scooted around her.

Ethan gave him a sour look before they both started walking out of the building. In the wake of their departure, the mistress was screaming about getting the portraits off the walls. The sound of approaching sirens encouraged them to pick up the pace.

"Was that necessary?" Ethan asked.

"Not in the least, but it's the most fun I've had since—well, a while."

"I know these people are hacks, but someone is bound to have some real magic."

"And then what?" Efrat tossed a tiny ball of electricity forward like a child might toss a rock down the road.

"Don't do that. Someone could see."

"Help me understand what you are trying to do. Annette is dead, so you need to find another mentor to teach you magic, but why here?"

"I need a better understanding of magic."

"Why?"

"Because I do!" Ethan turned to face him. "Since when does no one trust my judgement! Since when am I the one everyone suspects is up to something?"

"Oh, sorry." Efrat stopped and saluted him. "Yes, sir, absolutely, sir."

"Knock it off."

"Isn't that why you brought me here, to give you somebody to order around?"

"No."

"Then I assume you needed help with something. What is it? What's the plan? Why are we seeking out a necromancer?"

"Because he wants to raise the dead," a voice chimed in from behind them.

Efrat looked back at the woman who had been glaring at him before they left the psychic's house. "Who the hell are you?"

She raised her chin proudly. "I am Mistress Safir."

10

"Y ou're Mistress Safir?" Efrat asked. "Why were you playing backup to the bad actress, then?"

"The actress is a friend of my mother's. They started the business together. Lonnie runs the front room." She looked them over. "I run the back room."

"Why weren't we offered the back room?" Ethan asked.

"Because you are obviously tourists, and tourists get the front room. The front room is the show, the experience. It's where people who don't really believe in magic go."

Ethan stepped closer to her. "Well, we aren't non-believers."

"No, I gathered that when your friend here almost burned down my house."

Efrat snickered. Ethan elbowed him in the side. "Sorry about that," he said, though he still couldn't stop smiling. "I don't get out much. My social skills aren't as honed as they used to be. Assuming they ever were."

Safir narrowed her eyes at Efrat—no doubt trying to figure out if he was borderline crazy. He was wondering that about himself too. Life outside the prison was strange to him now, and he couldn't seem to wrangle the ten-year-old boy inside of him that wanted to break bottles with rocks and play with firecrackers. He was certain he would get over it—assuming he didn't move on to worse behavior.

"What are you?" Safir asked.

"I'm an elemental," Efrat answered.

"You are not," she said flatly.

"Afraid so." Efrat waved his hand around, gathering a small electrical ball before letting it dissipate again.

Safir watched the display with interest. "Something isn't right about you. Your energy is all wrong."

"Efrat is a military experiment. He's only an elemental because he possesses the hands of an elemental."

"How in God's name did they do that?"

"I'm pretty sure God was off duty the day of my surgery."

"Still, you're speaking about a surgical procedure that grafted meat and magic."

Efrat shrugged. "What can I say? The military is full of mad scientists."

"Efrat is not the reason I came to see you," Ethan said, perturbed.

"I know why you came to see me. The same reason all men come to me during times of grief. Because they cannot accept what Death has taken from them."

"I didn't come here because I'm seeking a necromancer. I came here because I'm seeking a witch."

"Well, you're in luck, my friend, because this city is filled with witches. Good luck to you." Safir pointed to Efrat, a stern maternal finger. "And you, stay away from my house." Safir turned to walk away.

"Mabel Annette is dead."

Safir stopped and looked back at Ethan. Suspicion grew in her eyes as she looked him over. She glanced at Efrat, but her interest in his elemental power must have waned. Ethan was now an anomaly. Her eyes skirted his body, as if she were searching for his aura. "How do you know Annette?"

"She was a friend of mine. I was introduced to her by Danato Calibria."

Safir shook her head. "Who are you?"

"My name is Ethan Xaviar Pierce. I am the warden's successor."

"Or was," Efrat mumbled, drawing a glare from Ethan.

"I must confess, I always thought the prison was just a rumor. The containment facilities here are much more limited."

"That's because they don't have a bubble," Efrat offered cheerfully.

"A bubble?" Safir frowned, obviously uninformed about the details of the prison and why it exists in the first place.

"Never mind that," Ethan scolded Efrat, trying desperately to keep them on topic. "Annette was one of the most powerful Earthen witches in the world. She—"

Safir snorted. "Only because she had access to dragon blood on a regular basis."

"Nevertheless," Ethan said with dim resolve. "She taught me a lot about magic before she died, but not enough. I need to learn more. I was told that there are powerful witches in New Orleans. Are you one of them?"

Safir considered his words for a moment. "I did feel Annette's presence leave this realm. I'm sorry for your loss. And to answer your question, I may be a rather talented practitioner, but at best, I am only third or fourth on a very short list of local witches. I believe the woman you are looking for is Aldine Traber. By rights, with or without dragon blood, she is and has always been the most powerful earthen witch in the world."

"Do you know where I can find her?"

"You can usually find her wandering around the swamps, but if you're looking for a mentor, I would advise that you aim lower. There is a reason Aldine is such a strong spellcaster. She's dabbled a little too deep into the earth magic and... well, let's just say her manners and hygiene no longer classify as human."

Efrat frowned at the thought of searching the backwoods for some stinky old woman. He glanced at Ethan and found the same wary expression. "What about third best?" Efrat asked both Ethan and Safir. "You must know a little something about magic, and you appear hygienic."

Safir crossed her arms. "As touched as I am at being chosen for that illustrious honor, I do have better things to do than to teach you boys the ins and outs of conjuring magic."

She turned to walk away again, but Efrat threw out a net of electricity. With his mind in alignment with his hands, it took little more than the thought of containment to create the webbed force field around her.

Safir observed the ensnaring orb before turning back to face Efrat. She gave him a vampish smile that he couldn't help but return. Then she spoke one word. "Reverse."

The energy that surrounded her ricocheted back toward him. He couldn't account for the sudden shift in power, and nearly a full dose of his own weaponry impacted him. Had he been a born elemental, he would have been immune to it, but his body was still human, and it launched him across the road into someone's picket fence.

Ethan rushed over to check his status. Efrat waved him away since nothing was broken beyond his ego—and the fence. He stood back up and dusted himself off.

"If you two idiots knew anything about magic, then you would know that elemental magic is just an offshoot of earth magic—and a weak one at that."

"Weak?" Efrat was just pissed now. He had spent years trying to reign in his power, to put a stopper on the storm raging inside of him—his hands and his mind. "I'll show you weak."

Electrical energy snapped as he approached her, but he kept his hands down and back—the way he did before he regained control. Safir didn't flinch as he came nose to nose with her. It surprised him to find that she was, in fact, nose to nose with him. She was taller than he thought. On closer inspection, her eyes were not the brown he would have expected from her skin tone—they were a beautiful light green with unnatural turquoise highlights. Even in the dimming light, her thin, twisted braids shimmered.

All of a sudden, Efrat forgot about his anger. Looking into her eyes flummoxed him. Every scathing slur died on his lips as he inhaled the smell of patchouli and peppermint. He would have preferred to believe that this was some kind of spell she was casting, but it wasn't. This was the first time he had been so close to a real woman in years, and it was tripping him up.

Not that Cori wasn't a real woman. She was attractive, but she lacked the feminine ideals that put Efrat into a pubescent stupor. She more often smelled of dirt than perfume. Her hair was almost always thrown together—and forget makeup. As if Danato would ever find room in the budget for high-end cosmetics.

And of course, there was Gypsy, but good lord, the only thing feminine about her was her anatomy. Her aggression alone was enough to turn him off. He didn't prefer easy and self-assured women. He wanted to work for it. Flirting used to be one of his better skill sets. If he couldn't at least feel that he had charmed the woman, then it felt cheap to him.

"I'm waiting," Safir said in a singsong voice. "Or were you literally intending to show me what weak looks like? In that case, you are dead on."

Efrat looked down at his hands, which were no longer pouring with energy. But they had been. He still bled energy when his emotions spiked. Compared to the progress he had made, it was a minor inconvenience, except in one aspect of his life.

Since one of the benefits of his reduced output was his ability to touch his own body, Efrat had been experimenting with himself like a horny teenager. Unfortunately, even the prospect of pleasuring himself ignited his hands and tamped out his raging hormones. His celibacy thus far was still inescapable.

As pathetic as it must have looked to Safir, Efrat backed down from her. He had no desire to show her the full extent of his power—which he knew was well above average for an elemental. He knew any performance he put on now would just be to overcompensate for his other shortcomings.

"Was that really it?" she asked him, baffled by his surrender.

"Yeah, that's it," Efrat grumbled and walked over to join Ethan—though he kept his back to him, not wanting to show the array of disappointments on his face.

"If we are quite finished...?" Safir confirmed to announce that she would once again be leaving them in the dust.

"I need your help, Safir," Ethan said, though it wasn't the plead of a desperate man. He was telling her in no uncertain terms.

"I can't help him." Safir motioned to Efrat. "That connection is unnatural. Whatever issues he's having—"

"Not him. Me. I need you to help me understand the magic I possess."

Safir blinked at him. "Ah, honey, I don't know what you've been smoking, but you don't have any magic. You are dry as a bone."

"You're wrong."

Safir took in a breath as if she were containing her own torrent of slurs. "I think we've already established that I am at least the fourth most powerful witch in this neck of the woods. And I may be young, but I certainly wasn't born yesterday. So, I would know if you possessed any magic."

"Not if I'm a mage," Ethan said resolutely.

Efrat turned to look at him. This was the first he was hearing of this. Truth be told, he had no idea what a mage was. Despite the magical influence seeping into the walls of the prison like mold, that was never the focus of its operations. Containment was all they focused on. The fact that Cleos was trying to profit off it was at least a step forward for them.

However, judging by the blank stare that Safir gave Ethan, a mage was something pretty fantastical. How the woman didn't sense it was Efrat's first question. And why he had never seen Ethan perform a single act of magic was his second.

Before Efrat could ask any questions, though, Safir's reserve broke, and she roared with laughter. She continued the somewhat false display long after her humor could have reasonably warranted it, and well after Ethan had rolled his eyes and stomped away from her.

11

"What's happening?" Riley yelled over the gale-force wind emanating from the glowing orb in the back lot of the prison. It was only about the size of a luggage trunk, but since it was sitting over the grave of a now-deceased sorceress, it had the men running for help.

"I don't know," Cori said for the third time, with notable annoyance. She had said as much when Travis arrived and then again to Duke upon his arrival. The poor Texan had just gotten out of the statue and was about to contend with the looming threat of a magical breach. Not that anyone knew what that meant. It was anyone's guess what would pop out of this little light show. "Ask Levi." Cori bobbed her head at Levi without taking her eyes off the strobe light on the northeast side of the building.

She probably should have put more distance between her and the electrical storm crackling off the ball, but she had been around Efrat long enough to know that it didn't matter where she stood. If that magical explosion was as worrisome as everyone made it out to be, it didn't matter what she put between her and it.

"I think it's time," Levi shouted for them all to hear.

"Yeah, thanks, sport," Riley said sarcastically. "Time for what?"

"That question goes double for me," Duke said. "Do we need to clear this place out or what?"

Levi glanced around the compound. "I'm not really sure what it will do, but the dragons should protect us."

"Should?" Cori didn't like his uncertainty.

"The barrier that prevents us from accessing them should work to retain any magical runoff as well."

"So, those big dumb lizards are gonna keep this storm at bay?" Riley asked.

Cori glared at him for the insult. She was still getting used to his personality, and she didn't always appreciate his cynicism. Danato had all but thrown him back into his previous position, which was more than a little insulting to her. Not just because it represented replacing Ethan, but because she was still doing most of the work. The prison had changed a lot since he had been in the statue, and she was effectively training him on top of her other duties.

She hoped Danato would allow Duke to take the lead, but so far, Riley was clinging to his familial claim like a leech. Everything happening in the prison was either going through her or him. Why Riley wanted the burden of leadership so much was a little lost on her, but she had no room to talk. She was a glutton for punishment when it came to this place. There was nothing and no one who would tear her away from the prison now.

Cori looked at Levi. "Can you do anything?"

Levi's eyes widened as if she had just pulled down his underwear in front of everyone. Though he had no choice but to reveal his true identity to Danato, the specifics of his magical origins were still a matter of rumor for most of the staff. "I... They will—"

"Can you do anything?" Cori asked more firmly.

Levi was still a young man, at least so far as his numerical age claimed, but he had experienced a great deal in his life as a human. His apprehensive behavior resulted from his ill-treatment in captivity, and not because he was bashful. Despite his secretive nature, Cori trusted him. She knew that revealing his powers to her was an enormous leap of faith for him. Performing magic around other people would be another hurdle for him.

Levi's face shrank in terror as the men looked at him for some heroic supernatural rescue. Cori wasn't entirely sure when everyone started relying on Levi for "the weird stuff," but it was almost uniformly agreed that he was the resident expert on magic. Even Danato, who preferred to keep as much of the occult away from the prison as possible, had consulted him on a few long-standing problems.

Levi succumbed to the peer pressure around him and looked toward the orb that had now grown to the size of a house. Cori's immediate concern was for Belus's A-frame cabin. It was about to be swallowed up by the anomaly. Her mentor would be livid if he had to shack up with Danato.

"Come on, Levi," Cori said soothingly. "If there's anything you can do to help. Now is the time."

Levi looked at her with determination and nodded. "I can split the magic. Loop it back and forth through alternate layers of time. It's what I've been doing with Gypsy to keep her sane...ish." He added, since Cori's personal assassin had been berserk since she had asked her to do the unthinkable. Cori had thought nothing of it at the time—dismissing the woman's lacking humanity as permission to treat her like a trained dog. As much guilt as she felt for Gypsy's condition, she in no way regretted asking her to do it. It was a necessary evil when choosing between greater ones.

"I don't know what that means, but if it avoids an explosion, go for it," she responded.

"Well, it's not exactly..." Levi shook his head. "Never mind, I'll just..." He pointed to the breach and turned to move that way. He stopped and came back to her. "Can you hold on to this?" Levi pulled something from his back pocket and handed it to Cori. She nearly dropped the thin lock of braided brunette hair when it tickled her hand like a spiderweb.

Cori blinked at what she could only assume was Adrianna's hair. "Levi, is this dangerous?"

Levi grimaced. "There's a slight chance that the rapid shifting could leave me trapped in a superimposed state across several timelines."

Cori blinked at him, wondering when every explanation started sounding like a physics lesson. "What does that mean?"

"It means I could end up present in multiple timelines simultaneously."

"And you can survive that?" Duke asked.

Levi looked at him, his eyes searching him even as his mouth searched to form a sentence. "No." His eyes turned to the ground rather than meet hers, and he walked away.

"Well, don't do it if—" Cori went after Levi, but Riley grabbed her by the wrist. She yanked her arm; but Riley's renewed regime of dragon juice had left his grip too tight to break free. She fumed and was already forming the words to denigrate his manhood when he turned a stony gaze on her. "You asked him whether he could do something. He's doing it. Part of being a leader is delegation. The other part is being an audience to the results of that delegation."

Cori's lips pinched tight, fuming at the condescension in his tone. She definitely didn't like this aspect of his personality. She was used to Danato, Belus, and Ethan telling her what to do, but there was no way she was going to take it from this over-privileged—

"Look out!" Riley yanked her wrist hard, and she fell toward him. Unable to catch herself, she landed against his chest. She detected the faintest smell of soap and aftershave before she pushed away from him.

"What is your problem?" He nodded toward the fire-singed ground that she had only seconds ago been standing on. Feeling a little chagrined, she mumbled, "Thanks." He barely acknowledged the gratitude before turning his attention to the sphere.

Levi's efforts to displace the energy were inadvertently releasing bursts of magic. Apart from the elemental fireballs, lightning strikes, and icy rainbows streaking out of the orb, there was an occasional transformative fragment that worried Cori even more.

A purplish blob of energy launched across the sky and hit the prison's exterior wall. High on the fourth level, an impromptu oasis grew out of the side of the concrete. Complete with a palm tree and spiky plants with red flowers, the foliage didn't seem to mind the wintry temperature or that it was growing sideways on a building.

Another blob of energy, this time an orange one, landed near Cori's feet. Everyone took a step back. Cori felt a tug on her wrist as Riley urged her into the movement, even though she was already surrendering. She glanced down at the contact, wondering why he still had hold of her. "You mind giving me my hand back?"

Riley looked away from the cocoon of energy and down at the contact, as if he hadn't remembered he was holding her captive. He yanked his hand away as if she were made of acid and even went so far as to wipe his hand on his pants. "Just... watch out," he grumbled, as if saving her had been a huge inconvenience to him.

Cori ignored the many ways that Riley annoyed her and watched the orange blob give birth to a gigantic tortoise. Once again, she worried about the cold climate affecting this poor creature, but he didn't balk at the icy ground beneath his feet as he roamed away from them to explore his new home.

"Mother of God," Duke exclaimed. Levi had gained control of the breach, preventing any further discharges, but it seemed to be a sacrifice. His body was still standing in the same place, but there were streaks of movement to his left and right, as if he were smeared.

Though Levi had always claimed to be unmagical, he was a magical being. His specialty was dampening, amplifying, or balancing magical forces. Since he was not technically from this realm, he was immune to most magic and could play with it like a game of chess. Unfortunately, also like a game of chess, there were a nearly infinite number of games to be played, and each one, though similar, was different. Even as he manipulated one vein of energy, another was yet to come.

"Boss, I think I'm seeing something in that big ball," Duke said.

Cori narrowed her eyes, trying to see past Levi into the center of the orb. She moved closer to Duke so he could point to exactly where he was looking. She had expected to see a form emerging, but it was something coming up out of the ground. Something was rising... from the dead.

"Oh, shit," Cori whispered. "Is that an arm?" She asked, trying to distinguish the first appendage that had broken out of the dirt from Addy's final resting place.

"I don't suppose we can reevaluate the run for our lives option." Duke's face filled with dread. Cori wasn't sure what was more frightening to him. The prospect of a real live zombie crawling its way out of the ground, or a potential sorceress coming back to life to get revenge on the lot of them for killing her.

After the two arms revealed themselves, a head popped out of the earth, shaking off the excess filth. A short, tremendously slender body slid up from the grave with the help of gangly arms. Shortly after, the legs of the animated corpse arrived on unhallowed ground next to its own grave.

Duke made the sign of the cross, and Cori mimicked him, since they might need all the help they could get to survive this resurfaced threat.

As the sphere eased its fluctuations, Levi's blur turned into a flicker. Three images of him danced in Cori's vision, only one slightly stronger than the others.

"He's stuck," Riley announced what Cori was already suspecting.

"Looks like we've got another Pooh Bear stuck in a honey pot," Duke jibed.

Cori refused to let this be the end of Levi. He was a good guy and obviously useful. Since that was running short these days, she wanted to do anything she could to save him, including something stupid.

Her specialty.

She jumped into a run before Riley could grab her again. He called after her and even followed her, but slowed to a stop when it became clear that he wasn't willing to be that heroic.

Cori whispered his name, but Levi didn't move. She touched his shoulder furtively, unsure if he would shock her or explode on contact. Though he appeared to be vibrating, she could feel his body as solid as her own. The only difference was the effusion of energy that both repelled and called to her. She suspected that if she pressed her body against his, she too would be transported through the veils of reality with him. Something she was not likely to survive any more than he would.

Just beyond the barrier of the bubble, Cori saw the zombie within wobbling toward them. It was just a few feet away now. A shadow staring out at the reflection of its former life. Even without visible eyes, Cori sensed the being was staring at Levi.

There were probably a thousand rules about standing so close to a zombie-producing magical orb, but Cori didn't care anymore. Lately, every step she took to save someone was hurting someone else. Maybe that was all she would ever be capable of.

Saving lives and breaking hearts.

Cori slipped between the zombie and Levi. From her perspective, he was frozen, but she understood he was moving very fast. His face reflected the sheer exertion and possibly the pain of what he was attempting to do. Though Cori had benefited from magic many times, she still hated aspects of it. At least with physics, there were hard and fast rules. What goes up must come down.

Then again, maybe Newton knew more about magic than they realized. If an object in motion will not change its motion unless another force acts upon it, then Cori would just have to be that force. She tentatively pressed her hands against Levi's chest. The longer she pressed, the deeper she went, as if she were melting into him.

"I wouldn't do that if I were you, boss," Duke warned from the safety of twenty yards away.

Cori considered her options one last time before letting her reckless nature transform into heroism. She should consult with Danato and Belus prior to acting against this magical process. If she was wrong, it could kill her, kill Levi, or potentially exacerbate the breach. However, as with all the other times she had disobeyed the long-standing rules of the prison—there just didn't seem to be enough time.

Levi's face had shifted into an even more constricted expression. This was definitely agony. He was killing himself to do her bidding.

Be an audience to the result of her delegation? What a bunch of bullshit.

Cori slapped away the good little angel in the form of the prison's rulebook. She put her foot back and braced her stance. She pulled her hands back and, with as much speed and strength as she could muster, shoved Levi out of the path of destruction like a mini linebacker.

Cori was foolish to think that it would be as easy as two physical bodies colliding. Even when Levi was present, he wasn't really present. She wasn't pushing the man so much as pushing through him.

Cori gritted her teeth as unpleasant sensations took the place of Levi's magnetism. She felt the world around her shift and warp into something nearly unrecognizable. Levi was no longer the smeared image. Instead, it was the background of the prison that bled into beautiful watercolors.

This was not good. She couldn't even tell if she was still moving. Was she frozen between one second and the next, or was she about to be thrown completely out of her timeline? As much as she enjoyed the idea of being a time traveler, she was almost certain that doing so would cause a cataclysmic shattering of reality.

Then she felt Levi's hands touch her back, embracing her. His face was a mixture of shock and amusement. The outside world was still a mesh of colors, but she was able to detect the descent in their bodies. They were falling ever so slowly away from the bubble and toward the earth. Though Levi had trouble staying put in this place, Cori, however, was forever bound to it by gravity. As is the burden of all bipedal apes.

Just before they landed, voices inundated her eardrums with the words of her past.

"You're right, Mr. Nose. I have no intention of being compliant." Her voice said.

"You need to settle things with your husband," Cleos's scolding words echoed across the veil.

"You stupid girl! You did this to yourself!" Efrat hissed.

"I know not of gods and monsters..." The genie's voice wrapped around her like a warm blanket despite her history of horror with him.

"I only have one option," Ethan's anguished voice spoke from someplace far away. *"I have to kill Cori."*

The energy emanating from Levi and the bubble shattered. Prisms of magic shot out into the courtyard. Several of them impacted an unseen barrier in the courtyard, spreading energy across the thin air. Cori tried to focus on this anomaly, but time was returning to normal speed. The beautiful watercolor she had been enjoying solidified into the drab tones of her true reality. As disappointing as that was, it was Newton's third law that really got Cori into trouble.

When two objects interact...

Cori had expected to land on top of Levi since that was the direction she had been heading, but instead, she flew across the yard. Propelled well past Rodan's cage by the ramifications of interfering with competing magics, she hit the barrier surrounding the prison's property. She flopped to the ground like roadkill in front of the cement wall and struggled to breathe. For a split second, she thought the impact might have killed her because her eyes were flaring with stars that she confused for the pearly gates.

Heaven was just steps away until a pair of lips pressed against hers. A hot burning breath was forced into her lungs, making her cough. She rolled to her side, exhaling the forced breath and retrieving her own natural one. When she turned back over, she saw Riley and Duke standing over her. She wasn't sure which one had administered the mouth-to-mouth, but she just mumbled a blanket "thanks" to both of them. "Levi?" she asked.

"He's still getting his bearings." Riley nodded to where Trevor was helping Levi up.

"Wait." Cori wiped the rank flavor of waxy Chapstick off her mouth and moved to observe the disrupted ground of Addy's grave. "Where is she?" Cori asked.

Everyone's face held a slight grimace as they looked around for the missing body. It was certainly necessary to find it, but no one wanted to see its condition. Even with permafrost mummification, the poor woman was bound to look horrific. "Hey?" Trevor called to them. He and Levi were staring at something on the other side of Belus's house. "What the f…" Trevor's curse fell away as his mouth draped open in shock.

Cori moved forward, dreading to see what ramifications lurked around the corner of the cabin. She had hoped she would make it through this life without encountering a proper sorceress, but perhaps that was the inevitable destiny of all who tampered with magic. With that in mind, she drew her gun. There was a small chance she could end this catastrophe quickly and avoid any bloodshed.

Other than Addy's, of course.

Again.

"Don't." Levi's words hit her ear as if he were right beside her. She flinched, but by the time she glanced back, he was already back in his original position—if he had even left it at all. He locked eyes with her and mouthed the word, "Please."

Cori didn't want to kill the girl. She didn't want to kill anyone, really. She never had, but there was still plenty of blood on her hands. There were just so many dangers when it came to people with power. It made her a hypocrite, of course. To save lives, she had to take them. But it was getting harder and harder to see the morality of those choices. She may have purported to be the antithesis of the prison's strict rules, but more and more she found herself reaching for her weapons instead of her brains.

"Please," Levi's voice was back in her ear, whispering clearly, despite the distance between them. She could feel her will to fight melt away as his essence of peacefulness lulled her into submission—yet another facet of his *non-magical* skills. She lowered the gun but kept it at her side as she crept around the side of the cabin to sneak up on the potential sorceress.

Riley and Duke were right on her heels, armed and ready to attack if necessary. She held up a hand, signaling for them to hold off on the bullets until she knew what they were dealing with.

Cori peeked around the corner and saw the last thing she would have expected. Her residual desire to fight or kill—or even verbalize a strongly worded scolding—evaporated. She holstered her gun and stepped fearlessly out into the open. Riley and Duke followed, slightly more apprehensive until they saw what she was looking at.

"Well, I'll be damned," said Duke.

"Is that a dragon?" Riley asked.

Cori shrugged and nodded, having no other clear definition for the chubby blob of purple and green leathery scales that was struggling to walk on four very brand-new legs.

"It's a baby dragon," Levi said, joining them.

"How did that happen?" Travis scratched his head, glancing back at the adult dragons as if searching for evidence of the immaculate conception.

After a short pause, Levi erupted into raucous laughter that bordered on manic.

"You care to share with the whole class there, bud?" Duke leaned over to glare at him.

"She's been purified by the Earth," Levi said, elated by this idea. Everyone stared at him, waiting for further information. "She's become a guardian."

"What?" Riley asked, with notable impatience for the young man.

"Adrianna has risen from the ashes as a dragon."

As if recognizing the name, the baby dragon let out a quiet squawk and attempted to move toward Levi.

Cori let out a sound of adoration for the spectacle. She had always been fond of Penelope, but the small, round, baby-fat version of her was an absolute treasure. The whelp lolled its tongue off to one side of its mouth, letting it hang there like an overheated puppy. "Oh my god, can we keep her?" Cori said without thinking.

"What?" Riley's head whipped to look at her, his brow creased.

She looked at him, suddenly realizing what was about to happen. Addy was a dragon. An aberrant addition to the eight in existence. The eight that no one ever let breed, although they never replicated beyond the original two.

Riley was a by-the-book kind of guy. He would report this to Danato in an instant, and he would either kill the dragon for fear that it still possessed powers of sorcery, or he would send it away. She didn't want that. She wasn't sure why. It probably had something to do with how much time she had lost with her own child, but she wasn't interested in the psychoanalysis of her motherly cravings.

Riley grimaced at her, already seeing the abject and urgent plea forming on her face. "You know Danato will have a fit about this thing being here?"

"We could hide her in the stables. He never goes in there."

Riley rolled his eyes and scoffed. "It's not a dog. She's going to grow. He'll eventually notice a two-ton lizard in the back lot."

"You might be surprised."

"I hate to burst everybody's bubble," Duke interrupted, "but this here dragon is not a girl." Duke looked at Levi. "Not unless I'm misinterpreting that sack by her caboose."

Everyone successively leaned to the right and tipped their heads to look at the undercarriage of the creature. The dragon mirrored their behavior, tipping her head to the side as well. As Duke had said, there was a very telltale waggle of excess tissue between the animal's legs.

Addy was a boy.

"That's...ah..." Travis rested his hand on Levi's shoulder. "I guess Addy is... She..." Travis struggled to find the appropriate words of solace, but eventually, he gave up on trying to be delicate. "Yeah, dude, your girlfriend's got balls."

The dragon pranced around in front of them, happy to be using *his* brand-new legs. The sounds he emitted reminded Cori of a newborn baby discovering his voice for the first time. When he finally settled, the dragon approached Cori and licked her hand. She whimpered and turned to Riley.

He did a double take at her pitiful face and nearly smiled before controlling himself. He looked out at the sky, which was turning pink over the false horizon of the prison wall. "Whatever, you're the boss," he grumbled and walked away. "Just keep me out of it. I'm not going to help you hide a flippin' dragon from Danato," he said firmly.

Cori snorted and touched Levi's shoulder. "Do you want to help me with... her?"

Levi glanced at Cori. "It's okay. I know this isn't the real Addy anymore. Whatever she was, is gone. This is just the power she possessed in its proper form." Levi swallowed hard. "The dragons just used her. They used all of us."

Cori knew he was including Ethan in that statement. She wasn't sure whether he deserved the pardon. However, whatever falsehoods her husband had doled out about his time in China were so far from her top concerns that she almost didn't even care anymore. She had told far greater lies and kept more hurtful secrets than he ever had.

And now she had one more secret to add to her list. The only question was, how did one hide a tubby little creature that loved the sound of his own voice?

12

E THAN HADN'T EXPECTED TO end up in a dive bar with Safir and Efrat, drinking beer and listening to zydeco music. Sometime after laughing him out of the street, Safir had caught up to him and offered an apology in the form of drinks. He was certain the woman didn't believe his claim, but she was at least intrigued enough to continue their conversation.

Once they reached the bar, however, Safir was more interested in drinking than chatting. Efrat was more than happy to participate in the libations. It only took a few beers for him to raise his enthusiasm to meet Safir's boisterous personality.

Ethan watched them on the dance floor. Despite having just met, they had developed a good rhythm. When a particularly fun song came on, Safir shimmied up to Efrat, demanding a closer dance partner. Ethan could see Efrat's movements slow as he became unsure of how to place his hands without actually touching the woman. Efrat still didn't trust himself to touch anyone or anything freely. When he did it, it was done cautiously—as if it took great concentration to do so. Ethan didn't discourage the behavior since the elemental was still a very dangerous man. That was, after all, why Ethan had insisted he come with him.

Ethan's eyes shifted to the darkest corners of the bar, searching for unwelcome eyes. He assumed that a busy tavern would be a safe place to hide, but the longer he stayed away, the more paranoid he became. Soon enough, glancing over his shoulder would not be enough to dispel his fears of the things that go bump in the night. He would eventually have to look under his bed for bogeymen before he could relax enough to drift off to sleep.

Ethan reached into his pocket and pulled out the gold ring he had ripped off Cori's finger when they last spoke—or rather when she had spoken to him. He flipped it between his thumb and forefinger, watching the diamond glitter from the strobe light on the dance floor. He regretted taking it from her. He regretted many of the things he had done to her, but he still couldn't forgive her. Not in any way that counted. His every thought of her was now tied to the worst day of his life. A day that he was slowly burying, one day at a time.

Efrat finally shifted away from Safir's unwelcome proximity on the dance floor and gestured to the table where Ethan was sitting. He mimed the universal symbol for drinking before he moved away from her. She scoffed at his suddenly soured mood and continued to dance by herself. It didn't take long for another lone dancer to move in and take Efrat's place. A man who had no qualms about putting his hands all over Safir.

Efrat slumped down in the chair across from him and took a long guzzle of his beer. When he came up for air, he noticed the ring in Ethan's hand. He looked him over, his mouth almost forming a question, or perhaps he just wanted to contribute some thoughts about the events of weeks past. He was always careful not to bring up the subject of Cori. He would mention Danato or the prison, but he never used her name.

"She seems to like you," Ethan said before Efrat could muster the bravery to speak.

Efrat looked back at the dance floor and frowned at the man who was now up against Safir. "I guess," he said indifferently and returned to nursing his beer.

"You still don't trust your hands, do you?" Efrat looked everywhere except at Ethan, refusing to answer. "Don't you think it's time to test your boundaries?" Efrat still didn't respond. "I'm sure if you took things slow, you might be to—"

"Yeah, we're not having this conversation." Efrat pinned him with a hard glare.

Ethan nodded slowly, acknowledging the line that was apparently not to be crossed. They had made great strides in their friendship over the last few weeks, but they were both still holding fast to their personal boundaries. Efrat had been burying his feelings far longer than Ethan, so there was no point in trying to dig them up now. Lest he have to deal with Efrat's skeletons too.

"Why are you two sulking in this corner?" Safir's hands landed with a smack on the tabletop, spilling some of Ethan's still brimming beer. He reached for a napkin to mop up the mess, but Safir grabbed his wrist. "Your turn."

"What?" He looked at her coquettish smirk.

"Dance with me. Efrat is being a spoilsport."

"I'm not really in the mood."

"You're not in the mood for beer. You're not in the mood for dancing. Why did you agree to come here?"

"Because I thought at some point, you might agree to help me."

Safir threw her head back. "Fine. I'll answer a few questions, but then one of you is going to dance with me. Deal?" She pointed an accusing finger at each of them, and Ethan nodded. She plopped down in the chair between them and leaned over her knees. Her low position made her look like a little girl sitting at a grown-up's table. "What's that?"

Ethan barely registered what she was asking about before Safir ripped the ring from his fingers. He moved in a flash, grabbing her wrist and yanking the ring back from her. Efrat jumped up ready to defend Safir, but Ethan had already released her, leaving her somewhat cowering in her chair. Efrat glanced between them, and Ethan only met his gaze enough to assure him he was under control.

"I wasn't going to steal it," Safir objected.

"I'm sorry," Ethan mumbled. "It's just…" he trailed off, not explaining his reaction.

"Family heirloom? Must be valuable."

Ethan took a deep breath as he looked down at the ring pinched between his fingers. He gritted his teeth and shook his head. "No. It's worthless." He tossed the ring in with the keno cards like it was nothing but scrap metal to him. He felt a pang as he heard it hit—as if his heart could rip even deeper than it already had. He didn't want to give up the ring, but it was time for him to let go. To accept once and for all the fate he had chosen. To give up all hope of repairing what Cori had broken in him.

Efrat looked at him, his mouth wanting so badly to form some kind of objection, but it wasn't his place to decide Ethan's future. He had already had his life decided by other men; he was done being a victim of circumstance. From here on out, he would be the one driving his actions—not men, not women, and certainly not dragons.

Efrat sat back down, snatched his beer off the table, and swigged it. He brought it back down on the table with a smack—as if he still needed to get some demonstration of his irritation out.

Safir seemed to sense the tension but wisely didn't ask about it. She scooted up to the table and took a sip of her beer. "So, what does the great and powerful mage want to know?" she asked sardonically.

Ethan frowned at her. "Why don't you think I could be a mage?"

"Because you're not..." Safir twisted in her chair to face him. "Do you even know what a mage is?"

"I was told that mages are natural-born witches."

"Mmm." She stared at him as if deciding whether the judges would approve of that answer. She reached over and grabbed a napkin from the pile on the table. Instead of mopping up his spilled beer, she flattened it out and started searching for something. "I need a pen."

Efrat volunteered to find one and left to speak to the bartender. A moment later, he returned with a ballpoint pen shaped like a gator. Safir took it from him and drew a circle in the middle of her napkin.

"Let's go over the basics so we are all on the same page." She looked at each of them for agreement. Though Ethan was certain Efrat had little to no interest in magical edification, he nodded.

"First off, there is no such thing as magic."

Efrat glanced at Ethan before hiding his smile behind his beer. They both knew very well that magic existed. Both of them had experienced more magical energy than either preferred.

"When people speak of magic, they are referring to something that happens inexplicably without a known cause. But there is *always* a reason, and that reason is energy. Everything has energy, starting with—" Safir tapped the circle on her napkin. "—the Earth. It is the single most powerful tool freely available to witches like myself. How we access that power comes from a different energy."

Safir drew a bigger squiggly circle around the first circle. "Dark magic, also known as human magic. While most mammals possess a low-level energy that practically mirrors Earth's energy, humans have something else. We are special and can therefore wield other magical energies as tools. Witches, for the most part—" Safir drew a few little stick figures just inside her squiggly circle. "—operate just outside the boundaries of dark magic and as close to earth magic as they can sanely get. I mentioned Adeline earlier. Well, she's very powerful, but that just puts her into the blurry area of sanity."

"I thought dark magic was the one that made everyone insane," Ethan said.

"It will, but only if you try to hold on to too much at a time. Dark magic is natural to humans, but too much is like an overdose of medicine. A smart witch doesn't reach for outside dark magic but rather tries to access and enhance her own. However, earth magic is also problematic in high doses. It pulls you away from your base energy. Snaps the tethers to your human existence. You... forget that you are human."

Ethan shifted uncomfortably as the details of Adeline's existence formed a new picture in his mind. "So, what about a sorceress then? How is that achieved if it takes high doses of both?"

"Creating a sorceress is forbidden."

Ethan clenched his fists under the table. He was sick of hearing that phrase from everyone. "I know, but there has been sorcery in the past. Before that level of power was banned."

"Sorcery wasn't banned because it was too strong. It was abandoned because it was no longer possible to create a full-fledged sorcerer."

Ethan frowned at that explanation. "But—"

"I know that Annette tried to—on more than one occasion actually—but she was never successful. She always aimed farther than she could see."

"What about the wizards?" Efrat asked, no doubt trying to figure out where they landed on the spectrum. "I thought they were the baddest of the bad."

"They got an overdose of dark magic during their attempt to create a sorcerer," Ethan answered.

"A teaspoon of salt can flavor, Cher. A tablespoon can ruin." Safir summed up.

"Ogana repelled most of the dark magic," Ethan said. "But I think the years inside the bubble just naturally drove him to the edge."

"Why can't sorcerers be made anymore?" Efrat asked.

"A sorcerer is effectively a busbar between two very powerful energies. Earth—" Safir drew a dot on the Earth circle. "—and human magic." She plotted a dot on the dark magic squiggle and connected the two dots with a short line. "When everything is balanced, the energy flows freely between the two, giving the user access to the core energy of the Earth as well as the sum total of humanity's souls."

"And why can't somebody still do that—become a busbar?" Efrat asked.

"Because the energy is no longer balanced." Safir mimed a set of scales with her hands, illustrating the instability.

"The earth is too strong?" Efrat asked.

"No, humanity is. Humans are killing the Earth."

Efrat glanced at Ethan, searching him for further proof, but he didn't have any knowledge of this.

"You mean global warming, rainforest depletion, and cow farts?" Efrat probed the subject further.

"That's the scientific answer, but the truth is that the dark energy surrounding the Earth has become so powerful that it is overriding the world's natural immunity to us. We have become a parasite to the organism we are supposed to be living in symbiosis with."

"What are we supposed to do about that?" Efrat asked.

Safir shrugged. "I don't know, recycle. I'm only telling you why sorcerers can no longer be created."

"You're saying..." Ethan shifted forward and rubbed the bridge of his nose. "Even under the best of circumstances, if a ceremony was used to create a sorceress, it could never be successful."

"No, not since the 19th century."

Ethan shifted uncomfortably as his anger simmered. "And any magical being would know this. Even an extremely stupid one."

Safir glanced at Efrat, trying to understand his sudden mood change. Efrat certainly knew the story of Adrianna, but he didn't share it and pointedly looked away from her.

"Never bloody possible," Ethan said to himself. He was livid and, for the first time since he left the prison, he wanted to go back. He wanted to pick another fight with those fucking dragons and make them pay for using him. For lying to him and forcing him to do something that ultimately started the fuse of his self-destructive path.

"Are you—"

Ethan picked up his beer and guzzled it down as fast as he could. He could sense the discomfort at the table even as he drank. He brought the glass down hard against the table—too hard. The glass shattered. Safir jumped and shifted away from the table.

Ethan noticed blood pooling beneath his hand and lifted it to find a large shard stuck in the meat of his palm. Safir gasped and reached forward—no doubt to assist him with his glass sliver. Efrat cut off her reach, blocking with his arm. "I got it," he said and returned to the bar. There was some discussion with the bartender, resulting in a shocked and angry look from him, but eventually, Efrat returned with a clean towel.

He carefully removed the shard from Ethan's hand and pressed it to the wound. He peeked at the wound before instructing Ethan to put pressure on it. He reached into his back pocket and pulled out a twenty and tossed it on the table. "Come on, I'll take care of that outside."

"I'm not done drinking," Ethan said bitterly.

"Yeah, you are," Efrat said, leaving no room for demurral as he pushed Ethan away from the table. He picked up Safir's napkin and handed it to her. "Bring that. He's gonna have more questions." She nodded and led the way out of the bar.

"You okay?" Efrat asked when he caught up to him outside. He wasn't asking about his hand.

"They lied to me," Ethan said acerbically. "They all fucking lied to me."

Efrat gave him an empathetic look and squeezed his shoulder. "Welcome to my world."

13

ETHAN GRITTED HIS TEETH as Efrat seared the wound on his hand. He hadn't really felt the cut at first, but now he felt every bit of it. Yet another reminder that he needed to control his temper. He remembered a time in his youth when he had felt as unsettled as he did now. He wanted to be in control of his life, but he couldn't, and it made him lash out at everyone. His time at the prison had given him purpose and focus, but now that it was gone and his heart was in tatters, he couldn't keep that teenage boy away. The desire to punch the brick wall he was leaning against was almost irresistible.

"There." Efrat twisted his hand to check the cut. "The bleeding has stopped. Just don't flex it too much."

Ethan turned to Safir. "Where to next?" he asked, hoping against hope that his injury hadn't soured her mood for company.

She stared at him a moment before her eyes drifted to the concrete. "There's a bar just down the street. It's quiet, and the clientele are less apt to question our topic of conversation."

Safir once again led the way while Ethan and Efrat lagged behind. Ethan continued to scan the shadows of the alleys and streets. There were plenty of people to keep the bogeymen away, but that didn't mean they weren't being hunted.

"How much longer do you think we'll have—until they come for us?" Efrat asked. He was far from oblivious to Ethan's observant manner and, either by instinct or habit, the elemental had been mirroring his worry. Every time they stepped out into the night, they scanned the buildings around them, searching for spots that could conceal a hunchback man or two... or three.

"Not long," Ethan answered. "I'm actually surprised they haven't found us already."

"Must be difficult to track over an ocean."

"I'm not really sure how they travel," Ethan said. He had never really delved into the specifics of the collectors. Mostly because he didn't think it was necessary. He valued them as anyone might appreciate a device—so long as it worked, it didn't matter *how it* worked. Then again, now that he was in this situation, he wondered if his lack of knowledge was intentional. There were no books about the collectors, no manuals. He not only didn't know what they were, he didn't know where they came from, or who was in charge of releasing them. Danato had always handled it. And because of that, he didn't know if they had any weaknesses.

"Maybe we'll luck out and Danato won't send them."

Ethan snorted out a laugh. "Since when are you the optimistic one?"

"Since I'm not looking forward to getting my head bashed in by hellhounds."

Ethan nodded. "Well, maybe it won't have to come to that."

"What do you mean?" Efrat glanced at him.

Ethan shrugged. "Like you said, maybe Danato has offered us some leniency."

"Yeah, 'cause he's such a flexible guy," Efrat said with a mocking tone.

"Over here, you two!" Safir hollered to them from a basement stairwell they had almost just walked past. Neither of them had been paying attention enough to see where she had disappeared to.

They both paused and looked at the creepy stone descent. "Yeah, this doesn't look ominous at all." Efrat mumbled.

Ethan looked up and down the street, trying to decide if this was still a commercial district or if Safir was taking them to someone's house. A small sign hanging over the door to the establishment read "The Grave."

Ethan lumbered down the stairs and followed Safir through a door with its top corners clipped. It was meant to look like a coffin, but it just looked like the building designer had screwed up. The darkness within alarmed Ethan, but after a moment for his eyes to adjust, he could see the candlelit room ahead of them.

The harpsichord playing in the distance was his first hint that this place did not cater to tourists. If anything, it seemed to hide from them. Once he made it through the narrow hall to the main establishment, he saw why this was not a tourist destination.

Ethan tensed as pale faces looked up from their conversations to see who had just arrived. Years of interacting with photophobes had left him with more than a few prejudices against the species as a whole, but these were not the slobbering, clawing fiends he was familiar with. These were Hirudo vampires—one of very few non-violent vampiric species. Much like the leeches they were named after, the Hirudo would slowly suckle blood from their prey like a parasite. Ethan wasn't sure the distinction of non-violent made them any less dangerous, but for the most part, Hirudos did not seek to kill their prey.

Ethan noticed a young woman sitting on a plush red couch between two attractive male vampires. He eyed the two oval patches of blood on either side of her neck with disgust. He had never been a fan of the romanticized world of blood drinking. He couldn't claim any high status as a meat eater, but at least he didn't seduce his meal before digging his fork into it.

He heard a stuttered laugh followed by a groan and saw a young man on another sofa across the room. He was being feasted on by a small female Hirudo. Judging by the man's odd noises and the ever-changing expression on his face, he couldn't decide if the vampire's "kiss" tickled, hurt, or felt good. Since the Hirudo had serrated ridges instead of fangs, Ethan could only assume it was less painful than an outright bite, but he wouldn't volunteer to find out anytime soon.

Safir found a table near the bar, but away from the harpsichord, which now belted out a more modern song—proof that the instrument was meant to be left in the past. Ethan sat down at the round table, and Efrat followed, opting to sit across from him.

"Which descendant of Dracula owns this place?" Efrat asked.

Safir's eyes widened as the bartender arrived just in time to hear Efrat's dismissal of the establishment. He glanced at Efrat but said nothing. He laid out three napkins and three beers, which he popped the tops off of before returning to the bar.

"What, did you call ahead to order?" Efrat frowned as he picked up the bottle that had been placed before him. Ethan noted that none of the bottles matched. They were different brands and different brews.

"No need." Safir picked up her beer and took a small swig.

Ethan did the same and found that it was just the type of beer he would have ordered, had he known what to ask for.

Efrat took a drink, and his brow perked. "Oh, that's good."

"The Grave never fails to deliver."

"Psychic bartender?" Ethan asked.

Safir smiled at him but didn't answer. "This place is a little more aware of the real world. It's a pleasant respite from the act."

"The act?" Ethan asked.

"Mistress Safir at your service." She waved her hands emphatically before dropping them to the table. "It's a living, but some days it's just too demeaning. Not when I could show them real power." She said the last part to herself and almost as a threat—as if she had considered it a time or two already. Ethan already knew what the result of her flaunted power would be. He wasn't sure two to four years in jail was worth it just to prove herself to a few nuisance tourists.

"Tell me about death magic," Ethan asked when she didn't readily get back to her lesson.

She looked at him for a moment before digging around in her pocket for the illustrated napkin. She placed it on the table and found the pen she had confiscated behind her ear. She drew another circle around the Earth and the dark magic squiggly line. After that, she scribbled a jagged line around the whole image making it resemble a sun. Ethan frowned, not following her visual very well.

"This—" she pointed to the jagged outside circle. "—represents cosmic power. This—" She poked her pen into the drawing and turned to look at each of them before continuing. "—is the strongest source of power that we know of. It is the source of all life and therefore raw, unattainable, and untamable energy."

"Except by a genie," Ethan said somberly.

"That is a very rare exception. Back in the days when sorcerers were able to balance the power of the Earth, they used their power to lasso up pieces of the cosmos and tether them to the earth with the sum total of humanity's dark magic. It's a very complex process that involves a lot of sacrifices. The price of which would be far too expensive by today's measure of morality."

"Are you speaking metaphorically or literally?" Efrat asked.

Safir glanced at him but didn't address his question. "A genie is a manifestation of cosmic energy in the same way that dragons are a manifestation of the Earth's energy."

"I thought dragons..." Ethan paused, trying to figure out exactly what he wanted to ask. "Annette told me that if male and female dragons were brought together, they would effectively kill themselves to bear new offspring."

"They will. I don't really understand why, but that's just their life cycle."

"But you're making it sound like they originally came from the earth."

"Well, technically we all came from the Earth, and the Earth came from the universe, but yes, despite their origin, they will mate and reproduce just as all mammals do."

"Why bother if they will never increase in number?"

"They don't need to. The Earth requires the exact number of dragons that it has."

"Why does the Earth require dragons?"

"We don't know for certain, of course, but we suspect that they are observers or sentinels."

"Guardians of the Earth," Ethan murmured.

"Precisely."

Ethan considered asking her more about the dragons, namely, why they had communicated with him. But since she didn't believe he was a mage, he doubted she would believe another outlandish declaration from him. "Where does death magic come into play?"

Safir poked the circle between the represented cosmos power and dark magic. "Death magic lies between humanity's power and the cosmos. This is how the concept of heaven came into being. The belief that there is something that lies between us and the endless expanse of the universe's blank slate. Of course, there's no real proof of that. We know the power exists, but we can't access it while we are alive. So, in truth, death magic is more of a theory than an fact."

"But what about voodoo?" Efrat asked. "Aren't you a necromancer?"

"Voodoo and necromancy still fall into the category of standard witchcraft. I can summon the dead to communicate with them, but I can't access their power."

"No one living can use death magic?" Ethan asked.

"No."

"Never ever in history."

"No, only the dead can use death magic, and again, the only evidence I have that the power even exists is from my interactions with spirits. If I'm being completely honest, death magic is useless to a witch. It is much too weak when it's used on Earth. That's why we get flickering lights, doors shutting, and temperature drops. That is the full extent of what the dead can do in this realm. Death magic could well be the second most powerful energy source in the universe, but we will never see it because the dead operate on a different plane of existence. If any one of us were exposed to such a powerful form of magic, it would kill us—instantly."

Ethan exchanged a glance with Efrat, seeing if he was thinking the same thing he was. "How do you know that? I mean, this is all theoretical, right?"

"That's true, but think about it. A genie is just a fragment of the cosmos. A pinch of fabric was dragged down to the Earth by very powerful men. To keep them contained, genies are surrounded by so much dark magic that just touching one would drive a mortal man instantly insane. If you could somehow reach past the veil of that spell and touch the universe, it would surely destroy you. So, it is with no great leap of intelligence that death magic would do the same."

"But no man could ever wield death magic, right?" Efrat asked.

Safir looked between the two of them as if they were simpletons. "No, of course not. The very nature of the netherworld is to end life. It would be impossible for a mortal to possess that power. For a man to walk the earth and possess that power... He would have to be a god."

"Or a monster," Efrat mumbled.

Ethan glared at him, but Efrat just shrugged. There was no denying that Daniel's power was a frightening one, but he would never believe him to be a monster. He, much like others before him, was just trying to do something good with what was ultimately a horrific skill. But could it be—had Daniel been wielding death magic all along? If that were true, then why was he dead? How does a god die?

"What about Death?"

"What about it?"

"No, Death as in the angel of—the grim reaper. Could he be an example of a manifestation of death magic?"

"Not every fable and fairy tale are true."

Efrat scrunched his face up in feigned disappointment. "So, no unicorns?"

"What about mage magic?" Ethan interrupted before Safir could offer a sarcastic retort. "Where would that land on this diagram?"

"A mage isn't a classification of magic. They are considered to be manifestations, like dragons and genies. They are just as rare too. The chance of you being a mage is like—"

"Show me," Ethan snapped, pushing her napkin closer to her.

She gave him a disappointed frown before drawing a line through all four circles. She turned the napkin for him to see. He glanced at her, waiting for the explanation, but he could see she was going to be stubborn—to remind him that this information was being given freely... for the time being.

"Are you saying that a mage possesses all four magics?"

Safir frowned and looked at her drawing. "Well, no, I just can't erase pen. Death magic would still be inaccessible to a mage, and to be clear, a mage cannot possess the magic as a sorcerer would; he can only wield it."

"So, a mage is a witch that can wield three of the four magical energies."

Safir's face crumpled again, and she looked at her drawing. "Oh, sorry." As a pièce de résistance to her ornate napkin diagram, she added an infinity sign across the entire drawing. "Chrono-magic. The power of time."

"A mage can affect time?" Ethan asked.

"No, I just forgot to add the fifth magical energy."

"Who gets to play with time magic?" Efrat asked.

"A genie, of course, possibly dragons—that's still up for debate—and..." Safir's face blanked. "The fae."

"Fairies can manipulate time?"

Safir bit her lip. "Not all the time—at least we don't think so. The fae stay hidden almost all the time, so we don't really understand them. They might be a manifestation of time magic like the dragons, or they might just be an entity that uses time magic to hide themselves."

"How powerful are they?"

"I've never even seen a fae, and those that do, usually don't remember it well. The magic they use is weak here, but it makes no difference. So long as they have the power to subdue any threat against them, they are still stronger—albeit benignly."

"What?" Efrat frowned.

"They can't be affected by magic in this realm because they are not technically here. I don't really understand it either. Studying the fae is a waste of time because none of us will ever interact with one. At least not while we're still sane."

"So, getting back to mages," Ethan said. "You were saying that a mage is a witch that can wield three of the five energies."

"No—I mean, yes, but a mage is not a witch." Safir groaned and flipped over the napkin and drew a stick figure. "A mage is effectively a manifestation of dark magic."

"You keep saying manifestation, but what does that mean? Are you saying that a mage isn't real?"

"Real is very difficult to define."

"A genie is created, a dragon is birthed, is a mage birthed or created."

Safir bit her lip. "That's not a fair assessment because genies are a false creation. There is not meant to be a manifestation of the universe."

"Oh, for the love a Christ, woman," Efrat complained. "Is a mage a human being or not?"

"Yes! But a mage is also an aggregate of magic, so that is why we would call them a manifestation. A natural pooling of dark magic."

"Wouldn't that make them insane?" Efrat asked.

"No, because they don't possess it; they are just connected to it. Will you guys pay attention!"

"Trying to, kitten," Efrat grumbled.

"Okay, remember how I said if a witch gets too deep into earth magic, they become sort of feral."

"Yes." Ethan nodded.

Safir drew an arch through her stick figure and then one above and below, making it look like it was standing on the center line of a rainbow. "Imagine a witch that was so grounded in human magic that she could reach down and scoop up a handful of earth power—" Safir drew an arrow from her stick man down to the lowest arch. "—while simultaneously reaching up into the cosmos for a tiny sliver of its power." Safir drew an arrow up from her stick figure. "She would be the most powerful witch in existence, but be completely sane—and arguably almost as strong as a sorceress."

"A witch grounded so deep in dark magic must be difficult to recognize since they would just come across as human," Ethan said.

"Yeah." Safir scoffed as if that were an understatement. "In fact, you could be sitting right across from a mage and not even know it."

Safir smiled introspectively, but then her amusement dimmed. She looked up at Ethan, something curious now showing in her gaze. Her eyes once again skirted him, searching him for evidence. Her mouth gaped slightly, and she shook her head. "Why do you think you are a mage?" she whispered.

Ethan opened his mouth to speak. What remained of his denial lifted like a veil. The stitched rift between the truth and his ambiguous explanations had finally healed, leaving his mind free to think and feel as he pleased. "Because the dragons told me."

14

"**H**EY, KID," A VOICE called to Cori from one of the transmorph cells.

Rather than the usual entourage of tormenting faces, Cori found Belus staring back at her from behind the bars. His hands were looped through the cage as if he were merely leaning on a counter instead of standing in captivity. It reminded her of how Mezula behaved in her confinement—as if the world around her was meaningless.

It might have been the same transmorph that had been impersonating him during her new arrival tour, but he was in a different cell now. There had been quite a bit of shuffling in the transmorph sections since Efrat had freed up space—care of his impromptu executions.

"Belus again, huh?" Cori scoffed. "That's a rare choice."

"It is," he admitted. "Transmorphs prefer to torment you with your lovers—or people that you've killed."

"I guess you qualify then, don't you?" Cori raised her hand into a pretend gun and clicked her tongue as if firing it, before walking on.

"I'm sorry I wasn't there for you."

Cori stopped and hugged her clipboard to her chest. "There for me?" she asked, even though she knew she shouldn't engage.

"I heard about your son. I heard what you had to do."

Cori nodded, examining the subdued emotions on the transmorph carefully. It didn't impress her that he knew about the death of her son. News traveled just as fast through the prisoner population as through the guards. However, the news of his revival had been intentionally slowed, due to their initial concerns about the genie. The fact that she could remember his name outside the bubble gave her hope, but she still wasn't ready to bring him out yet. Regardless of the genie, her son was far safer in the bubble than in this prison.

"Nothing a little voodoo can't help," she said flippantly.

"Voodoo?" His brow furrowed in thought and then his mouth dropped open with realization. A slight smirk touched his lips. "You remembered." He thumped his fist against the bars. "He's okay then?" he asked as if he needed to know for sure.

She knew she shouldn't play this game. She shouldn't reveal too much, but she was rarely a mystery to these creatures. "Oliver is fine."

Belus's eyes bloomed, and he took in a breath. "I remember that. You had asked me about his name. You wanted to know if Danato would approve."

Cori blinked at the transmorph. She also remembered that conversation. It was a private one, between her and Belus. She had never told Ethan about it, and she could only assume Belus hadn't either.

Seeing that the amusement of this game was waning, she turned to leave again.

"Cori, you remember that I'm immune to psychic infiltration, right?"

"Yes, I remember," Cori said. "Lucky dog. Half the prisoners in this place know what color my underwear is before I even put it on in the morning."

The Belus transmorph ignored her joke and continued. "So, you know that it would be difficult for a transmorph to impersonate me." He locked eyes with her and didn't relent until she acknowledged what he was saying.

Cori smiled and crossed her arms. "Oh, I don't know; you're doing pretty well, actually. You've got the tone just right."

"What tone is that?" he asked.

"The tone that says, I have a secret and I'm eventually going to tell you, but not just yet."

"Mmm, I see. Do you think if I were behind these bars for real and there was an impostor out there pretending to be me, you would be able to tell the difference?"

Cori shrugged. "It might take some observation, but yes. I think I would be able to tell the difference."

"Then you better start watching," the Belus transmorph said humorlessly.

Cori stared at him for a moment before glancing down at the cells she had just passed. Every cell now contained a carbon copy of Belus, each with a look of disapproval. She had never been good at this game, but playing or not playing was rarely an option for her.

She brought her attention back to her current Belus impersonator and walked over to his cell. She placed her toes on the very edge of the yellow line. He looked down, noting the proximity as well. "And what exactly will I be watching for?"

"They know you by heart. They know how I make you feel." Cori narrowed her eyes at him, questioning the phrasing of his statement. "They know how frequently I don't live up to your expectations. The transmorph will use that to his advantage."

"I'll bite. How?"

"There is a fine line between advising and lecturing. And an even finer line between cautioning you and chastising you. I've struggled with it for years, but he'll screw it up entirely. He thinks he understands me because he sees me through other's eyes, but he's wrong. He'll do whatever he can to damage the relationship we've cultivated over the years. Lash out at you unnecessarily or pick a fight with you when he should just let it go."

"Sounds like a Tuesday for us," Cori mocked.

"No," he said defiantly. "This will be different. He'll say or do something hurtful. Something... inappropriate or unforgivable, and he won't apologize for it."

Cori resisted the urge to remind him that Belus rarely apologized for his actions, even when he was wrong. "Why? Why bother? Belus is already an enigma. A few odd behaviors could go unnoticed for weeks, maybe months."

"Obviously," he said sternly, motioning to his containment. "But he's not trying to hide from you. He's trying to break you."

"Break me?"

"Break us. They know that you trust me. They want us to be divided. To keep the truth quiet as long as possible."

"Why?"

"So, they can finish what they started. They are waging a war against us, Cori, and it started with Daniel McGrath."

Cori clenched her jaw, not wanting to think about Daniel lying dead in his own blood, but it was indelibly branded on her memory—as it was on everyone's. "So, tell me, if you really were Belus. How would you prove to me it was you?"

"I would advise you to search your memories and use the education you already possess to suss out the real Belus."

"I think I can do that." Cori held two fingers up to her forehead and dramatically scrunched her face in concentrated thought. "Oh, I've got something. Yes,

yes, here it is. Page one in the prison manual." Cori dropped her theatrics and stared at Belus. "Don't trust the transmorphs!"

Cori scoffed at his disappointed face and walked away. "Forget the manual."

Cori stopped in her tracks and wheeled around. "Oh, sorry, Charlie, you just gave yourself away. Belus would never tell me to go off the book." The transmorph cleared his throat, stepped away from the bars, and paced the short length of his cell. "Belus taught me well, and he taught me not to believe a word that comes out of the mouth of a transmorph. He would be very disappointed in me if I made an exception just because one of them was wearing his face."

He stopped and looked over at her. There was a small smile perched on his lips. "You're right, I would be disappointed. Unless, of course, you had a very good reason to trust me."

Cori watched him, watching her. The intensity in his eyes was alarming, like he was testing her. Even now, knowing she was winning by not falling for his bait, she felt like she was losing. Even as a transmorph, Belus was difficult to please.

She raised an accusing finger at him. "You're good; I'll give you that." She walked away, but this time she didn't stop when he called to her.

"Cori! Remember what you already know. He doesn't know what I know. He knows only what others know about me. Look for the clues in what you and I have shared and no one else. Don't let him fool you!" She reached the section break and froze with her hand on the door. She almost turned around to question him further, but then she glanced over at the wall where the faded words Doth Seola still stained the white paint.

He was right about one thing. This was no longer a game. This was a war. And she would not fraternize with the enemy, no matter who they looked like.

15

HEATON RANG THE DOORBELL of the third address in Sophie's little black book. They had been traveling for over a week, hopping from state to state in the hopes of either catching word of Nevia or finding evidence of transmorphs. So far, all they had accomplished was frightening two innocent families who claimed no knowledge of their home's former residents.

Though he had no wish to play the part of the bad guy, Heaton was well aware of what he had looked like sitting in the living room of a middle-class family with two bodyguards at his side. He might as well have been a member of the mafia to them. There was enough fear pouring off them that Callin hadn't needed to be more aggressive, but Heaton was wondering if he shouldn't have pushed a little harder. He could have gotten the name of the real estate agent who sold them the house. He could have questioned them for the previous resident's information.

He rang the doorbell several times, outright demanding the resident come to the door.

"Heaton," Callin said quietly behind him. "There's someone inside."

Heaton looked back at the glint in Callin's eye. He was pushing air through his mouth like a cat, tasting the smell. When he was done, his gaze twitched to Heaton, and opened his mouth to speak.

"He's dead," Mace interrupted from his vantage point in the flower bed, staring through the front window. They both looked over at him, and he shrugged. "No reason to smell what your eyes can see plain as day."

Heaton ignored the growl from Callin as he kicked open the front door to the house.

"You may not want to..." Mace trailed off as Heaton marched inside, unafraid of whatever crime scene he was about to witness.

But he was wrong.

The smell of putrefaction was so intense Heaton wondered how he hadn't smelled it coming up to the house. There should have been vultures taking residence on the roof by now. However, based on what he saw inside, he could have assumed scavengers had already arrived.

Heaton stopped in the entryway leading into the front room of the house and stared at the body splayed on the oval coffee table. He knew what he was looking at. He understood it completely, and yet his mind continued to circle, asking all the questions that civilized people must ask when presented with such morbid displays. Why? How? Who?

All three were answered with a single name.

"Christ almighty," Callin rasped as he stepped up behind Heaton. "This is worse than what she did to the hybrid."

"Wait, this was Jordan?" Mace moved deeper into the room, unfazed by the nearly dissected body on the display. "How the fuck..." He trailed off as he looked up at the sprays of blood on the ceiling. It covered the room, but it was always startling to see it on the ceiling. The power of the fearful heart.

Mace leaned in and examined the corpse. He reached down into it, and Heaton groaned. "Mace," he grumbled.

"Relax," he said. "He's no different from a slaughterhouse pig now." He pulled something out of the body cavity to examine it. "We ain't no better than our dinner when we're dead." Mace narrowed his eyes at the object and then moved to examine the man's mouth. He probed the orifice with his finger, tugging the cheeks this way and that.

"What the fuck are you doing, Mace?" Heaton asked.

Satisfied with his examination, he turned to Heaton and held up a small white object. "Your girl lost a tooth."

Heaton took it from him. He examined it carefully, noting that it was not simply a broken tooth, but rather a fully intact root and crown. He turned to Callin. "What does that mean?"

Callin shook his head. "She's not a full werewolf."

"What would it mean if she were?"

Callin didn't answer.

"Werewolves are polyphydonts like gators," Mace answered for him. "During their change, teeth can get damaged, so they have replacements." There seemed to be a consensus of surprise at Mace's knowledge, but Heaton ignored this.

"Does that mean she's changing?"

"No." Callin shook his head.

"Are you sure?"

"It's impossible. A true change would rip her to shreds."

"What do you mean true change? Is there another kind?"

"You have to understand human hormones—"

"Fuck the science lesson, Callin!" Heaton pushed up into his space. "Is Nevia changing?"

Callin's eyes flickered over him, with the same glint in his eyes as on the doorstep. "Honestly," he whispered and leaned in close enough for his breath to hit his face. "I have no bloody clue. She's an aberration on a good day. Who knows what the fuck she is now that she's gone feral."

"She's not feral!" Heaton insisted, though everything was pointing to that.

Callin smiled broadly. "We need to go."

Heaton frowned at his sudden shift to amusement. He glanced out the window to see if anyone was pulling into the drive. "What is it?"

"I'm getting thirsty." Callin took a deep breath and moved away from Heaton. "As much control as I have over the average wolf..." He looked at the body on the coffee table. "That body is starting to look appetizing," he grumbled as if embarrassed to admit that his animal instincts surmounted his base understanding of rotting food.

"That's disgusting," Mace said.

"Says the man with viscera on his fingers," Callin snapped.

Heaton checked the time and realized they were getting dangerously close to Callin's required check-in time. Unfortunately, being so far from home meant that he would need to use a local, aka, unauthorized caging facility. Something that none of them were looking forward to.

"Come on." Heaton slapped his shoulder and led the way out. He climbed into the driver's seat of the rental car, with Mace in the passenger seat and Callin in the back. Before he could start the engine, Callin was sucking down the water from a gallon jug. They had bought a case in anticipation of this event, but judging by how quickly the water was going down Callin's throat, there was a chance they hadn't bought enough.

"How far away is this facility?" Mace asked.

"About an hour," Heaton said. Callin smashed the plastic jug and grabbed another.

"Maybe you better drive fast," Mace suggested.

"That's the only way I know how to drive." Heaton backed out of the drive and sped off toward their destination. As worrying as the werewolf in his backseat was, he was more concerned about that goddamn tooth.

He knew the analysis of hormones and the complexities of the werewolf drives, but he also understood that Nevia was special. She was far stronger than people gave her credit for. As evident from the body, they had just left behind.

"Wait," Heaton nearly slammed on the brakes as his thoughts came to a halting stop. "Callin, you said that what we saw in there was worse than what she did to the hybrid."

"Didn't you think so?" Callin said before letting out a cavernous burp.

Heaton glanced in the mirror as he debated asking what he hadn't thought to until now. "You meant that she did worse to this hybrid, right?"

Callin paused the jug of water at his lips and frowned at Heaton's reflection. "I'm sorry, mate." He shook his head. "That man wasn't a hybrid. He was human."

16

As Cori passed through the aquarium section to check on the state of the water breathers, she found their most recent acquisition, a mermaid, happily circling her tank and nibbling on a fresh tuna. That was certainly almost as tasty as seal. Rather than linger and aggravate the female's meal, she headed over to the Kraken.

Though the creature was mostly harmless, he had taken a liking to playing in the bubbles of boat motors. With ample sightings of the "sea monster," the *powers that be* decided to take him out of the wild. Much like their resident monkey, he was only here to ensure he didn't accidentally harm others.

She snagged a piece of fish kibble from a nearby bin and tossed the baseball-sized blob into his tank. The animal squealed and clicked as he swallowed the treat whole. One of his long tentacles reached out of the tank and tapped the top of her head. At first, she thought he was just exploring the strange blob outside his tank, but then he began petting her. Apart from the odd sensation of wet kisses on her forehead from his suckers and mussing her hair, she appreciated the gesture.

"You're welcome, buddy." She reached up and tapped his tentacle before drawing away. He retracted his gratitude and squealed loudly as he continued to knead the edge of the tank in a self-soothing way.

Cori moved to the wall behind the aquarium and grabbed a towel to wipe the moisture off her face and hair. She noticed an empty tank nearby and moved to inspect it. It wasn't unusual for the tanks and cages on this level to be empty. Most of their residents had short lifespans—especially in captivity—but there was something particularly familiar about this tank. Cori remembered she had demanded that they outfit it with an aerator. It was technically at Danato's command, but regardless it was completed to the satisfaction of the inmate. A debt paid for her service battling the elementals during their most successful escape attempt.

Cori grabbed the roster. The last entry listed the occupant as "found deceased." First Onna and now Erin. Cori wasn't especially close to the cephalopod, but considering she was on a first-name basis with her, she felt something for the woman's loss. Apart from the grief at losing yet another familiar face, she was feeling suspicious. Onna's sudden suicide had never made any sense to her, and now Erin's abrupt death was concerning. Had she too committed suicide? If so, how?

Cori found herself right back in the infirmary seeking the autopsy records for Erin. The nurse didn't question her and seemed almost eager to have something to do.

While waiting at the front desk, the doctor arrived from the back hall with a nurse on his tail. Cori made it a point to turn away since she preferred not to converse with him. She had never been on the best of terms with the medical staff, but she was on this man's shit list. No doubt because she had frozen off a man's genitals. She regarded him with the same disdain, since he didn't think a forced penectomy was an appropriate sentence for rape. Granted, she was certainly biased on the subject. But she was also the only one between them who had first-hand knowledge of the trauma incurred by such events.

"I don't care what he says!" the doctor yelled at the nurse. "I need those parts!"

"I've put the requisition in three times," the nurse firmly stated.

"Then put it in again. I can't run this place properly without my fucking MRI machine." The doctor stormed into an operatory and slammed the door.

"Sure, no problem," the nurse mumbled. "I love pissing off Danato." As she walked back down the hall, she passed by the older nurse returning with Cori's records.

"Okay," she said as she arrived, opening the folder. She clicked her tongue and shook her head. "I'm sorry, dear. They didn't perform an autopsy on that inmate."

Cori frowned. "But that's protocol."

The nurse looked up at her with a worried expression. "Yes, that is protocol," she said, readily agreeing with Cori.

"So, who signed off on the cremation without an autopsy?" Cori asked, prepared to berate anyone who had a history of sticking her with needles.

Rather than answer, the nurse slid the document onto the counter and pointed to the signature line that granted the cremation. Cori's ire slipped down into her stomach where it soured into an ache. The heavy-handed R and B were about the only parts of the signature she could recognize, but that was enough to give her the information she needed.

Cori looked at the nurse, and they both seemed to sense the futility of this conversation. Neither of them had any authority to question Belus or his motives for skipping the autopsy, except perhaps Danato.

She was about to leave when another thought occurred to her. She turned back and rested her hands gently on the counter. "Can you get me another file?"

The nurse's face flickered with more worry, but she nodded and smiled pleasantly. "Certainly, dear."

17

"**U**GH! WHAT'S THAT SMELL?" Heaton shifted away from the entrance of the so-called wolf sanctuary. He was surprised such a high-risk facility was sitting in the middle of a metropolitan city, but sometimes in plain sight was the best policy with places like this.

"Desperation," Mace mused as he looked around and paused his gaze on a scantily dressed woman smoking on the other side of the street. Clearly a prostitute, she waved at them and asked if they wanted to have some fun. When none of them responded, she slid her tank top up, revealing her naked breasts. She caressed them candidly.

Mace, surprisingly, looked away, disgusted by the display. Though Heaton was certain that he was heterosexual, he had never been able to get a bead on what his preferences were. Well, beyond any inferiority complex, Mace seemed to hate women purely on principle. Daniel had once joked that the only woman Mace would be comfortable screwing was a dead one. As time went on, it was less and less of a joke and more and more of a concern.

"I like fun," Callin purred as his eyes locked onto the woman.

"Easy, Cal." Heaton shifted into the man's path, but his eyes did not waver. "Come on, man. We're not even at the 24-hour mark. You have more control than this."

"I am in control." Callin's predatory eyes shifted to Heaton. "I am always in control." He grabbed Heaton by the neck and with little to no effort lifted him off the ground.

Despite the pressure in his head and his dangling spine cracking, Heaton resisted the urge to retaliate. Fighting Callin this close to a full moon would only ensure his death.

"Oh, shit," Mace mumbled. "Don't run, you fuckin' idiot."

Heaton couldn't see what was happening, but the shriek that tore Callin's attention away from him told him enough. His back hit the pavement after Callin tossed him away. Mace lunged after the werewolf as he darted toward the fleeing woman.

Heaton agilely flipped himself back up onto his feet and joined the pursuit. Mace's initial attack had missed, and Callin was gaining more distance. Fortunately, Heaton was faster than most men—including werewolves. He caught up with Callin and, with virtually no other options available to him, jumped on his back.

Callin wheeled around, trying to fling him off, but Heaton grabbed on tight. "Callin, for fuck's sake, calm down!"

Mace arrived shortly after and knocked Callin's legs out from under him. Callin swiped at him, grabbing his leg and yanking him down to the ground with him. He tried to get on top of him, but Mace kicked him in the face. Callin's head snapped back, hitting Heaton in the jaw. He jumped off Callin as Mace's second kick came barreling toward them.

For a while longer, all three of them scrambled on the ground trying to get the better of each other. Though Callin was stronger than both of them, he seemed unfocused.

"Hey!" a voice bellowed over to them.

They all looked up and saw three men standing at the door of the sanctuary. The largest of the three stepped forward. His head was shaved and tattoos peeked from beneath the short sleeves of his t-shirt. "Are you going to come inside or just wait to change in the street?"

Callin's gaze locked onto the man and for a moment just stared at him. The muscular man did likewise. "How old are you?" Callin didn't answer. "You better not be breaking, boy. I don't do disposal services."

Callin brought himself back to his feet and dusted off his clothes. "I'm not breaking. And don't call me boy."

"I'll call you whatever the fuck you want *after* I get paid," the man said fearlessly. "Now get your asses in here before the locals call the cops. Bribes come out of your pocket." The man headed inside, leaving his two guards to hold the door for them.

Mace offered Heaton a hand up as Callin headed inside. He took it and dusted himself off before moving to the door. He glanced around the neighborhood, which was on the poorer side. Part industrial, part residential, the tall brick buildings blotted out what was remaining of the setting sun's light. As much as Heaton had considered this an odd location for a secret facility, he wondered if it wasn't perfect. No one had come running for a screaming woman or the three men brawling in the streets. There weren't likely to be any concern for the howls of pain coming from this building either.

The smell was worse inside the facility. A mixture of bodily fluids combined with wet dog and burned hair. Heaton had never really considered how much fur had to be burned after a werewolf returned to his normal, mostly hairless body. Despite repeat customers, Danato's prison never smelled anything like this place. It was no surprise since he was such a fastidious man, but it was also a much larger building.

Between Heaton's group and the three men who invited them in, the front office was at maximum capacity. There was a small receptionist desk taking up the remainder of the space, but no one was there to greet them.

"Names Grady," the leader said to them but offered no hand to shake. Before any of them could offer their names, he continued. "I'll be your caretaker for the next..." He checked his watch. "56 hours. You will be provided with the basic necessities for your change and nothing more. This facility is not part of the unnamed prison and has no connection to any of the North American werewolf factions. As such, you will be expected to pay a fee for your stay and accept the risks incumbent to your transformation as it pertains to this establishment."

Grady held out his hand to Callin. The werewolf slowly reached into his back pocket and pulled out his wallet. He pulled out a solid black credit card with no number or name on it. Heaton was familiar with it since he used something similar for work-related expenses. He tried to hand it to Grady, but the man dropped his hand.

"I told you, Wolf, we aren't part of that network. You want containment, you pay cash." Callin rolled his eyes and pulled cash from his wallet sleeve. Grady's brow wrinkled as he looked at the 50-pound notes. "I don't take Monopoly money either."

"It's worth more than your American dollars," Callin defended.

"I don't do banks, dipshit."

"For fuck's sake," Mace pulled his wallet out. "How much?"

"How much you got?" Grady salivated over the green bulging from his overstuffed wallet.

"I got stripper money. You want me to stuff it down your thong?" Mace pulled a pinch of bills from his wallet and handed it to him. Grady counted it and looked back at the wallet. Mace pulled a wrinkled one-dollar bill out and waved it at him. "I wasn't kidding."

"Good enough. Sign this release form on the desk." Callin moved to the desk and signed the form attached to a clipboard. "Welcome to the Shangrila. This way."

Grady guided them through two swinging doors at the back of the room. The smell of wet dogs worsened as they entered a large concrete space with open shower stalls and multiple drains on a concave floor.

"Strip and wash off with the orange soap." Grady pointed to one of the shower stalls.

Callin didn't move. He just stared at the room with the sneer of a man who had never been exposed to a true prison lifestyle.

"What's with the shower?" Heaton asked.

"Procedure."

Heaton wanted to argue that this facility was what needed to be disinfected, but he wasn't in a position to argue with the man if he wanted to keep Callin safe during his change.

Callin looked around the room. "I don't suppose you have shower shoes available?"

Grady snorted. "Nope."

Reluctantly, Callin began removing his shirt. He folded it in half and looked for a hanger to place it on. "Would you mind...?" he asked Heaton. Understanding his displeasure at seeing his clothing touch the floor of this place, Heaton offered his arm for Callin to loop his clothing over.

As he removed his pants, Heaton did his best to keep his eyes to himself. He had enjoyed the view the first time, but it was sullied by suspicion. Callin smirked at him as he looped his pants over his arm. "This is the second time in so many days that you've gotten me naked. People will be talking."

Heaton tensed his jaw, refusing to indulge in Callin's flirtation. The full moon was not far off, and he understood more than ever before that the cravings of a werewolf could become very tangled at this stage. The sultry gaze that Callin was giving him was more likely a sinister one.

Callin headed into the shower stall and turned on the water. Before beginning to wash himself, he turned his head into the stream and drank as much water as he could.

Callin's naked and wet body was enough to make Heaton embarrass himself, so he turned his attention to examining the room. The walls were built after the warehouse, so they didn't go directly to the ceiling. Somewhere beyond the walls was the sound of barking dogs. Heaton questioned why anyone would bring dogs into a werewolf facility. Despite a presumed common ancestor, he had yet to meet a dog that didn't go nuts at the smell of a werewolf.

"This place is janky as fuck," Mace murmured beside him.

Heaton grunted in agreement.

"This way," Grady announced once Callin was out of the shower.

The werewolf was not offered a towel, nor did he ask for one. Paying no mind to his nudity, he shamelessly followed Grady into the next room, which turned out to be a hallway. They maneuvered through the small passageways, turning multiple times, before entering a space not unlike Danato's prison. There were several small cages that fed into larger ones. Heaton didn't have to know that the reinforced bars were strong enough to hold werewolves. No one with half a brain would start a facility like this if they hadn't at least invested in proper containment.

"Your room, sir," Grady said mockingly as he motioned to Callin's human cage.

The werewolf entered voluntarily, and Grady closed the door.

"I'll be back to herd you in about twenty." Grady checked his watch again. "I'll show you two out." Grady moved toward the entrance, but Heaton and Mace didn't move.

"Actually, we're going to stick around," Heaton said.

Grady stopped and slowly turned back. "The hell you are; this isn't a hotel."

Heaton shrugged. "It's not a prison either."

Grady looked at either side of the room. "I can see how the bars confused you." He moved back to Heaton. "Let me put this another way. Get the fuck out of this facility. You can come back to pick up your friend in 56 hours."

"Or we can wait right here and monitor his treatment."

"Listen, Brit—"

"No, you listen. You've got an unauthorized facility that houses werewolves in the middle of a civilian population. As grateful as we are for your hospitality, you and I both know that it only takes one phone call and the Council of the Moon will not only shut you down, but they'll put you down."

Grady snorted. "Council of the Moon doesn't give a shit about us."

"Then you haven't met the new leader. She's very interested in protecting all her constituents. I'd be happy to tell her that you're mistreating the father of her son."

Grady's eyes widened, and his jaw rolled. He examined Heaton, no doubt searching for signs of deceit. Even if Heaton was exaggerating Leona's interest in American affairs, Callin was certainly valuable to her, and he was certain that she would kill anyone who hurt him.

Grady looked at Mace, who was standing stoically by his side, arms crossed. He wasn't as intimidating as he thought he was, but Heaton still appreciated the united front. "Fine, but you stay in here. And don't expect special treatment. There are no beds, there's no food, and you piss in the grates like the wolves do." As sullen as he was pissed off, Grady stormed out of the room like a snarky teen.

"Thank you," Callin said.

Heaton moved to the cage and offered him his clothes. Callin waved them away. "By the time I start to change, I won't have the competency to take them off. Better to leave them off so I have something to wear out of here."

Heaton stacked the clothing nicely on the floor outside the cell and started pacing the room. It was going to be a long night, especially once Callin started to change. He had not witnessed many changes, certainly not the entire change. He was not looking forward to watching his friend endure the agony of the transformation.

18

"WHAT'S THE PROBLEM?" DANATO asked as he perused the documentation Cori had borrowed from the infirmary. He didn't immediately see what she was so concerned about.

"There was no autopsy performed."

Danato's brow creased and he flipped through several pages of notes looking for the missing documentation. He let out a curious, "hmm" before sitting back in his chair. "That's... unusual."

"Unusual? It's completely against protocol and Belus is the king of following the rules."

Danato looked at her, his eyes crinkling as they narrowed on her. "Wait, are you upset about the lack of documentation or Belus's actions."

"Both." Cori shrugged not seeing a difference. "Onna and Erin have no explanation of death listed. I just don't understand why he skipped autopsies on two inmates."

Danato folded his hands over his chest and thought for a moment. "Why don't we just ask him about it?" He turned his head to the door just as Belus entered the office. "Belus, just the man we need."

"That's never good when someone needs me." He closed the door behind him and moved to the desk. "What's the problem?"

"Did you sign off on these cremations?" Danato handed the paperwork to him.

Belus glanced between the two files briefly. "That would be my signature." He looked up and noted the concern and suspicion being passed between Cori and Danato. "Is there a problem?"

"Why no autopsies?" Cori asked.

Belus turned his attention to her. "I deemed it unnecessary."

"Why?" Cori asked.

It was apparently a loaded question because Belus's stony expression turned even colder. "Since when do you take an interest in the medical care of our inmates? Don't you have enough to keep you occupied?"

Cori's mouth gaped and she started to rise from her seat. Since she was usually the one being accused of behaving childishly, she was more than happy to turn the accusation on Belus.

Danato cleared his throat and leaned forward quickly. He raised his hand to her but turned his attention to Belus. "I think what we are asking, is why you chose to deviate from protocol."

"Deviate?" Belus looked legitimately confused now. "I'm following protocol. Don't you remember the memo from the board? Just after the first of the year, they requested a reduction in all unnecessary medical procedures. I've adjusted the testing periods as much as I thought possible without being negligent. The autopsies didn't seem necessary to me so I canceled them. Onna was clearly asphyxiated in the ice and Erin was ill. She was becoming increasingly more anemic. The staff tried iron supplements and transfusions, but nothing helped. It's all in the logs."

Danato flipped through the paperwork and then read a few lines before raising a perturbed gaze to Cori. She had not noticed that on her initial scans of the paperwork—probably because the scribbled handwriting of the medical staff was nearly impossible to read. She had been so focused on the missing pages, that she didn't try to determine a less mysterious cause of death. "I see." Danato's words were primed for a lecture to come. "I guess that explains everything." He slapped the file folder shut. "Sorry, Belus, I completely forgot about that memo. Thank you for taking care of that." Danato darted his eyes toward Belus and Cori cleared her throat.

"Yeah, sorry about that."

Belus looked between them, searching for a better explanation for their odd behavior. He started to leave but paused next to her. He leaned in slightly to speak to her. "Why did you think I was signing off on the cremations?"

Cori let out an embarrassed chuckle and shook her head. "It was nothing. I think I'm just overly tired."

"Tired," Belus said the word almost as she did. "I've noticed that you have a history of being tired when you're hiding something very important." Belus rested his hand over hers, which was gripping the chair arm. It was a sweet gesture, but it nearly made her jump since Belus rarely touched her. "If you're so tired, then maybe you should cut back on your time in the bubble."

"What?" Cori wasn't so much asking as she was expressing her shock. Belus knew that she couldn't do that.

"Belus," Danato objected on her behalf.

"We don't know what the long-term effects of living in the bubble could do to her, Danato. Look what happened to the wizards."

"That was the dark magic," Cori said.

"We assumed as much, but regardless the bubble isn't exactly a natural environment for humans."

Cori looked at Danato who gave her a slight head shake, reassuring her that he wouldn't prevent her from spending time inside the bubble. She looked at Belus and tamed the emotions that were peeling off her. "I was upset that another prisoner I was personally associated with had died. I thought I was seeing a pattern and then the paperwork was missing. I thought someone was trying to hide something from me. Your name came up and I just latched onto the mystery I wanted to solve."

"And what if Danato's name were on the paperwork?"

"I would have asked him about it," Cori answered immediately.

"Right." Contention seeped into his voice. "So, when *his* name is on the paperwork you ask him about it, but when mine is on it, you still ask him."

Cori hadn't even seen the trap being laid. She had eagerly jumped into it thinking that she was helping her case. She opened her mouth to defend herself on points of proximity and timing, but she stopped herself. There had been a lot of tension between her and Belus since the day her son had died. Partly because he hadn't supported her decision to sacrifice him under her own terms, but also because he had cut her deeply with his accusations.

Not that he was wrong. She was selfish. She had acted rashly to keep control of the situation, but Cori had always made it clear that mother trumped warden. If anyone was surprised by how far she would go to protect the ones she loved, they weren't paying attention.

The time inside the bubble had served to heal her wounds, but her heart was scarred now. In a way that even the traumas of her past life couldn't compete with. She now looked at the world around her differently—not with indifference as Belus did and not with the abject devotion Danato did. She looked at it like an endless ocean that was, in one moment, serene and, in the next, trying to swallow her up. She finally understood now, that if she fought too hard, she would drown. So, she had to pick her battles and only fight the ones worth dying for.

"You're right," Cori said.

No one ever knew what was going on inside Belus's head, but Cori imagined she had some knowledge of his inner thoughts and motivations. Lately, however, she was getting her aim wrong and it was making their interactions more pragmatic than usual. As he stood before her now, he bore no emotion—his gaze purely analytical. She suspected he didn't trust her surrender.

Cori glanced down at the contact between their hands. She moved one of her fingers to brush against the side of his hand. She looked at him from beneath her brow—as submissively as she could without slipping down to her knees as she frequently did during earnest conversations with him. "I didn't come to you because I didn't want to piss you off. I'm tired of pissing you off."

Belus's brow perked slightly. "You are?"

Cori resisted the smirk that was tugging on her lips. "Yes."

"Well, rest assured, this would not have pissed me off. It's good to see you following up on your suspicions." He leaned a little closer. "No matter how outrageous they are." He released her hand. "Maybe next time you should do more investigating before you confront your suspect though," he said before exiting the office.

She looked back at Danato her lips wrenching down in a deep grimace. He picked up the files and handed them across the desk to her. She took them and stood up to leave.

"He's right, you know?"

"I know, I just said as much."

"No, I mean about the bubble."

Cori stared back at him. "I can't," she whispered, tears drawing to her eyes at the thought of returning to the real world permanently.

Danato's face mirrored some of her pain. "I know, but the time is passing so much faster now. I don't want..." He rubbed his forehead and cleared his throat. "I don't want to lose you, Cori." His eyes now started to show signs of tears. "You're all I have left."

Cori knew Danato missed Ethan more than he was admitting. His loss was like that of a son more than an employee. And though she was no longer in danger inside the bubble, the time away would eventually draw her closer to old age. It was unclear if she could stave off death like the wizards, but neither she nor Danato wanted to find out.

"I..." He trailed off and looked away. Cori moved to him and rested her hand on his shoulder. He looked at her just as a tear dribbled out of his eyes and disappeared beneath his chin. She wondered in that moment, if she had ever truly seen him cry. She had seen his grief and it was awful. It was the anguish of a wild animal instead of a man. This was Danato at his most vulnerable. "I think you should start restricting your time there."

Cori nearly recoiled from him. The very thought of adding more time back to her real life seemed almost impossible now. It was true that with the wavering timeline inside the bubble, the schedule became problematic. She couldn't follow a consistent day and night routine, but that shouldn't have mattered. The whole point was that she could catch up in the bubble. Not that she ever did. "Danato I can't—"

Before she could answer he engulfed her with a hug and dragged her into his lap. He clamped onto her as if for dear life and held her. She was helpless against him so she just held his head against her chest and stroked his hair. For a long while, he said nothing and just held her, his thumb rubbing along the skin where his hand touched her back.

When the touching moment was too much, even for her, she spoke. "Chuck is working on a little side project. He's predicting that he can use wave interference at a specific point in the bubble to deflect the acoustic barrier and reduce the penetration resistance."

Cori could feel Danato's brow dip. He drew back and looked at her. "What?"

She bit back her smile; thankful she wasn't the only one baffled by Chuck's technobabble. "He says he can make a door. If it works I'll be able to just walk out of the bubble instead of being pulled out. It will even minimize the auditory feedback."

"Really," Danato looked flummoxed but intrigued. "Fascinating." He stood abruptly, nearly dropping her off his lap. He scooted around her and moved to the door. "I should talk to him about that," he mumbled as he left.

Cori stood behind his desk, feeling a little rejected. Apparently, the heartfelt moment was over and Danato was no longer concerned about the effects of the bubble. She chuckled to herself about the attention span of men when it came to new toys. He would no doubt listen to Chuck babble on about things he didn't understand for an hour just so he could be included in the process.

She sat at the desk, daring to occupy Danato's chair. It no longer poked her the way it used to. It was surprisingly soft now. She flipped open the file she had brought to the office and read through the preceding documentation on Erin's treatment. Since food, medical care, and sanitation were all logged on the same schedule it was no wonder Cori had missed the iron supplementation. She scanned through the blue and black ink noting that all the iron supplementation followed a blood draw, which made sense. They would check her levels before giving her another dosage. Nearly the same two nurses performed every blood draw and dosage, except the last one.

Cori knew it didn't matter who signed off on the supplement or took the blood. All the nurses were qualified and even most of the guards were trained on basic first aid. Apart from the life-saving techniques that she had benefited from more than once, they could start I.V.s, set bones, place sutures, and on a very bad day, they could assist the doctor with surgeries. Cori was told once that the nurses were trained in emergency surgical techniques. On top of their usual duties, they could extract bullets, perform C-sections, and potentially even repair internal injuries from stab wounds. Naturally, the rules of the real world didn't matter here. Titles and degrees meant nothing when a life was on the line and the doctor was already busy with another patient.

As Cori rubbed her finger along the embedded initials of the last nurse, she considered how easy it would be to cover up a murder in this place. Not that she was considering such a conspiracy, but the thought was a little unnerving. It wasn't as if the prison had any cameras to monitor behavior. The only witnesses would be unreliable or untrustworthy. Who could have stopped Nurse B.L. from giving Erin a final dose of poison disguised as an iron supplement? She would have even taken it voluntarily.

Cori shut the file and drew away from the desk. She wouldn't allow herself to go down this rabbit hole. The one where she questioned everyone around her and made enemies of her friends. Whatever earworm had started this vein of suspicion needed to be quashed now before she really made an ass of herself.

Leaning forward to stand, Cori noticed something under the desk. On the left side, under the center drawer, the wall of the drawer cabinet had scribbles on it. She reached out and touched the deep scours in the metal. She looked closer trying to understand what she was seeing. It was graffiti that had been scratched out. Cori nearly snorted when she realized that someone must have gotten into Danato's office and scratched a profanity into the paint of his desk. Someone was obviously not a fan. She couldn't discern the words past the aggressive scribbled gouges, but Cori suspected it involved a four-letter word with a specifier.

She looked to the other side and found another attempt at graffiti there. She could see why it had been abandoned. The paint on that side was chipped off in chunks and wouldn't retain the words. Cori chuckled at the immature nature of the deviant responsible for this and stood to leave.

As she reached the door, the clock on the wall began to tick loudly. She looked at it, feeling her heart thumping in time with it. She was certain that ticking clocks were not capable of volume, nor were they capable of judgment or communication of any kind. And yet that blasted device was staring at her with the eyes of a devil—demanding something from her that she couldn't quite provide.

Cori looked around the room to see if there was something she was missing. Something that the entity might want her to know about before she left. She knew it was not wise to start interacting with her instincts as they related to the bubble's entity. That was the real danger Danato was concerned about. She was already intrinsically linked to her now. Traveling in and out of the bubble with such frequency was liable to strengthen that bond. What happened when she and the entity were so in sync that she wasn't sure who was influencing who?

She moved back to the desk to examine the graffiti closer. Maybe she could determine the letters behind the scratches. Rather than bend over she crawled under the desk to inspect the lines. Nothing was legible. It was all gone, even the tips of the letters were obscured.

From the corner of her eye, Cori saw something else written on the underside of the center drawer. She leaned back unable to understand the letters as they were written. She was baffled by the phrase, but also because it was backward. Why would someone go to the trouble of writing this and then write it backward?

Cori moved out from under the desk, suddenly feeling claustrophobic. Something felt very wrong, but she didn't even understand why. She was afraid, but there was no threat. At best, it was just a creepy feeling drawn up from memories of horror movies and nightmares.

As she leaned over the desk to calm herself, the breath that was supposed to calm her hitched in her throat. The dread of the monster in the basement was pooling inside her and making her heart race. Suddenly the transposed letters made sense. She could imagine them right there, calling out to her from under the desk. From above, they made sense—as if they had been written on the underside of a piece of glass. To Cori that meant only one thing. The writer of that graffiti had sat in Danato's chair while they scratched the words into the underside of his desk.

It was all just an awful joke and one she wouldn't allow herself to be concerned with. She stood up and walked away from the mystery. She didn't want the answers to this one. She didn't want any more clues. And most of all, she didn't want to know why the occupant of that chair had scratched the words "help me" into the underside of Danato's desk.

19

"Y OU'RE NOT GOING TO find the answer to that question inside that cage," Mace said.

Heaton barely heard him over the constant rumble from the beast before him. Callin's transformation had been slow and agonizing as usual, but the beast before him was not nearly as volatile as he expected. Callin's wolf seemed to be hunting him rather than haphazardly lunging at the bars as if he knew that he was only one stupid human mistake away from having his supper. As hungry as Heaton was 24 hours without food, he couldn't imagine the hunger that was gnawing at this creature.

Heaton turned slowly to look at Mace. The hours had ticked by slowly waiting for Callin to change. With quite literally nothing to entertain them, they were both getting pretty punchy. They had taken turns sleeping, but neither of them had much luck on the cold concrete floors. "What?" he asked.

Mace chuckled. "You may not be ready to admit it, but we both know what's going on with your partner."

Heaton bristled at Mace's presumption to know about anything about Nevia. "Is that so?" Mace chuckled again. "What the fuck is so funny?"

Mace stopped laughing and stared at Heaton for a moment. He pulled himself off the floor and approached him. "You know I get that you never liked me." Heaton rolled his eyes. "It's fine. I get it. I'm just a hick from down south."

"It's not because you're a hick. It's because you're a dick."

Mace smirked at him. "I thought your kind liked dicks." Heaton narrowed his eyes on him. "Yeah, I knew. Even if I hadn't you've been looking at Callin like he's lollipop since this all started." Heaton wasn't sure what to do with this information. He had spent so much time keeping his personal life out of his work life that he wasn't prepared to answer for it—especially to a guy like Mace. "I don't care what you do, Heaton. I'm just trying to make a point."

"And what point is that?"

"That sometimes we have a better view of people when we don't like them." Mace pointed to the wolf beside them. "This is the way that werewolves are supposed to work. One day they're men and the next they're monsters. You can see the change, but sometimes it's more like Dr. Jekyll and Mr. Hyde. Which I never understood, because Jekyll sounds like the bad guy to me."

"It doesn't matter, they were both bad." Mace looked momentarily confused. "Never mind. Could you please just cut the bullshit and say what you want to say?"

Mace paused a moment. "She killed a human, Heaton," he said rather softly, almost sympathetically. "She's gone feral."

Heaton shook his head even though it was the same conclusion he had been wrestling with for the last day. "She had to have a reason."

Mace scoffed. "Reason to kill, sure. Reason to eviscerate a man and eat his insides. No, Heaton, we gotta face the facts. Your girl's gone crazy."

"She's just grieving and angry."

"She wasn't grieving when she took a bite outta my neck. I know you don't want to hear this because we both know what it means. But there are rules for a reason." Heaton scoffed, surprised to hear Jack Macey toting the company line despite repeatedly playing jump rope with it over the course of his career. "If this were any other werewolf we would be calling the local she-bitches and you know it."

"Well, it isn't just any werewolf. She's my partner. And besides she's only a quarter wolf."

"That doesn't seem to be making a difference."

Heaton took a soothing breath. "What do you want from me, Mace?"

Mace considered this. "I know it doesn't look like it. But this is me, trying not to be a dick. I guess I just wanted to make sure that you're prepared."

"To lose another friend?" Heaton snapped. "How could anyone prepare for that?"

Mace nodded and backed away—surrendering to the fact that Heaton was not ready to give up on Nevia. Even if he didn't care for her as a sister, his obligations to Daniel indebted him to the duty of protecting her.

The wolf beside him began to growl louder. Heaton checked his distance to make sure he wasn't about to get a paw to the face. Something clanked behind him. He and Mace exchanged a glance before looking at the double doors leading into the next room. They had briefly explored the area, but the way forward had been locked. Their only option was to return the way they had come in.

Another loud clunk resulted in the double doors slowly swinging open. The darkness on the other side disguised who was inside, but as the shadow within shifted, Heaton felt himself go completely cold with shock. The outline of the large beast shifted just as Callin's wolf began to roar.

"Run!" he heard Mace shout.

Suddenly awake and remembering that he did indeed have legs, Heaton sprinted after Mace to the door they had entered through. Mace arrived just before him and yanked at the knob. It was locked but Mace just broke the knob off with his fist and retracted the inner mechanism. They both pushed forward, but there was a chain on the other side, leaving only enough room to extend a hand through and flip off whoever was laughing on the other side of the door.

Heaton cursed as he saw the loosed wolf barreling toward them in leaping steps. He didn't have time to contemplate his death before Mace shoved him to one side. Heaton landed and rolled a little too close to Callin's cage and narrowly missed getting clawed.

"Shit!" Mace yelled as he dove and rolled under the hind legs of the werewolf. When he stopped he looked at Heaton. "Get to the shit!" he said.

Heaton looked at Callin's conjoined human cage and saw what remained of his pre-change evacuations. Pools of blood, puke, piss, and shit that the caretaker had not bothered to hose down after transferring Callin.

"Hey!" Mace shouted and waved to the werewolf, trying to draw his attention away from Heaton, but he was the closer target. The werewolf drooled as he shifted down onto all fours, prepared to lunge at his prey.

Heaton looked at the mess as any sane man would, but in the face of being eaten alive, there was no comparison. He less than gracefully flopped into the befoul deposits before him and rolled over them, covering his body in everything distasteful and disease-ridden.

Callin roared pounding against the bars to his left. The new werewolf approached the open cage, teeth bared and with a hunger only a carnivore could understand. As his head entered the cage, he stopped. He sniffed Heaton.

His fear was at its peak. Though his sweaty body and pulsing heart must have been appealing to the wolf, the fact that he smelled like vomit and feces was enough to put him off his meal. He turned away, no longer interested in him. Even Callin stopped banging at the cage since he wasn't interested in eating what he had only recently given up.

The wolf turned his attention to Mace, who was slowly backing toward the next room. He was probably hoping to lock the doors again and stay on the other side, but there wouldn't be time. And now that the wolf knew that he was there, he would tear down the concrete walls just to get to him.

Heaton grabbed a particularly solid specimen and scrambled to his feet. He ran safely past Callin's cage to get a better view of Mace. When he was in view, Heaton lofted the hefty turd at him. It arrived as a brown splotch on Mace's chest, startling him slightly since his attention was on the beast before him. He looked down at the shit, looking offended that Heaton had assaulted him with the filth.

When the werewolf leaned in to sniff Mace, he had the same disinterested reaction as he had with Heaton. The animal seemed almost annoyed as he growled and brushed past Mace. Whatever meal had been so appetizing to him before was now spoiled.

Mace stood in the doorway looking stunned. Heaton could only assume that the man had prepared himself for certain death. The fact that he had saved Heaton's life with no expectation of surviving himself was surprising. Jack Macey had never been the gallant type. He tended to consider his actions with regard to his own benefits first. But perhaps he hadn't had enough time to be selfish.

Heaton moved to him and looked him over. "Are you okay?" he asked.

Mace locked eyes with him and his confusion faded. Anger grew in his features like an ember growing into a flame. It fanned Heaton's own fury and they turned to the chained door that had blocked their escape. Without discussion, they walked toward it. Their steps increased rapidly and soon they were both running.

Two heavy bodies colliding against the door was too much for the chain and it snapped open. Heaton barely registered the first face he saw before nailing him with a hard punch. Mace was right beside him bloodying the face of a second man. The caretaker, Grady, arrived just as they finished subduing the men. He pulled a gun, but Heaton leaped forward and twisted his wrist. His misdirected shot hit the wall. Mace punched him in the stomach and the man doubled over. Heaton yanked the weapon from his grip, nearly dislocating his trigger finger.

Despite the size disparity, Mace managed to unbalance him and push him onto his back. He kneeled on one arm, while Heaton pressed his foot to the other. He pointed the gun at the man's face, seething with anger. He wanted to ask just who the hell he thought he was dealing with, but this man didn't care about labels like hunter or soldier. All he cared about was money.

"What is this place?" Heaton asked.

"Fuck you! Go ahead and shoot me."

"We ain't gonna shoot you," Mace drawled just before grabbing the man's crotch. Grady screamed as Mace twisted his genitals. Heaton resisted the urge to remind Mace that the threat of pain was usually enough to get people to talk.

"Okay, okay, okay!" Grady begged.

"Talk!" Mace yelled.

"We run a wolf fight! It's an underground blood sport!"

Heaton glanced at Mace before aiming the gun at the man's forehead. "Show us."

20

Heaton and Mace followed Grady through another winding hallway to a set of rickety metal stairs leading down into a basement. He grabbed Grady's shoulder to stop him and gave it a good squeeze. "What's this?" Heaton asked.

"Would you rather take the wolf entrance?" Heaton rested the gun on his shoulder, reminding him that murder was still on the table. "The games are in the warehouse across the street in a dug-out basement. These tunnels are the only way in."

Heaton didn't like the idea of walking into such a flankable position, but if they wanted to see the operation, they were going to have to go down the scary dark staircase. Mace glanced behind them, no doubt thinking the same thing. Heaton offered him Grady's gun to him, since he still had his own. Mace looked at the firearm a moment before taking it from him. He had never been a fan of guns, though perhaps not for the altruistic reasons that most people weren't. However, he wasn't lacking the skill to use one. And given the situation, they were going to need more than fists to protect themselves.

Heaton gave Grady a shove and they proceeded down. The temperature dropped as they entered what felt like a cave. The natural dirt walls around them were propped up with wood like an old mineshaft. It didn't inspire confidence, but it was a short trip to the basement of the next building.

As they exited the tunnel, Heaton had difficulty understanding what he was seeing. Though they were standing on the concrete floor of a basement, just ten yards ahead of them, beyond heavy metal bars, the floor descended into a dirt pit. What was even stranger was that the ceiling—the floor above—had also been gutted. The main supports at the center of the building had been bisected by numerous and mostly likely unapproved metal beams.

Adding to the engineer's nightmare, were a series of bleachers surrounding the grand pit. The audience that was cheering on the dog fight currently underway, was safely contained behind the same bars that were protecting Heaton from the residents of the pit.

"A dog fight?" Heaton nodded toward the two pit bulls savagely biting each other.

Grady looked over at him. "The opening act."

Mace peered up at the spectators. "All this to gamble?"

"Some are just here to witness two amazing creatures rip each other apart."

"How do you explain this to the wolves? They have to know they've been in a fight when they come out of it."

"That's assuming they wake up," Grady smirked at Heaton. "It doesn't matter what they know. Once we get them in a cage, they never get out again."

Heaton narrowed his eyes on Grady as his words sunk in. "You keep them?"

Grady chuckled. "This isn't exactly Grand Central Station. And wolf fights are hard on the body. They die pretty young around here. I expect I can get another four or five moons outta your mutt."

"You're not getting one moon out of him," Heaton warned.

Grady smiled. "What? You think holding me at gunpoint will stop the show? I'm just the hostess."

Heaton looked around at the men standing guard around the perimeter of the cage above them. They were no doubt there to keep the audience in line, but he saw more than a few holstered guns. Despite the one Mace had held on Grady, it wouldn't take much for this situation to turn sour.

A horn sounded and the audience cheered. One of the dogs in the pit was now dead while the other was very nearly. Covered in blood and panting hard, he paced the pit with a slight limp in his step.

The audience started to clap in rhythm and someone with a loudspeaker announced it was time for the main event. Before Heaton could consider what to do, the werewolf that had nearly eaten him charged into the pit and pounced on the winning dog. The yelp made Mace flinch. His face screwed up tight and he stared at the dog being gobbled up. Even Heaton, with no particular affinity for animals, cringed at the sound of the poor animal's bones snapping between the teeth of the wolf's jaws.

This was nature, he reminded himself.

This was the circle of fucking life.

As if that wasn't enough carnage for the night, Callin's wolf came running in and started eating the loser of the fight. Suddenly aware that his second course was being stolen the first wolf lunged at Callin. His teeth sunk into his neck.

Heaton shifted back to examine his surroundings, searching for access to the pit. Grady laughed at him. "What are you gonna do, sport? Jump in the middle of a wolf fight?"

Heaton glared at him but realized he was right. There was nothing he could do to stop this fight. Callin would have to fight and survive on his own if he wanted to make it out of this alive.

As it was, Heaton wasn't sure how to handle their situation. He couldn't just shoot Grady. Assuming Callin did survive, they needed to get him out of there. That meant using Grady as leverage or as a hostage.

"How long do these fights usually last?" Heaton asked.

"Depends on the age of—" Grady's face expelled blood. The resounding gunshot was barely audible over the sound of the cheering and roaring. Heaton looked back at Mace and the smoking gun that was still aligned with the back of Grady's head.

Heaton lunged for Mace even as Grady's body collapsed to the floor. He shoved him against a brick wall, twisting his fists into the fabric of his shirt. "What the fuck, Mace!"

"Oh, don't tell me you give a shit about that asshole."

"We needed him!"

"What we need is to shut this place down."

"Please tell me you didn't shoot him just for that fucking dog." Mace rolled his tongue behind his lip, as if checking for residual tobacco that he might spit in his face. Heaton blinked at him, taking in his incorruptible indifference to murder. He imagined that he had worn the same expression a time or two in his life, but he had to believe that it was for a greater purpose than to satisfy his own convictions.

"I'm taking this place down. You can either help me or fuck off." Mace shoved him back and he toppled over Grady's downed body.

"Damn you, Mace!" Heaton jumped up and followed Mace as he stalked along the bars. "You can't just open fire in here! These people may be lowlifes but they're civilians."

"Not according to the council. They're already dead. We're just saving time."

"That's not how it works and you know it. We don't have the authority to do this."

"And who says that?" Mace swung around to face him. "The board says that werewolf matters are to be handled by the council. But the board has been taken over by a bunch of transmorphs and they're trying to eliminate loose ends one toe tag at a time. Are you really gonna start quoting protocol at me?" Mace didn't wait for a response before continuing up another set of metal stairs to the audience level.

Heaton knew that at the very least he should call the council. However, the figureheads needed to approve immediate action in a situation like this, were incapacitated by the full moon. It would be at least another 24 hours before they had permission or backup to arrest these ingrates. By then the entire operation could be evacuated. Not to mention, the option for conventionality went out the window the minute Mace shot Grady. Heaton cursed and checked his bullet clip before following him up to the audience level.

Mace's second gunshot didn't get much more fanfare than the first one. He just walked right up behind a man with a rifle and buried a bullet into his back. He dropped like a rock, not technically dead, but on the verge of seeing the white lights of salvation. Mace moved on while Heaton grabbed the rifle and swung it over his shoulder.

Mace shot the next man in the face and the crowd nearby finally took notice. The gray area between right and wrong went out the window as people began screaming and leaping from their seats. Unsure of where to find safety from the psychopath circling the arena, they scattered left and right, running into each other and falling off the bleachers.

A large man in a suit mistook Heaton for the shooter and barreled toward him trying to be a hero. He deflected the man sending him straight into the protective bars. Though he respected the man for trying to protect his fellow patrons, he still bashed the butt of the rifle into his face to make sure that he would be incapacitated for the rest of Mace's perceived mengamuk.

The fleeing audience members brought as much attention as the next gunshot and everyone clamored to the exits. Screams overrode the sound of the werewolf battle below them. Heaton could barely keep up with Mace. The guards searched for the source of the disruption and fired at the two strangers carrying guns.

Heaton leaped up into the stands to get clear of the pile of people that had developed in Mace's wake. Gunfire pinged off the metal near him and he found the source of the attack and put him down with one shot. He sprinted across the bleachers, jumping the gaps to catch up with Mace. He shot two more men climbing the bleachers to get a better view to shoot from.

Mace slowed after the last man was put down. The majority of the people were gone, except those who had been injured in the melee. They just whimpered and cowered where they lay, trying to hide in plain sight so they didn't get shot.

Mace turned to observe the room. He spotted Heaton and abruptly raised his weapon. The shot fired before Heaton could determine if he was meant to be the victim. A thump sounded behind him and he turned to see the man who had tried to attack him earlier sprawled across a bleacher bench. Still clutched in his right hand was a gun, no doubt appropriated from one of the guards. Heaton dismissed any guilt he felt for not giving him a harder hit to the face. There was only so much he could do to protect bystanders, especially when Mace was the one driving the chaos.

Regardless of who got hurt, Heaton would have to help Mace finish this fight. It was the only way to ensure that Callin would be safe. And the only way to guarantee these assholes didn't start up another wolf fight the minute they left.

21

"HOW IS SHE DOING?" Cori asked from the door of the room Gypsy had been sequestered in since the incident. Gypsy was sitting on her bed, and Levi was crouched before her, holding her hands. The diagnosis of her condition, according to the doctor, was a mental breakdown, but that wasn't the right word for it. There were no words for what had happened to her that day. No description of the degradation of one's sanity due to magical influence.

Levi looked up from his concentrated efforts to disperse the dark magic that was clinging to Gypsy. She still didn't understand what he was doing for her—at least not any more than she understood the rest of the magical world. All she knew was that Levi was preventing Gypsy from slipping into a coma like Adrianna.

"Today is a good day." Levi released his grip on Gypsy's hands, and her eyes flapped open. She turned her attention to Cori.

"Tick tock," she whispered.

"How are you feeling, Gypsy?" Cori asked, though she wasn't sure she wanted the answer. She didn't want to know how deeply she had shattered the woman. Though Levi insisted that Gypsy would have reached this point eventually, she still didn't like the idea that she had placed the last straw on her back.

"Who am I feeling, you mean." Her eyes glazed, and she smiled sinisterly. "Everyone." She turned to Levi and earnestly asked, "Why did the mouse turn blue?"

Levi bit his lip and shook his head. "I don't know."

Gypsy narrowed her eyes. "How can you not know? Turn back the clock, little bug. Find me the answers."

Levi's shoulders rose with a heavy breath. "It doesn't work like that."

Gypsy abruptly slapped him across the face, knocking him to the floor. Cori gasped and rushed to aid him. "Gypsy, stop!"

"Worthless little shit!" Gypsy rose to her feet, towering over both of them. The darkness in her eyes was all her own, but the menace in her voice was something new. Something Cori was not familiar with. "I should have cut off your head instead of your wings."

This comment visibly disturbed Levi, and he slid back across the floor to get away from Gypsy.

"This is a good day?" Cori jumped up when Gypsy went after Levi. "Leave him alone," she said firmly.

After a long moment, Gypsy turned his aggressive stare to Cori. "If we don't know why the mouse turned blue, then we can't know what's happening inside that clock." She spoke gravely, as if her babblings were of the utmost importance. "What if we can't turn him white again?"

"We'll figure it out. I'll help you," Cori said, not simply to placate her, but to remind her she was there to help her. Whatever she was going through, Cori would do her best to help her through it. It was the least she could do.

"I can feel them, you know?" Gypsy reached up and stroked her cheek. Cori flinched a little, but allowed the contact. "He's so angry."

"Ethan?"

Gypsy nodded.

Cori frowned. "Can you... communicate with him?" It was a long shot, but she had to ask.

Gypsy's brow furrowed as she contemplated this. "Hmm, I wonder."

"I wouldn't advise that." Levi jumped to his feet and fearlessly returned to Gypsy. "Dark magic connects us all, and while it would be theoretically possible for her to reach out to any living being, it would only serve to pull her deeper into the magic."

"I'm at the bottom of the ocean right now, Levi," Gypsy answered, remarkably cogent. "What difference would a phone call make?"

"You're at the bottom of the ocean in a submarine," Levi snapped. "It's the difference between being trapped under water or being crushed by it."

Gypsy looked him over, her gaze pausing on the red mark she had only recently left on his cheek. She drew away from them both and braced her hands on the wall as if waiting to be searched by a police officer. "Why hasn't Danato put me down?" she asked.

"I told him you can't wield the magic, so you won't be a danger to us," Levi explained.

Gypsy let out a low chuckle before turning back to look at Levi. "You don't think I'm dangerous?"

Levi swallowed hard, unnerved by the borderline alluring gaze Gypsy was aiming at him. "You're just a vessel, Gypsy."

"What if she wasn't? Just a vessel?" Cori couldn't help asking even though she knew the answer would likely be inscrutable to her.

"She..." Levi looked at Gypsy as if he didn't want to speak about an affliction in front of its victim. "Dark magic is by nature very weak. It is only through the sum total of humanity that the magic becomes so potent. The stronger it becomes, the more it can affect other magic. By design, the innocuous energy from the Earth stifles human magic. However, this degree of dark magic can degrade earth magic. That's why we had to perform the ritual on Adrianna. We needed a bigger dose of earth magic to balance the dark magic inside her. Unfortunately, it was too much. Her human form wasn't compatible with the earth magic we put into her, and so she had to be transformed."

"So that's why she didn't become a sorceress? She got a bad mix?"

"Yes. It was a foolish endeavor, since—"

"He won't let me see the baby dragon." Gypsy pinched up her face like a little girl emulating anger for the first time. "I think he's afraid I'll eat it." She chattered her teeth at Levi like she just might take a bite out of him. He recoiled and held out a barring arm to keep her from getting closer. Though it wasn't necessarily out of character for her to bite someone, she couldn't help but find some amusement in the odd pairing that Gypsy's condition had forced them both into.

A tiny snicker escaped Cori's throat, drawing Gypsy's attention. She did her best to hide the smirk that was tugging at her lips. Her former nemesis seemed surprised and pleased by her amusement.

"There are two theories as to why we can't create sorcerers anymore," Levi continued. "The most accepted belief is that the sheer number of humans is increasing the dark magic on Earth, creating an imbalance. That means we can't create sorcerers because there is too much dark magic being contributed to the merge. Too much dark magic dampens the earth magic and leaves the possessor insane."

Gypsy motioned to herself as an example.

"And the second?" Cori asked.

"The less favorable theory suggests that dark magic and earth magic were designed to be in balance regardless of the number of humans. That means that at one time in human history, millions of people shared the same amount of dark magic as the billions of today. It was just more potent back then. Which gave their magic more impact."

"If their dark magic was stronger, wouldn't that make it harder to use earth magic?"

Levi contorted his face in thought, obviously displeased by her interpretation, but unsure how to adequately correct her. She hated to tax his teaching skills, but he really was the only one to ask about such things.

"Dark magic is cold." Gypsy walked behind her, dragging a finger across her ass as she went. "Earth magic is..." She stopped behind Levi and leaned over his shoulder. "...hot." She rasped the word seductively. Judging by how Levi jumped, she had possibly pinched his buttocks as well. Cori was unaffected by the leering gaze Gypsy was giving both of them, but Levi seemed to be thrown by the woman's overt sexuality.

Cori preferred to stay out of the private lives of her colleagues, especially the temporary ones. However, she couldn't help wondering about Levi's backstory. He had been generous enough to share the basics with her, so she understood he had a history of captivity. She also understood that Annette had saved him from that abuse. However, he had been far less lucid about his time with Adrianna. It had been common knowledge that they were *together*, but he never spoke of her. At least not in any way that would divulge the degree of his feelings for her.

Seeing how alarmed he was at Gypsy's forward personality made it seem like he was either inexperienced with women or possibly disinterested in them altogether. Could it be that the subdued emotions he expressed on the topic of Adrianna had less to do with her death and more to do with the guilt of a disingenuous relationship?

Levi cleared his throat and shifted away from Gypsy's provocation. "One could consider dark magic to be like a set of oven mitts. The stronger the dark magic, the thicker the mitts and therefore, the more earth magic you could carry. Someone with access to a lot of dark magic could manipulate an equal portion of earth magic, making them rather powerful. Today's witchcraft is almost always done primarily with earth magic. It's supplemented with spells, potions, and fetishes, but not many practitioners can access their dark magic. At least, not without the help of a coven."

Cori considered Annette's history with her coven. They were unsuccessful in creating a sorcerer and ultimately the dark magic they accessed rebounded and made the coven insane. However, despite their insanity, they still had access to the dark magic. They could still hurt people. Thus, the rationalization for keeping them in the bubble.

Cori turned her attention to Gypsy, who was already looking at her. "How much dark magic does Gypsy have inside of her?"

"All of it," Gypsy answered. She moved to Cori and grabbed her neck.

"Grace!" Levi jumped forward and gripped Gypsy's wrist, not quite pulling her away, but reminding her she had to behave.

Gypsy panted as she stared at Cori. Her eyes watered, and she gritted her teeth. "I know you had to do it. I know you didn't trust your aim, but... fuck, Cori! This sucks!"

"I know," Cori whispered. "But I meant what I said. I'll help you. We'll figure this out, and we'll fix you."

Gypsy snorted. "Just like Humpty Dumpty." She paced the short expanse of the room. "He wasn't an egg, you know? He was a cannon. And he didn't fall. The wall beneath him crumbled." Gypsy stopped in front of her. "Do you know how useful a cannon is when it's not aimed at the enemy, Cori?"

"Pretty useless, I would assume."

"Exactly. So, stop worrying about fixing me and just get me back on the fucking wall!"

Cori nodded even though she had no idea how to do that. She looked at Levi, who shrugged. She wasn't the only one confused by the metaphor.

"You should go," Levi whispered. "I need to finish our session."

Cori nodded and left them alone. Though she was certain that Levi was doing everything that could be done to help Gypsy, there was possibly one other person who could help her. Someone who knew all about walls.

22

ORI HAD SPENT WEEKS avoiding Cleos, even to the point of taking the stairs, lest he surprise her in the elevator. She reasoned it was to avoid a long overdue confrontation, but she also suspected she was afraid to talk to him. Afraid that with Ethan and Efrat gone, she might fall back into old habits. The last thing she needed to do was rebuild a friendship with such a selfish being.

The elevator opened directly onto the top floor, revealing the museum-like exhibits. She headed down the north aisle, peeking into the offices and lab spaces that had once upon a time held prisons instead of desks and microscopes. She eventually came upon an area that had been completely restructured to accommodate a larger room with a raised ceiling. The dark interior seemed to fit Cleos's needs perfectly.

She stepped through the entryway and immediately felt the temperature drop several degrees. As her eyes adjusted to the dim blue lighting, she realized this was not an office space, but rather a preservation room. Tucked under glass and protected from light and heat were a series of books, documents, and logs. It didn't take more than a cursory knowledge of history to know that these items were old.

Very old.

How and why Cleos had them was just one question in a long line of questions regarding his motives. The man she knew was ever in pursuit of trophies, not knowledge. Though he could easily acquire information through his feasts, his priority was the manipulation of people. However, he was a shrewd businessman, and she had no doubt these books would ultimately make him money or give him power.

"Don't touch those," Cleos snapped from the doorway. "What are you doing here?"

"Hello to you too." Cori hadn't expected a welcome mat, but since he was the one seeking her attention, she had assumed he would be grateful to see her. Then again, it had been two weeks since he had stopped asking after her. Perhaps he had found someone else to satiate his cravings. "Nice collection. Is this Aramaic?" She pointed to one of the scrolls scribbled with glyph-style words. She had no clue what Aramaic looked like, but it seemed like a safe guess.

Cleos stepped into the room and took up a position on the opposite side of the center display. Beneath its glass was a map. At first glance, it appeared to depict the location of the prison. However, on further inspection, she realized it was the bubble being highlighted. She noted that there were several dots to the west, indicating the impermanent location of the wandering village.

"What do you want, Corinthia?" He crossed his arms, and she realized he wasn't wearing his matching suit jacket. His tie was missing as well. The first two buttons on his shirt were open. Was this casual for him? For years he had been subjected to prison jumpsuits, so it was still odd to see him dressed up, but she got the impression he didn't deviate from his fashion expectations frequently.

"I thought you wanted to see me," she said if for no other reason than to give him the opportunity to explain himself.

"Did I?" he feigned ignorance. "It's so hard to remember." He glanced at his watch. "I mean, that was several weeks ago."

Cori nodded. "I assume you've heard by know, about..." She glanced out the door. She was so close to the lamp here.

"Oliver," Cleos finished her sentence without ceremony. "Yes, I think I was the last to find out. Congratulations, you managed once again to save the day and piss off everyone in the process."

Cori pinched her lips together, holding back any insults that might fly out of her mouth. Since he wasn't wrong about her track record, she had no room to argue. "What did you want to see me about?"

"Nothing in particular. I just wanted to clear the air, so to speak." Cleos shifted his hands to his hips.

Noticing dust on his pant leg, he immediately brushed it off. He frowned when part of it would not surrender its occupancy. "We didn't exactly get off on the right foot when I got back."

"I was under a lot of stress." Cori hadn't meant to make an excuse for herself. Her anger at Cleos's arrival was still warranted. He had made it well known before he left that she had wronged him in an unforgivable way. For him to take grand strides to solidify his place at this prison was baffling to her. Though he certainly had higher reasons than revenge, it still felt like he was digging a knife into her back. Especially with the recruitment of Gypsy and Leona.

"Look. I don't want to rehash old issues. My life is hard enough without adding to my enemies list. Why don't we just call a truce?" Cori found it exceptionally hard to raise her hand. Even beyond her pride, she literally felt like a weight was pressing against her arm.

Cleos glared at her extended hand and veritable olive branch. "What do you want, Cori? I may have been gone for a while, but I doubt you've changed that much."

Cori frowned at the implication for her character. However, since she did have an agenda, she once again bit back her forked tongue. She dropped her hand back to her side. "Why haven't you helped Gypsy?"

"Gypsy is beyond my help."

"Maybe you can't cure her, but you could clear out the cache. Make a little room in her mind."

"You're missing the point. She is a lost cause. I could help her day in and day out for months and never make a dent."

"But you could feast."

"Ugh. Would you really subject yourself to the same meal over and over again?"

"Are you saying that you won't help her because it would bore you?"

"I don't expect you to understand, but people do come in flavors. And while I do enjoy harnessing Gypsy for a worthy cause, I find her to be a rather bland meal. Emotions play a huge role in my enjoyment of memories. Without them, it's like eating cardboard."

"She has plenty of emotions running through her now."

"You'd think that, but it's not the same. She's flooded with dark magic, and I can't just break off a piece of it here and there. One bite is a thousand. And as you well know, a little salt flavors; a lot becomes unpalatable."

"So, suck it up and swallow it, anyway. For her sake."

Cleos chuckled. "Give it up, Corinthia. I'm not going to waste my energy gathering rotten fruit."

Cori tapped her hand on her thigh, barely debating her next thought before it was out of her mouth. "What if I offered a chocolate cake chaser?"

Cleos's gaze locked onto her, and for a moment he didn't even move. "What exactly are you saying?"

"You've always been partial to my flavor." He smiled in a nearly lascivious way. "What if you wash down Gypsy with a bite from my mind?"

"Well, well, well, I never thought I'd see the day when you would prostitute your mind for the sake of an enemy."

"She's not my enemy. Maybe she never was. But it doesn't matter. She saved my son. I need to save her."

Cleos moved around the display and stopped in front of her. He reached out and, without touching her, moved his hand down her arm. She balled her hands into fists, resisting an almost uncontrollable instinct to run.

"It's a tempting offer, to be sure. But the answer is no." Cleos dropped his seduction act and walked away.

"Can't you just try?" she called after him.

"No! Now get out," he yelled from beyond the room.

Cori scoffed. She couldn't believe that even with the bribery of her mind, he wouldn't help Gypsy. Cleos had never turned down a taste of her mind. Perhaps her flavor was no longer palatable to him.

23

T HE SWIFT ARRIVAL OF several black vans and a slew of non-werewolf investigators following his call to the Council of the Moon's local chapter impressed Heaton. Several young men poured out of the vans, some armed with guns and medical bags, others equipped with laptops.

One such young man had cornered him and Mace, interrogating them about the evening's events. They went through the details, not leaving anything out.

"Why didn't you call us after you had subdued the first group of men?" the twenty-something man in too-tight slacks asked.

"It got done, didn't it?" Mace's usual condescension toward people drew an inquisitive look from the investigator.

"What my partner means is that we weren't expecting such a prompt response. Given the full moon, I mean."

It was Heaton's turn to get the man's inspection. "I'm not sure what kind of operation they run in Europe, but this faction of *the Moon*, is prepared for emergencies surrounding lunar events." He was speaking diplomatically, but he was also calling them both out on their idiotic intervention. "Given the association with the board, I see no reason to take either of you into custody. Frankly, you just saved us some bullets."

"Told you," Mace mumbled.

"However, you haven't exactly explained your presence here."

"Is that required for your report?" Heaton asked.

The investigator eyed Heaton before tapping a button on the screen of his laptop and folding it up. He tucked it into his messenger bag and crossed his arms. "I guess that depends on what the answer is."

"Maybe it's none of your business," Mace snarled.

The investigator glanced at him before returning his gaze to Heaton. "I could always check in with your comptroller." He reached into his coat pocket and pulled out a cell phone.

"You could, but she's dead," Heaton said sourly.

"And how did she die?" There was a slight accusation in his tone, but Heaton ignored it.

"Look..."

"Silas," he supplied.

"Look, Silas. Our reasons for being in the U.S. are currently discretionary and have nothing to do with werewolves."

"Are you sure about that?" Silas gave him a sly look. "I find it extremely coincidental that we got a report just this afternoon of a... shall we say... violent murder."

Heaton stared at him, revealing nothing.

"It wasn't very far from here." Silas pulled up a photo on his phone and showed it to Heaton. He looked at the splayed victim they had recently found but didn't react. "You see why we might be concerned about the arrival of a foreign werewolf and such a gruesome death."

"Callin didn't do that?" Heaton said.

Silas observed him for a moment. "You don't seem surprised to see it though."

"I'm ex-military and a hunter; I've seen it all."

"I bet you have." Silas put his phone away. "I'm sure you're well-versed in werewolf behavior too. You know that when werewolves start to go feral, they tend to be carnivorous even in their human form." Heaton swallowed hard, refusing to let even a glimmer of emotion trespass across his face. Silas moved in close to him, speaking quietly. "I'm sure you also know that failure to report a feral wolf is a punishable offense by both the council and the board."

"Callin is not feral," Heaton said firmly, comfortable with his lie by omission.

"And what about you, Mr. Macey?" Silas shifted his stance to look at Mace. "Do you have anything to add to Mr. Reid's statement?"

Mace eyed the nettlesome man, his mouth rolling around the fresh pinch of chew he had recently lodged in his cheek. After a moment, he nodded. "Yeah, I got something to add." Heaton stiffened as he considered what actions he could take to protect Nevia if the council found out about the murder. He could explain the transmorph situation to them, but that didn't change the fact that her behavior was abnormal. By all known definitions, she was acting like a feral wolf. And that was enough reason for them to put her down.

Mace leaned in and sniffed Silas's neck. "How do you stand that perfumy shit you're wearing? You smell like you just fucked Estee Lauder."

Heaton's reserve finally broke, and he smiled at Mace's inappropriate comment. He should have known better than to think he would rat Nevia out. Regardless of how little the man thought of virtually every human being on earth, he was still loyal to his partners.

Silas glanced at the blob of shit still residing on Mace's chest. Heaton waited for him to formulate a well-deserved insult regarding their odoriferous state, but he didn't stoop to Mace's level. "Let me know if you notice any changes in the werewolf." He handed Heaton a business card that displayed his name and number with the symbol of a crescent moon in the upper right-hand corner. Heaton tried to take it, but Silas held onto it tightly. "A feral wolf should not be trusted under any circumstances."

Heaton ripped the card from him and made a show of pocketing it. "I'm aware."

After Silas left them, he turned to Mace. "Thank you for not mentioning Jordan."

Mace shrugged. "She barely qualifies under their jurisdiction, anyway. Besides that man has no idea who the real villains in this story are. The way I see it, if Jordan is still going after the board members, then she's not completely bonkers yet."

"That's true."

"Maybe you were right. Maybe she had a very good reason for killing that man. Girl can't help it if she gets the munchies in the middle of a murder."

Heaton frowned, not preferring the casual way that Mace addressed his partner's cannibalism.

"However, I think one thing is very clear. We are gonna have to start moving faster if we want to stay ahead of her appetite."

Heaton nodded in agreement. His ultimate goal had always been to find Nevia, but now that he knew she had murdered a member of the board, he had a more pressing goal in mind. He needed to find her potential victims before she did.

24

C ORI PAUSED HER COUNT on the last cell in the section. The roster was a mess, and she was trying to get things organized again. Without Ethan or Duke around, the guards were taking more of a laissez-faire approach to prison management. So far, the paperwork listed three cells with the wrong transmorph I.D. and this last one didn't even have a photo available for her to confirm the identity.

She looked up from her clipboard and saw the transmorph that was impersonating Belus—or at least one of them. It was a different section than it had been the last two times, and she hadn't bothered to remember what the I.D. tags had been. If this wasn't the same transmorph, it meant that several of them were sharing this game to torment her more methodically.

Belus still seemed to be an odd choice, though. Not just because he was immune to psychic reading, but also because transmorphs generally didn't prefer to mimic shorter structured persons like children, or dwarfs. Apart from the loss of moisture required for the deception, compacting the spinal column was not particularly comfortable for them.

She moved to his cell and checked the floor for moisture, but there was none. It meant nothing, since he could have easily released the water into his privy. She considered asking him to turn around and lift his shirt so she could examine his spine for abnormalities. However, since she wasn't sure what Belus's back looked like to begin with, there was no point.

The transmorph noticed her examination and slipped off his cot. "Any problems?" he asked as if he expected a full report from her.

Cori looked him over, searching for the cracks in his facade. The way he stared back at her was difficult to bear, so she pretended to be suddenly interested in the other transmorphs in the section. There was not a direct neighbor to this transmorph, but further down the line, she saw several familiar faces, including Ethan's. She felt a pain claw at her heart as she looked at his face. It had been a long time since she had seen him. Longer than it had actually been. She looked away before she could display even a second's worth of her pain to the transmorph.

"You're starting to suspect something isn't right, aren't you?" Belus asked.

Cori tucked her clipboard under her arm and stared at the impostor. She didn't have to be here. She didn't have to converse with this parasite, but part of her was starting to believe his lies, and that scared her. "You know we could get to the bottom of this deception right now. Care for an acid bath?"

"Not particularly, but I'll endure whatever tests you want to perform."

"Okay." She called his bluff and walked toward the emergency station to grab her handy-dandy bottle of liquid transmorph detector.

"However, I suspect my photo is either missing or damaged."

Cori refused to acknowledge that he was right. She pulled the spray bottle out of the stash of crap that had nothing to do with emergency situations and more to do with being too lazy to walk to the trash chute. The bottle was light. She gave it a shake and determined that it was completely empty.

"Son of a bitch," she murmured to herself and made a note in the log to hunt down the safety supervisor and rip into him for not keeping up with his duties.

"That won't be the only thing missing."

"Of course, it won't. That asshole thinks safety checks are personal leave."

"There's been a lot of changes lately, haven't there?" Belus asked.

"Yeah, well, we're short on help, so we have to compensate." She checked her watch and decided that she didn't have time to waste tracking down the acid yet today. "You'll have to take a rain check on that acid bath."

"Did I ever tell you why I don't prefer to visit Danato's house?"

Cori had her hand on the door, ready to leave. She stared at her reflection in the glass. She wanted to know why she was being so stupid. Why couldn't she just follow the rules?

It wasn't as if she had never had a transmorph solicit her attention before. She had seen every manner of ghost in these cells. Perhaps it was different now because she was feeling lonely. With Ethan gone, she was relying on everyone for everything, and yet she still felt like she was doing it all herself.

Or perhaps it had more to do with the fact that she and Belus were not getting along lately. She knew better than to take anything the transmorph had warned her about to heart. However, it was interesting that their relationship had tarnished in the way he predicted. The transmorphs' psychic link may not have included Belus, but perhaps, like Cleos, he could predict the future with the knowledge of the personalities contributing to it.

"In the early days, if you remember, I turned down most of your dinner invites," Belus continued without her prompting.

Cori leaned forward and banged her head gently against the door before turning her attention to him. "I was under the impression Danato had not welcomed you back into his life. Or that you preferred to keep things professional."

Belus nodded. "I imagine I gave that impression, and neither of those things is untrue, but there was another reason. One I've never told anyone. Ever." Belus moved away from the bars and took a seat on his cot.

She waited for him to continue, but he didn't. It was such blatant bait that it pissed her off. He was just drawing her in. Using her losses and Belus's secret mind to appeal to her.

She closed her eyes and tapped her finger on the door handle before releasing it. "Okay, fisherman, you've caught me. I'm feeling nostalgic." She moved to the very edge of the yellow line, making it a point to look down at the position, before returning her attention to him. "Tell me why Belus rejected my invites."

"You already know that I have a past with the entity."

"Don't we all?" Cori mumbled.

"It's difficult to explain, because at one point, the being we think of as the house was just that—an emotional presence, satisfying our needs and desires as best it could. But after it took over Olivia, it was different. It stopped being an *it* and started being a *she*. She stopped being a force in the background of our lives and started to be ubiquitous. There was no longer a distinction between the woman we loved and the entity we feared because *she* saw no distinction. As far as the entity was concerned, she *was* Olivia. She had her memories and her body, so to her that was enough. She had no concept of an essence—a soul."

Since Cori already knew all this, she lost interest in his story and looked around. She noticed the transmorph a few cells down was in his natural form. His pale, nearly featureless face was staring at her. She narrowed her eyes at this oddity. At no point had a transmorph ever revealed himself to her voluntarily—at least not without a face full of acid or a reflection impulse.

"After I killed Olivia," he continued, and Cori's attention gravitated back to him. Belus didn't prefer to speak about Olivia, let alone his murdering her. However, since this wasn't the real Belus, it didn't matter what he said. "The entity, which was effectively Olivia, rejected me. I had to ask permission just to walk in the front door." Belus shifted off the cot and moved to the bars again. "But it was more than that. The chairs that I sat on were uncomfortable—to the point of the wood leaving splinters in my skin or sharp springs making me bleed. The air around me—and me alone—was particularly cold or unbearably hot. I'll spare you the stories about my bathroom mishaps."

Cori allowed herself a small smile, but only because she knew Belus would never acknowledge a history of comical plumbing issues. "And you never told Danato about this?"

"No, because most of what was happening was partially his fault. You see, it wasn't just the entity that didn't want me there; it was also Danato. He couldn't stand looking at me after what happened. What I had done. What I reminded him of."

"So, why did you…" Cori cleared her throat, refusing to let this game get out of hand. "Then why did Belus start coming around more often? Enough calluses on his ass to endure the pain?"

Belus grew a small sly smile and perked his brow. "Well, that and… you."

Cori took a breath and looked away from him. This was the trap. Seduction was a regular occupational hazard in the prison, but the transmorphs were the best at it. Nevertheless, she wanted or needed to be seduced. "Me?" she probed, noticing that the faceless transmorph was reaching out to her as if he were asking for help. His mouth was moving, but no words were coming out.

"I imagine it was a combination of things," Belus said. "Your presence made Danato happier. It lessened his pain and resentment. But also, as the house became more connected to you, it started to accept me more. She recognized your love for me."

Cori barked out a laugh even though she was tearing up. She collected herself before taking a bold step up to the red line. Belus noted the proximity. She crouched down so she could speak to him face to face. The burning in her eyes was no longer from tears, but the fire she had relit behind them. "Do me a favor. Save the heartfelt confessions for another face." She waved her hand over Belus's general being. "It just doesn't suit him."

Cori glanced over to the faceless transmorph as she moved away from Belus's duplicate. He had given up his odd performance and was now solidified as Daniel McGrath. She stopped in her tracks, ready to throw her clipboard at the creature. It was probably a good thing that the acid was gone because she would have sprayed the creature out of pure spite.

"There is a plan for every eventuality, Cori," Belus said.

"What?" she asked, trying to rein back her temper before she considered alternative punishments.

"Check the manual."

Cori rolled her eyes and headed to the door. "I've read the manuals, you twat."

"Not the ones I wrote."

Cori clamped her hand around the door handle as if it were this creature's throat. "Belus didn't write any manuals."

"Yes, I did. Because I was not satisfied with the prison protocols regarding certain contingencies." Cori looked at him, silenced mostly by her disbelief at his audacity. "Let's just say I didn't think bombing the prison was a necessary outcome for every scenario."

She let out a frustrated groan and backed away from the door again. "Okay, where's this manual?"

"For obvious reasons, I can't tell you." He nodded toward his neighbors. "I'm afraid you will just have to figure out where to find it."

"I don't have time for this," Cori whispered mostly to herself and checked her watch again. The minute hand had moved substantially, but it was her clipboard that had surprised her. Below her notation about the safety officer was another note. Written in hard-pressed pencil lead was the word "run" three times over. Cori stared at the words, knowing that she had not written them, but understanding very well that she *had* written them.

"What is it?" Belus asked, no doubt noticing the fear in her expression.

Rather than answer him, she did as her inner mind was demanding and ran.

25

"DON'T FIGHT IT, ETHAN." Safir pressed closer to him, pushing her ample breasts into his chest. He could hardly concentrate with her so close to him, but he couldn't force himself to push her away. She smelled of lavender and flint. Despite his desire to maintain his marriage vows, he couldn't help but admire her smooth sienna skin and the long, black, glossy waves that cascaded down her back. He wanted so much to touch them, but he knew he wouldn't stop there. Nor did he want to do anything to disrupt his lessons. Regardless of his stray thoughts, he still wanted the magic more than he wanted her.

Safir's previous disinterest in his delusions of grandeur had melted away the moment he had admitted to hearing the thoughts of the dragons. Apparently, hearing the creatures was a distinctive honor—only held by a mage. He assumed that was why he had been unable to tell anyone about his connection with them. Whether it was by his own will or the dragon's, hiding his ability to hear them was key to keeping his identity a secret.

But why? Why was it so important for him to stay in the shadows—hidden even from himself?

For two weeks, Ethan had spent practically every minute with Safir. He was eager to learn from her and hone this skill set that had been hidden so well from the world that even Annette had not sensed it. Unfortunately, his understanding of magic lent nothing to his ability to wield it. He assumed he might be able to focus his mind on a single thought and make it happen by sheer will, but the harder he concentrated, the farther away his goal seemed to get.

Despite making little to no progress, Safir was still eager to teach him—even to the point of exuberance. After all, it wasn't every day that a witch had an opportunity to train a mage. Even just interacting with Ethan seemed to thrill her. Her draw to him was not sexual, but rather like a fan glomming onto a celebrity. He was the new, hip thing in magic, and she wanted to be a part of it.

"There you go." Safir smiled at him, though he wasn't sure what he had done differently. "You have to let go of your assumptions about yourself. Once you embrace who you are, you will be able to access parts of yourself that you never even knew existed. You will become a whole new man."

Ethan's thoughts caught on that idea. He understood the idea of shedding his previous image of himself—to envision himself as a magical practitioner instead of just a man. But did he really want to become a whole new man?

Did shedding his old self mean forgetting his past? Forgetting wasn't that easy. If it were not, he wouldn't still feel an ache in his heart every time he pictured Cori's face. His fists wouldn't bunch up every time he remembered his son's cold, pale body.

He definitely didn't like the direction his life had taken recently, but was he ready to leave it all behind? He told himself he was. And every action he took, pushed him farther and farther away from his old life. He was barreling at a brick wall, and if he couldn't break through it, it would stop him dead in his tracks—quite literally. Either way, he would be free.

"Okay," Safir whispered to him. "I'm going to let go so you can take over."

Ethan focused all of his thoughts on air, gravity, and space—just as Safir had instructed. It was all about intention. What did he want to achieve? What did he really want to do?

Float. He demanded the word to press into his mind as if he might just stamp it in hard enough to make it happen.

Ethan's knees hit the hardwood floor, and Safir landed just after him. She let out a disgusted sound. "What happened that time?" she asked as she rubbed her knees. The look on her face told Ethan the luster of his superior craft was wearing off. He suspected she might be doubting his claim again. And why not? It wasn't as if he could prove the dragons had spoken to him. As far as anyone was concerned, he may well be delusional. Maybe he was. The prison was full of all types of psychics and magical entities. Who's to say that one hadn't just whispered in his ear? But then, of course, there was China. Who was whispering in his ear then if not the beasts in that cave?

"I concentrated as you said. I visualized as you taught me," Ethan tried to defend yet another failure. "We can try again if you want."

Safir's ire simmered—revealing a particularly damning look of surrender. "No. That's enough for tonight." She stood, waving off his attempt to help her up. She moved into her kitchen nook and opened the refrigerator. For a long moment, she just stood there, staring into the glow of last night's Chinese food and a twenty-four-pack of cheap beer that was more than half gone.

Ethan glanced at Efrat to see what he thought of Safir's mood. The elemental was lounging in a bowl chair, watching him—or perhaps he was just staring past him. He had been a trooper the last two weeks—coming along for his lessons and patiently waiting for Ethan to take him to a bar or some other entertainment afterward. Since Efrat hadn't been set up with a fake I.D. before they left, he was at Ethan's mercy. To add misery to their circumstances, Ethan was running low on money. The emergency credit card he had taken had finally been shut off, leaving him with whatever cash withdrawals he had left, which wasn't much. There was some irony in the fact that he had never worked harder than at the prison, and he didn't have a dime of his own to show for it.

He wasn't sure he was ready to take up proper employment yet. That would, of course, mean getting back to his roots. Petty theft and B&E sounded like a step backward in his career path, but between his strength and Efrat's power, it would go much easier than it had for him the first time around. Still, he was hoping to be better than that.

"Maybe we should start with something easier than levitation?" Ethan called over to Safir, breaking her out of the hypnotic lure of Asian cuisine.

"You want a beer?" Safir turned back and leaned over the pass-through, giving him an ample view of her cleavage. He was certain that she wasn't trying to be seductive; he was just very sensitive to her at the moment.

"No thank you, we should get going." Ethan stood and looked at Efrat. The elemental was still staring at him. Ethan perked his brow, urging Efrat to either share the thought that was causing him to scowl or, at the very least, blink. "Right?" he asked.

"Right," Efrat chimed in mirroring agreement. He shimmied himself out of the bowl chair he had stupidly opted to sit in. He still didn't like touching soft furnishings. He wouldn't even sleep in a bed for fear that he might burn alive if he had a bad nightmare.

Even his mannerisms hadn't changed yet. He still held his hands perpetually six inches away from his hips and shifted them behind his back before getting close to someone.

Doorknobs had always been a challenge for him, so he was content to let Ethan play the gentleman to his entrances and exits. Not that Ethan really minded. More often than not, observers just assumed they were a couple and even smiled at the affectionate pairing. But he sensed Efrat was not as comfortable with these looks. Aside from any discomfort he had with the prospect of a male partner, Ethan assumed it was the general humiliation of frailty putting him on edge. The elemental had already endured a decade's worth of foreign hands assisting his day-to-day necessities, so further placing himself in a feeble or feminine role was trying, not just to his masculinity, but to his dignity.

Ethan assumed he would eventually adapt to his new normal, but so far, he was holding steadfastly to old habits. His efforts to encourage him to branch out had not only fallen on deaf ears but enraged the man in the process. It only took Ethan a few heated arguments to realize that, like Ethan, Efrat was not ready to forget the man he used to be. Not because he had even a sliver of fondness for that former life, but because he didn't know what the future held for him. They knew next to nothing about Cleos's mental manipulation, including how long it would last. Efrat was preparing himself for the worst. He was waiting for the day his wires would be uncovered again. There was no sense in getting comfortable with the new normal if it was only temporary.

Fortunately, Efrat had at least ventured so far as to handle his own bathroom trips. The early days of their travels had been rather awkward with both of them going into toilet stalls together. It was a small sacrifice in comparison to the benefit of Efrat's company, but still... A man has limitations on his compassion.

"The night is still young," Safir baited them. She leaned against the doorframe as Ethan opened the door to leave the apartment. He paused midway through, noting her playful smirk. Her interest in his magic had most definitely worn off, but she still seemed to be interested in his company. "We could play Beer Pong. Girls against boys."

"That doesn't seem fair, two against one."

"I don't mind, but we could do one-on-one if that makes you more comfortable." There was a slyness in her smile that told Ethan they were no longer talking about games. He hadn't spent a lot of time in the company of young women, but he wasn't blind, and Safir wasn't exactly being cryptic. Perhaps he was mistaken about her interest in his magic—or maybe she just wanted a consolation prize for his failed efforts to impress her.

He was certain he could impress her in other ways, and as his eyes lingered on her bottom lip, just barely caught between the grip of her teeth, he was tempted to show her.

But not tempted enough.

"Thank you, but I don't hold my liquor well," Ethan declined in a soft voice.

"Oh, that can't be true."

"It really is. Just ask Efrat." Ethan nodded to Efrat.

Safir looked to him for the answer. "Good night," Efrat said and pushed between them to get out into the hall. Rather than wait for Ethan, he headed down the stairs.

Safir stared after him before turning her attention back to Ethan. "I guess he's not into games."

"He..." Ethan trailed off, not sure that there was enough time to explain Efrat's hot and cold behavior. The man had become increasingly cool around them both since he started his lessons. Ethan had attributed this to his overall boredom, but he knew that there was so much more going on in Efrat's life than lacking entertainment. Much like him, Efrat had been thrown into a world that was now foreign to him. Though Efrat would never admit it, he was scared. The future was uncertain, and neither of them had any answers. "I should catch up with him before he—"

Safir braced her arm behind him and leaned in fast. Her lips captured his. He raised his hand to her shoulder—not pushing or pulling, just placing it there. Safir let out a soft moan as she tickled his lip with her tongue. He relented and returned the sensuous kiss, allowing the tingle in his lips to ripple down into his legs. He felt his body respond, and it surprised him. He pulled back and stared at Safir wide-eyed. "I can't," he said, even as he realized he could.

"Ethan," Safir whispered softly. "I know there is a story behind this." She reached down and touched the wedding ring that still donned his left hand. "I also know it's a sad story. I can see it in your eyes." She moved her hand to rest on his chest. "I don't want to take you away from anyone—except yourself." Her hand moved down. The slow movement was like a countdown. He was five seconds from submission—from letting go of his ideals. Was this the final step in letting go? The nail in the coffin? The nail in his coffin?

Ethan grabbed her hand before she could trespass below his belt. "I'm sorry. You're beautiful, but I'm not going to be able to get away from myself."

Safir's eyes dimmed with a new level of disappointment. Her association with Ethan was turning out to be a bust on both ends. "I understand." She put on a fake smile and reached for the door. "Have a good night?" She pushed on the door, effectively scooting him into the hallway.

"Tomorrow then?" Ethan asked, just in case his dismissal would affect his training.

Safir gave him a weary look that told him she no longer wished to waste her time. "Tomorrow," she reluctantly agreed and closed the door.

Ethan headed down the stairs to the front stoop. A young man had just come out ahead of him and was trying to light his cigarette with a stubborn lighter. He flicked the lighter several times before shaking it to get more fuel to the wick. Efrat was leaning against the railing, waiting for Ethan, and noticed the man's troubles. He reached over and touched the man's cigarette tip. It lit with a flame, surprising the man. Rather than be shaken, as he should have been, the man just laughed and offered Efrat a high five, which he did not return. The man eventually gave up the camaraderie and thanked him before walking on.

Ethan stopped next to Efrat and glared at him. "I've asked you not to use your power in public."

"They don't know it's real. They think I'm an illusionist."

"Still. We don't need any more attention than necessary."

"Yes, sir," Efrat grumbled.

They began walking back to their apartment. They didn't have to discuss the option of hanging out at the bar. Ethan could already predict Efrat would not be up for a public place tonight.

"What's got you in a mood?"

"Not sure what you mean, sir."

"I mean, why are you acting like an ass all of a sudden?"

"Aren't I usually an ass?" Efrat snapped his finger, throwing an errant spark and making the two women ahead of them on the sidewalk jump. They glanced back and upped their pace.

Ethan put his hand over Efrat's and pushed his hand down. He noted the elemental kept a steady tingle of electricity in his palm just to make Ethan uncomfortable.

"Seriously," he stepped in front of Efrat, blocking his path. "What is your issue?"

"I have several. Which would you like first?"

"Let's start with the one that has been making you grow progressively quieter over the last two weeks. Not that I mind the silence, but I prefer your yammering sarcasm over your murderous glares."

Efrat pulled his hands away and circled around to look for prying ears. "Oh, let's see, why don't we start with... What the fuck!" Efrat spat the words through gritted teeth, emphatically gesturing with his sparking hands.

"You'll have to be more specific."

"Mage." Efrat lifted one pointed finger. "Talking dragons." He threw up a second finger. "Why didn't you tell me about this?"

Ethan shrugged. "I couldn't at first."

Efrat narrowed his eyes. "Why not?"

"I don't understand it either, Efrat. Honestly, I don't understand most of what Safir has been telling me."

"You understand it a hell of a lot more than I do."

"Not enough to make a difference, apparently," Ethan mumbled.

Efrat looked him over like an anomaly. "How come you haven't been able to do anything?" he asked delicately—as if it might be an offensive question.

"I'm not sure. I really am trying, but..." Ethan shook his head. "I'm beginning to wonder if the dragons lied to me about this too."

"Why would they lie about you being a mage?"

"Why would they lie about creating a sorceress?" Ethan began walking again.

"Is that what they said?" Efrat followed a step or two behind, walking on the street instead of the sidewalk.

"What?"

"Did they ask you to create a sorceress?"

Ethan thought back to his first conversations with the enigmatic lizards. "Not in so many words."

"What did they say?"

"They said I had to save the girl. That she was important—to them and to me. So, I saved her. And then Danato killed her."

"What did the dragons have to say about that?" Efrat moved around a parked car.

"They acted like it didn't matter. They told me to bury her."

"So, you buried her and then the dragons arrived to commune over her grave."

"What's your point?"

"I don't think I have one, but maybe the sorceress wasn't the point."

"The point was to save her, and I failed," Ethan said firmly.

"You can't save everyone."

Ethan spun on his heel to face Efrat, who was already wincing at the stupidity of his befitting life lesson. "I think that goes without saying, Efrat, but thank you for reminding me of my inability to protect my family."

Efrat's mouth formed a few silent words before he got his sentence out. "You know that wasn't what I was referring to." Ethan moved away, but Efrat grabbed his arm. "Wait." Ethan turned back and once again waited for Efrat to build the courage to speak the words that he had been holding back since they left the prison. "It wasn't your fault."

Efrat's commiseration admittedly surprised Ethan, but it only served to stoke the embers of the fire that still burned just beneath his skin. "No, you're right. It's not my fault. It was her fault. The one to blame for the endless ache inside of me is my dear, sweet wife. The woman who created my son—also took him from me."

"She had no choice," Efrat spoke softly, trying to aim the petition under his armaments. Little did he know that Ethan no longer had space in his heart for Cori's excuses.

"She had a choice. She could have fought to the very last minute just like we did."

"I know you don't want to hear this from me, but..." Efrat trailed off as he looked at Ethan's fierce expression.

"Oh, don't stop. I'd love to hear this."

"I'm just saying that maybe what she did was for the best—for everyone else."

"You wouldn't be defending her if it was your son." Ethan turned away and continued down the sidewalk.

"And you wouldn't be condemning her so hard if you had ever killed anyone."

Ethan stopped. He took a steadying breath and turned back to Efrat. The elemental was back on the sidewalk, and for a moment they just stared at each other.

"What does that have to do with anything?"

Efrat raised his hands, baring his palms. "Do you think it's easy to be the bad guy? Do you think the blood just washes off in the shower?"

"I thought we were talking about Cori's bad choices."

"Don't you get it, man? It wasn't a choice for her. Somebody was always going to take your son from you. Whether it was Danato or Belus or that goddamn genie, you were going to lose your boy. She was backed into a corner, and while we were trying to kill each other, she did the only thing she could to protect all of us." Efrat took a tentative step forward. "Don't you see what she did? She stacked up all that guilt and grief, put it on her shoulders, and then braced herself for a tidal wave of anger and resentment from everyone around her."

Ethan closed the distance between them and grabbed Efrat's neck, pulling him down so he could speak into his ear. Efrat pinched his fingers into tight fists but didn't defend himself. "Do you really think I give a damn what she is going through right now?" Ethan released him and walked away. As far as he was concerned, they had nothing left to discuss.

26

T HE ALARM ON THE roof blared, and Cori dropped the prism she was using to tempt her cornered goblin into a cage and out of the heating vent he insisted on calling home. The creature screeched; ears assaulted by the loud noise that was also echoing up through the vent from the floors below. He lunged forward, barreling past the cage and right at Cori. She had no time to react before the creature's claws slashed across her face. She fell back, defending against the searing pain. Before she could retaliate with her taser, the goblin was gone. No doubt squatting in another vent that would require her attention later.

Cori touched the aggravated skin on her cheek and found a deep laceration. She cursed at the amount of blood she found on her fingertips. As she considered how many stitches she would need, a few drops of blood dribbled off her brow, crossing her vision before landing on her cheek. She touched her forehead and found the upper extension of the creature's scratch. She was lucky she hadn't lost an eye.

The radio on her hip chirped, and she flipped it to a private channel. "Yeah," she responded less than enthusiastically.

"I need you down here right now," Danato demanded.

"Can it wait? I've got a bit of a—"

"That's an all-man alarm, Cori. Get your ass to the dock now."

"Yes, sir," she said slightly sarcastically. "What's going on?"

"Now!" he barked into the radio before clicking off.

Cori missed the normal days in the prison—if there could have been such a thing. The stress of maintaining order was getting to everyone—especially Danato. He was getting progressively stricter with her. His demands on her were more frequent. She spent most of her days running around, averting catastrophes that could have been prevented with proper procedures.

It was easy for her to put the blame on the men. Even if they resented her as their subsidiary leader and despised her for the choices that put her into the position, there was a deeper problem running through the ranks. Morale had been low ever since Ethan had left. Even with Duke back, it still wasn't much better. Cori hadn't realized how much impact her husband had on this system. He was apparently the glue that held it all together. And try as she might, she could barely hold herself together, let alone the people around her.

When Cori reached the stairwell door, she noticed several of the guards had clustered at the roof's edge rather than head down. She initially moved to instruct them to join the others, but as if choreographed many times, the six of them broke apart and scattered across the west end of the building. There was a feral buzz among them as they pulled out their sniper rifles, loaded them, and propped them on the ledge.

Cori moved forward slowly, stepping up onto the edge between two broken merlons. She looked down at the courtyard that was filled with nearly a dozen jeeps and trucks. At first, Cori thought the board had returned in response to recent events, but it wasn't black-on-black that filed out of the back of the trucks. The marbled dark green camouflage made Cori cringe as she considered that the U.S. military might now be involved. However, it wasn't the correct red, white, and blue flag that was proudly displayed on the hood of the lead vehicle.

As the troops lined up and marched toward the entrance with their rifles propped high on their shoulders, Cori realized what this was. The neighbors were paying them an unscheduled visit.

The head honcho of the group stepped out of the lead vehicle. Awards, insignias, and chevrons riddled his dark green uniform. All signifying that he was someone important. He tugged on his uniform as he glanced up at the men lining the roof. His gaze paused on her. She wasn't sure he could see much of her at this height, but regardless, she probably stood out among the cocksure snipers that were keeping their heads low.

The man smiled as he walked toward the building, dismissing any threat that the roof guards might pose to him.

Cori leaped from her spot and barreled down the stairs to the elevators. The doors were wide open and waiting. In record—stomach-tickling—speed she was on the main floor. She ran down the hall to the docks and arrived just as the Russian general and a handful of his men entered the prison through the truck entrance.

In any other scenario, the stock-still prison guards lining the docks as if this were a daily event would have impressed Cori. Everyone seemed to have built-in military instincts except her. She slipped through the wall of men, keeping her late arrival as inconspicuous as possible. She must have done well because Danato didn't flinch when she stopped at his side, chest puffed and arms strapped at her side like a good little soldier.

Thankfully, she had opted for the traditional black-on-black uniform today, so she didn't stand out any more than she usually did in a room full of men.

The general looked over the line approvingly before descending the steps to the packing level of the dock. He removed his hat and approached Danato. After a brief pause, the man's face broke into a smile. "Danato!" He raised his arms, offering a hug.

"Grisha!" Danato opened himself for a hug, and the men slapped each other on the back as they embraced.

They both laughed as they parted, but Cori sensed there was some tension in Danato's half of the amusement.

"It's good to see you, my friend," Grisha said in a thick Russian accent. He frowned as he squeezed his arms. "Have you lost weight?"

Danato cleared his throat. "You remember my second Rutherford Belus and—" Danato turned as if to look for her, but found her right next to him. He did a triple take, first out of surprise to see her right there, second because he noticed her cut, and third because he realized how severe it was. "This is... Cori Reiger, my... successor."

"Christ, Danato," Grisha laughed as he looked Cori over. "What the hell have you done to her?"

"Technically, it's your fault, General," Cori said stone-faced. "Your arrival sounded the alarms, which disturbed the goblin I was in the process of catching."

Grisha's smile waned as his eyes searched her to determine if she was being earnest, sassy, or just funny. "A goblin hunter?" he turned his disbelief to Danato, who nodded to confirm Cori's claim of grandeur. "Well, I never..." Grisha stepped up to her and extended his hand for a proper handshake. She gave him a stiff-armed shake, but he held her hand a moment longer than necessary. "A pleasure indeed. Does that hurt?"

"Immensely, sir."

Grisha laughed and backed away from her. "I thought you had a boy for this."

"He didn't work out."

"With such competition, I can see why."

"Indeed," Danato nodded to the courtyard where three dozen additional soldiers were taking up space on his lawn. "Why the theatrics, Grisha? Since when do your social calls require fanfare?"

"Social call?" Grisha frowned. "Did I say I was here to socialize?"

"Cut the crap. Why are you here?"

Grisha clicked his tongue. "You Americans are always so eager to get down to business. You'll die young with an attitude like that. It's been a long trip. I'm tired. And your poor heritor is bleeding into her bra." Grisha laughed. "Why don't we pretend this is a social call and enjoy each other's company for a moment before the yelling and gunfire begin? Please, Danato. It is because I genuinely respect you I don't want to remind you whose land this prison sits on. It's because of our friendship I don't want to begin my negotiations with bloodshed." Grisha's expression seemed sincere. However, Cori suspected his threats were also sincere.

"You just want to get your hands on my liquor stash," Danato teased.

Grisha let out a belly laugh. "This is very true. You know me too well. Come! We will drink, and we will eat. Yes?"

"Yes," Danato conceded.

Grisha smiled broadly and pointed to Cori. "Her too, yes? Yes," he answered himself. "I like this one. She's got—uh…" His eyes lit with intrigue as he thought of the English words he wanted. "Star potential." Cori didn't like the smile that he gave her.

"Lead the way, my friend," Danato said, ushering his guest forward. He looked back, giving Belus a stern look before volleying his eyes to Cori.

"Let me look at that cut, Cori," Belus said rather loudly before tugging on her hands. She kneeled down so he could inspect it more closely. "Did Danato ever tell you about the last Russian visit?" he whispered, barely moving his lips.

"Yes," she said just as quietly.

"Then you know they've wanted the prison for a long time."

"Yes."

"What they really want is the bubble though, so under no circumstances will you say anything about spending time in there. They have no idea that the wizards are dead. If they know that thing is basically an open portal to raise armies in, they will stop at nothing to have it. Do you understand?"

"Yes."

"I mean it, Cori. Bloodbath."

"Yes, sir."

"Come on, I've got supplies at the house," he said a little louder.

Cori trailed behind him, watching the men disband to return to their regularly scheduled performances. The Russian soldiers also headed outside to join their comrades. Cori glimpsed Levi standing in a corner and waved him over. He rushed to join her in the hall.

"I get the impression this isn't going to be a quick conversation. Can you tell Riley what's going on and..." Cori winced at the thought of coming home to her sullen little boy. Lately, it seemed she was always being delayed. And although she had legitimate reasons for it, her excuses meant nothing to a child who missed his mother. "Try to smooth things over with Oliver."

Levi nodded. "What are they doing here?" he asked.

"I'm not sure, but the last time they *visited*, Danato had to forcefully remove them. Hopefully, it won't come to that."

"And if it does?" Levi asked.

Cori took a moment to consider what a foreign occupation would do to this place. How many of its occupants would be in danger? How many of its employees would be *relocated* or *dismissed*?

"I won't let it come to that," she assured him before walking away.

Despite the conviction of her statement, Cori was not confident she could avoid a takeover. Her reputation for getting out of complicated situations was downright legendary now, but there was no guarantee her luck would translate to the battlefield. And if the Russians really wanted the bubble, that was exactly what this place would turn into.

27

B Y THE TIME BELUS and Cori arrived at the house, Danato and Grisha were already sitting in the living room enjoying an expensive vodka. To Cori's surprise, both men looked genuinely relaxed as they enjoyed the warm fire. Grisha let out a sigh as he put his feet on the coffee table. Despite the faux pas of decorum, Danato did not scold his guest.

Belus guided her to a seat at the dining room table before retrieving the in-house first aid kit. She knew it was the type of injury she should go to the infirmary for, but apart from her non-optional invitation from Grisha, she needed to be here. She needed to know just how much danger the prison was in.

She glanced at her watch, trying to forget the fact that she was already past her preferred entrance time. The goblin had taken longer than she expected to find, let alone coax. Belus gave her a glare, already predicting what she was thinking. As she suspected, going back to the bubble now would draw undue attention to her and it. That was out of the question.

"Would you like something for the pain, darling?" Grisha offered, raising his glass to her.

"No," Belus answered for her. "But I might need it for disinfectant."

"Oh, you're right." Grisha rose and came around to watch Belus work. "Goblins are particularly... dirty critters. Have you ever had the pleasure?"

"Cori received an early introduction to goblins when she came to the prison," Danato said from his chair. "She handled herself admirably." Danato caught her eye as he gave the compliment. The swell of pride was enough to make her smile—though only until the pain became too much.

"I'm sure she did." Grisha was still looking at her with more interest than Cori preferred. She would have preferred to attribute it to some basic attraction, but she suspected Grisha was not the type of man to put his cock before his country. "May I?" He raised his glass again, directing the question to Belus.

It took Belus a moment before he realized what he was offering. He shifted away from her side and motioned for Grisha to step up to bat. Cori looked at Belus for something just short of heroics, but he just tipped his chin up, as if this were one of those times that she shouldn't get too emotional.

"Ready?" Grisha asked, shaking his glass. "Close your eyes," he instructed.

Cori did as he bid, and a second later the stinging disinfectant of fine liquor splashed across her face. Apart from the razor pain of having anything touch her wound, the alcohol was particularly harsh, making her want to cry out—but she didn't. She was the warden's successor now. She was not allowed to feel pain—let alone express it.

When she opened her eyes, Belus had returned to prepare for stitching. Grisha was still watching her, seemingly pleased that she had contained her pain. Had she known he would enjoy her stalwart resistance to pain, she would have groaned and cursed like she wanted to when Belus stitched the first pass of the thread into her cheek.

"I've heard a lot about you, Corinthia Reiger." Everyone seemed to have the same reaction to her given name. The same question perched in all their eyes.

"What do you mean, Grisha?" Danato asked.

"Danato thinks that I don't keep tabs on this place," Grisha said only to her. "He thinks that I am content with his semiannual reports. And though they are entertaining in their sufficiency." Grisha glanced back at Danato, attributing the compliment to him. "I have found other avenues to get the real gossip about the activities in this prison."

"Such as?" Danato finally stood and joined the conversation.

Grisha glanced at him with a deceptively amused smile on his face. "I have been particularly impressed with your resume." He moved to her and pressed a hand to her shoulder. She looked up at him from beneath her brow, so she wouldn't disturb Belus's stitching. "I heard about the recent trouble with the genie." Cori tensed at the topic. She hated talking about that day. She spent enough time thinking about it—over and over again. "I know that these people will harbor anger towards you. They will spit on you, but deep down they all know that you made the right decision." He stepped back again, saving her the trouble of shrugging off his mock condolences. "In Russia, we understand that protecting one's people is more important than an individual life."

"If you don't value individual lives, then what are you protecting?" Belus asked. Grisha looked at him, his satisfaction waning slightly as he examined the petulant man. "I think what you meant to say was that protecting one's sovereignty is more important than individual lives."

Grisha chuckled. "So says the man who shot his best friend's wife."

Belus paused his work to stare at the man, offering no retaliation to feed the man's mockery of him.

"He did that for love," Cori interjected on his behalf. "Just as I did what I did for love."

Grisha smiled warmly at her. "Yes, I know you did. So much of what you do is based on this foolish idea of devotion to this place... to this man." Grisha motioned to Danato.

"Why is that foolish?" Cori asked, curious about what his response would be.

"Because he doesn't see you!" Grisha motioned enthusiastically to his own eyes. "I see you, Corinthia. I see the potential within you." His eyes danced with possibility. "You would be a welcome addition to my team."

"She will not leave this prison." Danato stepped up to Grisha's side, bearing down on him with bodily threat.

Grisha paused, his face still trying to maintain its amusement rather than let the sneer from his eyes sink into the rest of his face. "And why is that?" he finally addressed Danato, face to face. "Because you need her to collect your monsters, to rally your troops, or is there another reason you want her here." Danato stared at Grisha, confusion seeping into his features. "As I said, Danato, I keep very close tabs on this prison. I know who is coming and going at all times. I know when there is a shift in power." Danato's face turned ashen. Grisha's contrarily brightened.

"I want to make it very clear to..." Grisha examined Belus again. "...both of you. I do not care who sits in the big seat. I do not care what monsters sit inside those walls. What I do care about is preserving value." Grisha looked back at her. "I will not allow you to waste... such a beautiful—"

"Her rings don't work," Danato said flatly.

Grisha's energy waned, and he looked at Danato. "What?"

"Ethan took the wedding ring when he left. If the set isn't complete, she can't wield contact magic."

"Oh." Grisha looked at her hands and the empty finger that was as much a slap in the face to her as Ethan's attempted murder. "Damn," Grisha grumbled, losing all interest in her star potential. "I guess it's on to new business then."

Grisha moved back to the couch and Danato back to his usual chair. Cori glanced at Belus, who was smirking as he snipped the excess threads on his handiwork. He tossed the scissors into the box as he leaned into her ear. "Don't look so disappointed; you'll hurt Danato's feelings."

Cori let out a breathy laugh and headed into the bathroom to get a quick sponge bath. She would have much preferred a shower, but at least she could wipe the blood off her neck and chest. She caught sight of herself in the mirror and nearly broke into tears. It obviously looked worse than it was with the swelling and the blood. Belus had done a fine job with the stitches, so the scar wouldn't be much. If she had time, she would try to see Penelope for some magical first aid.

She glanced at her watch and realized that she had been out of the bubble for an hour. It wasn't the first time she had missed her deadline, but she suspected that tonight would be well over her usual disruption in schedule.

She quickly took off her shirt and wiped herself down. In the button drawer of the vanity, she found one of Ethan's spare shirts. He always tucked one in the downstairs bathroom for a quick change in case he got something less than appealing on his shirt during the day. Despite being freshly cleaned, she pressed the cloth to her nose and smelled it.

Mixed with detergent and the familiar fireside scents of Danato's house, Cori could smell her husband. Though nothing much affected her these days—her heart had hardened into a lump of coal that only had room for one objective—she nearly broke into tears at the thought of Ethan being there with her. By her side, to care for her, to protect her.

She could not blame him.

She would not blame him.

But there was an anger deep inside of her—irrational and selfish, certainly—but she wasn't sure how much longer she could *want to* forgive Ethan and not actually forgive him. At some point, her love would fade, and her anger would be the only thing that survived the long days and longer nights.

Cori bit back her tears, as she always did when the thought of Ethan overwhelmed her. Much like withstanding the shock of a vodka disinfectant, she boarded up the nerve endings that were screaming at her.

She looked back in the mirror and saw a face from history staring back at her instead of her own reflection.

The woman reached forward, coming out of the mirror, and whipped a black riding crop across her face.

Cori gasped and jumped back, feeling the pain of the impact in real-time. She braced her arm to stop any further attack, but the image was gone. All that remained was her own reflection, defending against a memory. Though she rationalized the pain in her cheek was the same as when she had entered the bathroom, she could have sworn it felt worse.

It was all in her head.

Old memories rising to the surface.

But these were memories entirely disconnected from the bubble. Things she hadn't thought about in years—not since Cleos had tampered with her mind.

Though she was certain telling Danato would not help matters, she considered telling Cleos about this disruption. If his mental blocks were crumbling, then maybe she just needed a tune-up.

Cori composed herself as best she could and slipped on the new black shirt. When she arrived back in the living room, Grisha was waving his hands as if whatever he was saying should have been obvious. "I am not leaving here without the money, Danato. I don't want demurrals or I.O.U.s. I want my money."

"What money?" Cori asked.

"His bribes," Belus answered from the chair opposite Danato.

Cori propped her hands on her hips, waiting for more information.

"You see, petal..." Grisha scooted forward on the couch and turned to speak to her. "This prison resides in a territory that is neither useful nor advantageous to Mother Russia. However,... it still belongs to her. So, the board Danato answers to is obligated to pay us rent and... Let's call it hush money."

"Bribes," Belus repeated.

Grisha laughed. "What do you expect? It's an American-run operation with potentially damaging ramifications. Not to mention, we provide the safeguards that keep this place in line."

"Safeguards?" Cori asked, looking between Danato and Belus. Neither of them would look at her.

"Oh, don't tell me you didn't know about the..." Grisha made a clicking sound as he bobbed his finger. "...button."

Cori frowned. "You're the one responsible for destroying the prison?"

"Yes, of course. We are the closest and frankly, if an American missile came anywhere near us, it would be blown out of the sky." Grisha stood and moved to the liquor cabinet. He poured a very generous portion of something brown into his glass before returning to her. "Perhaps I'm negotiating with the wrong person." Grisha winked at her.

"I don't have any money here, Grisha," Danato said irritated. "You know that. The board is responsible for distribution."

"Why hasn't the board given him the money?"

"We discussed this possibility."

"No, we discussed the possibility of the board shutting us down. Is this—" Grisha reached toward her cheek. "What are you..." Cori dodged the man's reach, but eventually, she just let him touch her wound. His finger came back with a drop of blood. To her horror, the man licked it off—tasting it like a sample of food.

"Danato, are you sure the prison doesn't hold anything of value you could offer to tide me over?"

Cori was only beginning to formulate thoughts of vampires, siths, and cannibals when Danato appeared behind Grisha, his mouth so close to his ear that he might bite it off. "She... is... mine."

The words startled Cori more than Grisha's bloodlust. Danato was certainly protective of her, but for him to declare it in such a territorial way shocked her.

"Just try it, and I will end this machination and deal with you as I should have the moment you arrived."

Cori swallowed hard as she glanced to where Grisha was gripping the gun on his hip.

"My men will—"

"—follow the orders of their General," Danato said sinisterly.

Grisha's eyes widened, and he relinquished his grip on his gun. "You need to look at this more rationally, Danato." Grisha pulled away from Danato and moved past Cori. "I am your only connection. Without me, there is no one to tamp down the people who have no trust for this operation—or the people who want to control it. I suspect it is only a matter of time before my people can simply walk in and take it—or am I misreading the room?" Grisha stared at Danato, waiting for him to answer, but he didn't.

"No one is taking this prison," Cori answered for him, but Grisha paid her little mind.

"Regardless of what the future holds, it is the here and now that I am interested in. If I return home with nothing... then there is nothing for me to distribute to my colleagues. And unlike you, I would not lower myself to offering empty promises. So perhaps the question is not whether I will have possession of this prison, but rather, how soon will I have possession of this prison."

"I will end you, Grisha," Danato seethed.

"Yes, yes, threats. But you must know how Russia deals with your ilk. You must know that we are not afraid of you. I suppose it goes back to the idea of putting country before the individual." Grisha glanced back at Belus. "You see, we don't care who dies, as long as our enemies die too." Grisha cracked his neck and circled to the back of the couch. "So, I will ask you once again..." His words were slow and intentionally calm as he clenched his hands. "Do you have anything to pay your debt to Russia? Anything to stop me from taking… everything."

The house went cool as Grisha and Danato stared at each other. Cori knew Danato had nothing. The only thing of value in this prison was the prison—and the bubble. If Grisha went away empty-handed, he would be back with an army. He would indeed confiscate everything—including the bubble. She couldn't allow that.

She had already sacrificed too much.

She would not lose—

"I have something to pay you with," Cori said, breaking the stalemate and causing everyone to look at her.

Grisha smiled at her. "That is a sweet offer, but I'm afraid it will take more than your sweet kisses to keep Russia happy."

"Not me, you idiot," Cori snapped, perturbing Grisha with her bite. "A dragon."

"Cori," Danato scolded her, but she was past the point of listening to him. So far he had done nothing but threaten this man. It was time either to appease him or to end him. And she suspected bloodshed now would only result in a bigger attack later.

Grisha laughed. "The dragon? No, I'm afraid I can't do much with her. She's certainly a good source of magic, but she is far too old to be useful to us."

"What about a male dragon?" Cori asked.

The fire flared as Grisha's eyes turned hungry with interest.

"What are you talking about?" Danato asked.

"Would that be enough to satisfy the debt—for a while at least?"

Grisha moved to her, his sinister smile returning as he looked her over. "I was right. You were the one I should have been negotiating with all along." He cleared his throat. "You should know, though; I don't take kindly to deception. Don't offer me lies." Grisha touched his weapon to remind her he was armed.

"I can take you to him right now," she said with confidence.

28

D ANATO CAUGHT UP WITH her as she led them to the stables. He grabbed her arm, squeezing it much too tight. "What are you up to? If you are planning something, then you should know that Grisha is not a merciful man. If this is a trick..."

"It's not a trick, Danato. I lied about the breach. It wasn't entirely benign."

Danato's grip on her arm relinquished, and he looked away from her as he walked. "Why am I continually surprised by your deceit?"

"Stop killing things and maybe I'll stop lying."

He looked back at her, anger melting as pain took over his features. "That's not fair, Cori. You know that if I had any other options—"

"You wouldn't have seen them," Cori answered. "You didn't see them. And now we continue to suffer because of it."

Danato stopped, blocking her from moving forward as well. "I will not carry the blame for the situation we are in—at least not alone."

"Don't assume for one second I don't share that blame. But could you for once in your life learn from it and trust me?" she seethed. She glanced back at Belus and Grisha, who were nearly within earshot. "Yes, I'm sure, Danato," she said, disguising her volume as irritation.

She pushed his arm down and entered the stable. Past the sheep and the cows, and beyond the endless chicken roosts, was a ladder leading into the upper loft of the stable. Used to store extra food and hay, it was the perfect hiding place for her little pet. He didn't know how to use the ladder, so he remained confined on the upper deck out of sight from unapproved eyes—like Danato's.

Cori whistled and kissed, calling to her favorite little dragon. At first, nothing happened. She looked down at Grisha, who was stroking his gun tenderly. "Problem?" he asked.

"He's probably just asleep," she retorted.

She sat down, tapped her fingernails on the wood floor, and waited. She noticed that Danato was getting anxious as well. He was looking around, searching for weapons. Though she was certain that he could handle a pitchfork just fine, she knew it wouldn't be needed.

Even as she considered another way to call to Puff, a screeching yawn signaled he was waking. She smiled as the pile of hay he had wiggled himself under shifted. "Puff," she called to him, and his precious little tail poked through the hay and started wagging furiously. She couldn't help but laugh at his little round butt cheeks adding to the shaking of the hay pile.

He squirmed and hopped, freeing himself from the hay. He shook off the remaining grass and pinpointed her across the loft. His squeal of joy was enough to make her laugh, which made her hiss in pain. Puff let out a guttural noise that might someday be a roar. He ran to her side and immediately started licking her cheek.

"Oh, careful, careful!" Cori cringed at his lapping tongue but soon felt relief from her pain instead of an increase in it. She relaxed and let him do what his instincts demanded.

"How have you kept this a secret?" Belus asked. "How have you been—"

"Because she's clever. And you two are self-involved idiots." Grisha threw a hand up, effectively silencing Belus's questions. "Can he blow fire?"

"He usually just burps fire, but he's getting better at it." Cori patted Puff's back and he let out a burp that was mostly black smoke. "Do you think he will satisfy our debt?"

Grisha was practically drooling as he gazed at the dragon. "Oh yes, I think that will do fine." He climbed the ladder and touched him—as if checking to see if he were a mirage. Grisha grabbed Cori's chin and turned her head to check her cut. "He's an excellent healer too."

Cori moved her chin out of his grip. He continued to look at her carefully before his gaze slid to the two men below. "Come! I insist you walk me out." Grisha let out a grunt of surprise as he lifted the whelp into his arms and carried him down the ladder. Cori followed him as requested and walked with him toward his cluster of vehicles.

"What will you do with him?" Cori nodded to Puff, who despite the occasional uninvited lick was behaving very well for the General.

"It's best not to ask such questions, but I assure you we know enough about dragons not to wish them destroyed. They are powerful creatures and, as such, demand respect." Grisha called to his soldiers, and two of them came running over. They eyed the creature in his arms before accepting the heavy bundle. Puff squawked as they took him away, but his mewling became louder when he realized Cori was not joining him. She tried not to cry, but the pain of losing something so precious was a pain she wasn't sure she could endure.

Not again.

"Do not fret, Corinthia," Grisha drawled and wiped the tear from her good cheek. "I will do everything in my power to protect him from cruelty. I only wish I could offer you the same."

Cori stepped away from him, searching for an attack. When it became clear that none was coming, she frowned at him. "What do you mean?"

Grisha looked over her shoulder at Belus and Danato, who were only pretending not to take great interest in their conversation. "I meant what I said before." He pressed his hand to her back, urging her to continue walking with him. "You would make an excellent addition to my team. And as much as I would love to rescue you from this prison, I'm afraid your shackles are much too determined."

"I'm not a prisoner, Grisha," Cori assured him.

"Oh, that's the sad part. You actually believe that." Cori scoffed, not willing to entertain someone else's interpretation of her life. Grisha stopped at his vehicle and leaned against it. "What's worse is that you have no idea how much danger you are truly in." Cori frowned at this assessment. "If I were any kind of hero, I would snatch you up right now and take you away from here—even against your will."

"I suspect you wouldn't get very far." Cori narrowed her eyes at him.

"Indeed, not. Which is why I should not rescue you today. Perhaps the reason you *have* to stay is also the reason you *should* stay. I can see that you are a fighter." He plucked up her hand. "With or without your rings." He kissed her hand, which she allowed.

Puff's cry drew her attention, and her breath hitched. She regretted her bargain already. It was a risk, to be sure, but one that needed to be taken.

"Listen to me, Cori." Grisha stood and blocked her view of Puff as his men shoved him in the back of a truck.

"If things go the way that I think they will, this prison will need my help eventually."

"What?"

"This board that runs things—the one that is supposed to pay me. I think they are done contributing money to things they cannot see or understand."

"It's fine. We'll figure it out."

"No, I don't think you will. Not in time to keep the doors open. So, when the day comes that I return to offer my help, I hope that you will remember that I am not your enemy."

"No, you're just the man who takes bribes."

Grisha chuckled. "I know you've been here a long time, but surely you remember how the real-world works. Be happy that I am an easy man to please and loyal to the highest bidder. Then you will always know where you stand."

Cori scoffed. "Just because I have given you my dragon, does not mean I consider us friends."

"Certainly not. I can see it hurts you a great deal to see him depart. But we both know there is something far more valuable than dragons inside that prison. Something that my people have wanted for a long time. And just because I have decided not to rip it from your grasp, does not mean I consider *you* a friend." Grisha let his words sink in as he stared at her with dead eyes. "However, there is value in keeping our relationship civil. Not just to avoid bloodshed, but as a way to keep an honest exchange of information. Men of my status prefer interrogation and torture. I prefer conversation and vodka." Grisha looked back at Danato, who was downright leering at him. "Whatever dangers lurk ahead, just remember one thing. I monitor all the communication out of this prison. Should you require my assistance, you need merely ask."

"I can only imagine the price of your help," Cori said.

"Desperate times, my dear..." He winked at her before waving at Danato. "Do svidaniya, my friend."

Danato gave him a wave and watched him get into his vehicle. The soldiers loaded up as well, and before long the caravan was on its way over the lowered bridge. Cori stared after them, still hearing the high-pitched squeal of Puff even after the drawbridge had closed behind them.

Danato came up next to her and looked between her sullen face and the entrance. "What did he talk to you about?"

Cori felt an instant pang of sadness that Danato's first concern was their conversation. It was true he didn't fully understand what Puff was—or what Puff used to be. Had he known, she was certain he wouldn't have let her use him as a bargaining chip.

"He enquired after the bubble and tried to sell me on becoming a Russian spy." Cori wasn't sure she understood half of what Grisha was trying to say, but regardless, she understood he was not a trustworthy man. He may have considered his loyalty to money an asset, but she saw it as his downfall.

Cori walked away from the empty courtyard, and Danato followed. "I'm not sure it was a good idea to give the Russians a second dragon."

"Second?" Cori's eyes flashed to Danato. Yet another revelation uncovered after so many years of service. She knew they held the male dragons in separate locations across the globe. She just assumed Danato was as much in the dark about their locations as the rest of them. "Don't worry. They won't be getting a second dragon."

"What do you mean?"

"Puff may have been birthed from the breach, but she still has an adoptive mother."

Danato's confusion was there and gone. The loud thump of a heavy object drew his attention and put urgency in his steps. Cori increased her pace as well.

By the time she reached the outer hangar, the roar coming from inside was loud enough to be heard through the whole compound. She rushed inside and released the door so that Penelope could escape the confines of her false cave.

The dragon shuffled out of the space like a waddling duck. Her head bobbed to and from searching for her little Puff. Cori stepped out of the hangar, and Penelope wheeled on her. She raised her wings in a high arc as she lowered her head to meet Cori.

A low growl tickled Cori's eardrums, followed by an open-mouthed roar. The hot breath that pushed her hair back was without flame, but Cori sensed Penelope wanted there to be flames. She had wronged the mother. Another betrayal to add to her list of evil deeds for the year.

Cori stood her ground, accepting the blame for everything. Danato kept his distance, watching both of them cautiously, no doubt waiting until it was absolutely necessary to intervene.

"Then go get him back." Cori pointed vaguely to the south, where the vehicles most likely were, on their way back to more hospitable lands.

Penelope looked to the south and sniffed the air. All of a sudden, she seemed to realize it wasn't too late. She still had time to save her baby.

Cori shielded her face as Penelope's liftoff stirred up a storm of dust. She rose high before directing her flapping wings to the south. Danato looked at Cori with a mixture of worry and disappointment, but he didn't scold her for the obvious double-cross.

Grisha was right that keeping things civil between the prison and the Russians was for the best. But he was also right that Cori was a fighter—with or without her rings. If her feats had impressed him up to this point, he would be downright beside himself after this—possibly literally.

Cori tried not to think about the roar that Penelope let out as she dove on the south side of the compound. Somewhere beyond the wall, there was a sound of crunching metal. The gunfire began soon after.

Penelope rose again, wings flapping hard. Gripped in her talons was a metal box—formerly a jeep. She dropped it from well above a survivable height. Cori ignored the screams that eventually outnumbered the bullets being fired.

There was more crunching and the shriek of twisting metal. The explosion of one of the gas tanks sent a plume of fire and smoke into the air, well above the height of the wall. The gunshots eventually ceased.

Penelope returned to the eastern yard with Puff carefully gripped in her claws. Ever so carefully, she deposited a terrified Puff onto the ground, before flapping away again.

Cori ran to the whelp and checked him for injuries, but the blood that was on him had come from his mother. Much like any justified carnage, Cori ignored the guilt that surfaced because of these lost lives.

She urged Puff to follow her into the hangar so she could clean him up, but another ghost from her past blocked her path. Paul Hirem, the elemental she had failed to save, was standing before her in the courtyard. There was a bloody hole in his chest from the gunshot that had killed him. That fucking hole might as well have been in her own heart.

Cori gasped and stumbled back. She averted her eyes to the ground, holding herself up by leaning on Puff. He wasn't hers; she told herself. It wasn't *her* heart dying that day.

So why did that memory hurt so much?

"Cori." Danato approached her, touching her shoulder.

"I'm okay," she lied. She wasn't sure she even knew how to be truthful at this point.

"I think you should get to the infirmary right now. Make sure that goblin didn't give you more than a nasty cut."

"I don't have time to—"

"Cori!" Danato barked, and she looked up at him. He was holding out a handkerchief to her. She looked at it strangely, noting the concern on his face. "Your nose," he explained.

Cori touched her nose and came back with a finger covered in blood. "What the hell." She grabbed his handkerchief and dabbed her nose—more embarrassed than worried by the blood.

"Get yourself to the infirmary. I'll take care of... this." Danato glanced at the wall where most of the screams had stopped. Cori checked her watch. "That's an order. I'll come check on you later." Cori nodded and headed toward the nearest entrance.

"Cori," Danato called after her. She looked back, and for a moment he only stared at her, but then he nodded to Puff. "This was a good idea. It will probably bite us in the ass later, but... good idea."

Cori huffed out an attempted laugh and nodded. "You should know by now I'll do almost anything to protect what I care about."

His face dimmed slightly, and he nodded. "Yeah, Cori, I know."

29

T HE NURSES TOOK ONE look at Cori's cheek and jumped to life. They called for the doctor and had her in a patient room before she could explain why she was there. When the doctor entered, he took one look at her and snickered. "Please tell me Belus disinfected this before stitching you up."

"Yes—how did you know who—"

"I recognize his stitching. It's like a fingerprint." He sat down and wheeled himself over to inspect her cheek. He lifted his chin, examining her through the microscope lens attached to his glasses. "Did you go see Penelope?"

"No—I mean, yes."

"Well, I can't guarantee you won't scar, but it looks to be closing up nicely. I can check it in a few days."

"It was actually my nosebleed that brought me in."

"Oh." He stood and leaned her head back. Using his tiny flashlight, he inspected her nasal passage. "How long did it last?"

"Just a minute. It was done by the time I got up here."

"Have you had them before?"

"No."

"I suspect it's just a result of the dry arctic air."

"So, nothing to do with the bubble?" she asked hopefully.

"It's possible, I suppose, but I'd be more concerned if your ears were bleeding. I'm actually surprised you're not deaf after going in and out of that place so often." He moved to his clipboard and scribbled down a few notes. "How's everything going in there?" he asked.

Oliver was not frequently sick, but regular check-ups were part of the prison protocol, and Cori wanted to make sure that he was developing normally. Thankfully, the doctor did not oppose house calls regarding her son's situation.

"Good. I should probably get back in." Cori made a show of checking her watch, but didn't actually jump up to leave. She stared at the floor and fidgeted.

"Is there something else?" he asked, managing to sound interested.

Cori looked at him, debating how much she should share with him. Apart from their rocky history and her determination to keep the medical staff at a palatable distance, she wasn't actually sure she could trust him. "Do we have doctor-patient confidentiality?" Cori asked.

Sensing the gravity in her tone, he dropped his pen and returned to his chair. "That depends." He crossed his arms. "I am a prison doctor. I am obligated to report a condition that would put those around you in danger or compromise the integrity of the prison." He paused a moment. "But... I don't have to reveal the specifics of the condition. Especially if you are uncomfortable discussing it with your superiors."

Cori cleared her throat. "Sometimes when I come out of the bubble, I have a memory flash."

He frowned. "What do you mean, memory flash?"

Cori took a breath. "I guess it would qualify as a hallucination."

"Is this a recent or ongoing phenomenon?"

"Recent."

"I see." He leaned over his knees to speak to her. "One of the stupidest decisions the board ever made was not placing a psychiatrist in this program. The daily stress we are under is worthy of counseling from time to time. And you..." His gaze paused on her, and he leaned back again. "You've been through a lot recently. It would surprise me if you weren't experiencing some physiological or psychological reaction to it all."

"You think the hallucinations are from stress."

"Grief or extreme stress has been known to trigger a hallucination or two. But when my CT scanner gets repaired, I'll take an image of your brain—see if there is a screw loose." He smiled, letting her know he was joking.

She thanked him and slipped off the table. At the door, she looked back at him. "So, until you get your scan, Danato doesn't need to know about this, right?"

He narrowed his eyes at her. "Just keep me informed, Ms. Reiger."

She agreed and checked her watch. She was late—very late. She ran all the way to the bubble, hoping against hope that nothing much had changed since she had left.

30

E FRAT HAD OPTED TO give Ethan a little more space. He, of all people, understood that talking about problems you have no control over was next to useless. Not to mention, he was the last person Ethan wanted to talk to about such things.

Since Ethan's sessions with Safir were getting longer and apparently more fruitful, Efrat had taken to the streets to impress the tourists with his *magic*. It only took a few meager displays, and they were throwing money at him for more. He knew Ethan would not approve of the exhibition, but money was something they both needed.

After a rather lucrative evening, Efrat arrived at their apartment building and found Ethan standing on the darkened stoop, staring across the street in deep contemplation. Efrat didn't pay any heed to his silent treatment and headed inside. He wasn't in the mood to argue anymore. For once in his life, he wanted to let bygones be bygones. He knew he couldn't mend Ethan's relationship with Cori—and why would he even want to? The truth was, he was mad about Cori killing the boy too. Not as much because he thought it was wrong—it really was the only choice they had left—but because it meant that she was no better than Danato. She was turning into a cold-hearted devotee of the prison. She was becoming an ideal warden.

Efrat headed down the hall and pushed through the door of the much too colorful apartment that they had rented for their stay in New Orleans. It creaked open easily without the usual twist of the knob. He looked down at the damaged door jamb that had allowed him to open the door without resistance.

Someone had broken into their apartment—or some*thing*.

Efrat was only just realizing the light in the hallway was out when hot, stinking breath brushed the back of his neck, making the hair all over his body spring to life.

Efrat threw a torrent of electricity behind him to fend off the imminent attack.

An impossibly heavy body dropped onto him from above. It pressed his back against the floor of the hall. A wet, snarling mouth glinted above him, but he couldn't get away. The creature's feet pinned his arms down. He could feel the claws of the toes kneading his flesh with the dexterity of fingers. The creature reared up, and Efrat dreaded finding out whether the creature intended to punch him with a thick fist or headbutt him with its bald head.

A crash sounded from the front stoop, and something knocked the collector looming over him from his perch.

Down the hall toward the back of the building, two collectors were scrambling to get untangled from one another. One had apparently toppled into the other, effectively saving Efrat from a rather painful introduction to a collector's full strength.

Efrat looked back at the front entrance, where he saw Ethan standing in front of a large hole that had previously been a door. He panted heavily through his clenched teeth. Ethan had never seen him so angry. Rightfully so, since in the few seconds since Efrat had passed him, the man had obtained enough injuries to rip his shirt to shreds. The claw marks on his chest and stomach were bleeding heavily, and his cheek looked red from a recent impact.

Ethan turned his furious expression to Efrat lying on the floor of the hall. "Are you going to help me or not?"

Two more creatures emerged from the night's shadows and jumped onto Ethan's back. They weighed him down—forcing him to bend to one knee. With a genuine effort that reflected as much endurance as strength, Ethan pulled the chokehold of a thick bicep off his neck. He roared and gritted his teeth through the constant strain. Ethan's gaze landed on him again—the fire in his eyes was almost as intimidating as the collectors. "Bloody fight, you idiot!" Ethan screamed.

Efrat had never considered trying to fight the collectors when they arrived. He had prepared himself for the process of being bitch-slapped by the top of the food chain and going home with his dick between his legs like a beaten dog. That was the plan anyway. But apparently, Ethan wanted to put up a fight.

Pointless as it was, Efrat wasn't entirely against it. He hadn't been in a fight for a good long while. Oh, sure, there was that little thing with Callin, but that was nothing compared to what he used to do on the top floor. When the guards could deflect his bolts, he could give it his all. It was sometimes the only release he had, and in some ways, it was more about the pleasure of it than the anger that fueled it.

Efrat let the power inside of him rise. It felt good to have the strength raising the hairs on his skin. Since Cleos had reprogrammed him, he wasn't sure that he would have the same voltage, but it was all there—and then some. He had always felt a pressure in his knuckles as the power built up, as if they were begging him to release the energy building behind his palms. But now it was different. It was deeper. The power wasn't just coming from his hands. He felt it throughout his whole body.

So, this was what it meant to be an elemental—to have the power of a raging storm inside of you, ebbing over your muscles and swirling inside your gut. And yet with all that power, Efrat didn't feel angry or bitter or jealous. For once in his long life, he felt calm—body, mind, and soul. For a split second, Efrat understood he was not an electrical elemental as he had once thought. He had it all wrong. It wasn't the spark that fueled him and made his power so damn strong.

It was the air.

The space between heaven and the only hell he knew.

He was the breath they all breathed. He was the spark that fueled the fire, the clouds that carried the rain, and the wind that froze it on the way down. He was the reason a cold rock could sustain life and permit humans to thrive.

He was everything.

And he was about to get his ass kicked by two man-dogs if he didn't snap out of his ego trip.

The two snarling faces of the collectors lunged at him, ready to take over where they had left off. Despite the bluish trickle of his branched earth power, the creatures didn't back down. They had the instincts of werewolves. Fight, fight, and fight some more. Just short of death, they wouldn't stop.

Efrat released a thunderous bolt at the creatures, and it launched them toward the back of the apartment building. Their massive weight combined with the force of his power pushed them right through the drywall and wood studs of the duplex, adding to the damage Ethan had already done.

Before he could celebrate that victory, thumping feet pounded against the hardwood floors inside the apartment. Two more bald, pale-skinned collectors loped toward him.

He raised his hands in defense, but they leaped into the pooling electrical field before he could raise the strength necessary to hurt the brawny bastards.

They landed on his arms, one heavy body for each sparking hand. Despite his continued output of energy, they both just sat there growling furiously at the stinging pain he was causing them. He increased the output and consequently their pain. They roared louder but didn't retreat. Determined to a fault, they were holding him down despite the agony he was causing them.

Efrat looked back to see where Ethan was with his attackers. They had him corralled in a corner, trying to climb back on him, but he was throwing heavy punches at them to keep them at bay. Their pale flesh was turning puce and swelling from the damage Ethan was doing to them, but still they persisted.

Efrat tried to throw a bolt out to help him, but he couldn't aim with the creatures on top of him. "Ethan, we can't win this!" he yelled over to him.

"Don't give up!" Ethan continued to fight. Efrat admired his relentless spirit, but he was being ridiculous. Even he didn't have enough stamina to compete with the collectors. If they were capable of retrieving werewolves, then they didn't have a chance.

"Ethan, without frying these fuckers to death, I can't win."

Ethan locked eyes with him for the briefest moment between his punches. "Then fry them!"

Efrat heard the fury in his command, and it surprised him. He looked between the bellowing creatures holding his arms down and the two others creeping in from the backyard. One of them had a slight limp, but that was the only sign he had damaged either of them.

Efrat had little time to debate. The newly arriving collectors would surely knock him out, and then all six of them would turn on Ethan. They would be back at the prison in a matter of days—probably to sit in a jail cell.

Efrat took in a deep calming breath and drew back the strength of his electrical current. It was a relief to the collectors holding his hands down, and he could see that they were ready to accept his surrender—as all their prey eventually did. But it was a short-lived reprieve because he was only pulling back so he could land a stronger punch.

Efrat balled up every last ounce of anger into his stomach—not so much overwriting but rather combining with the Zen calm he had previously felt there. They should have been opposites—fire and water, tamping each other out, but that wasn't the case. Because, of course, fire and water create steam, and it can burn you just the same as the flame.

Efrat let out a feral scream barely audible over the explosion from his hands.

The lightning bolts from each of his palms, fed by the storm inside of him, lit the room with pure white light, momentarily blinding everyone. The bomb-level impact moved the air around him and threatened to shatter his eardrums just as it shattered the windows inside the apartment.

His head swirled with an almost euphoric high. He had always enjoyed using his power, but this was an altogether unique sensation. Instead of feeling the exhaustion of an endurance workout, he felt revitalized and... enraptured.

When he blinked away his stars, Efrat saw the result of his work. The two creatures holding him down were now slumped over, sizzling like fresh barbecue. Efrat scrambled to get out from under them—to free himself from the steaming corpses he had just created.

The two approaching collectors were not dead, but they looked scalded. Their skin was bloody and cracked—pieces were peeling off around their eyes, making them look like zombies instead of feral man-dogs. The ones attacking Ethan had since stopped their attack. Their backs looked red, but they weren't nearly as bad as the other two. They looked at their fallen comrades and then at Efrat. Their mouths dropped open, and they made a clicking noise that sounded like a stunted growl. He couldn't believe after two deaths and two severe injuries. They were still trying to fight. What belated survival instincts did these beasts have?

Efrat rose to feet and lit his hands—bright and threatening. "Fuck off!" he shouted at them.

Movement to his left drew his attention. Efrat eyed the wounded ones on their approach, but they weren't attacking him. They were dragging away the dead body of their kin. Ethan's attackers moved forward as well, but they too only reached out for the meaty corpse of the remaining collector. Their hands slid off the body several times as strips of cooked flesh gave way in their hands. Efrat lifted his chin and pinched his lips, denying the gag reflex that made him wonder if he would ever eat barbecue again.

He had done this. A sickening display of strength that resulted in two deaths. It wasn't his first kill, to be sure, but this felt different—like he had crossed a line. Apart from executing transmorphs, all his other kills had been fairly accidental. Granted, he had intended to aim his power at them, but they weren't supposed to die. That was just the result. This time, however, he had intended to kill these creatures.

Efrat watched the collectors carry away their dead and disappear out the back and front doors. They disappeared into the night, going God knows where to be picked up by God knows who. This might be the first time they would arrive at their destination with victims instead of prey. What would Danato think of that?

Efrat looked at Ethan, only to find him staring back at him. He was stunned by the event he had just witnessed. Efrat had just done the impossible. "We just fought off the collectors."

Ethan nodded. "I think that credit goes to you." He sagged back against the wall and relaxed. After a moment, Ethan laughed—a tired, lazy chuckle that sounded more like a cough.

"What is it?" Efrat tried to take a step toward him, but his legs gave out beneath him. "Whoa," he yelped as he landed on the floor again. Despite his exhilaration over the event, Efrat could feel the exhaustion catching up with him. He needed to get some sleep or food or possibly plug himself into a light socket.

"You okay?" Ethan asked, pulling himself off the floor to help him.

"Yeah, just ran a marathon though."

"No kidding." Ethan lifted him off the floor with ease and moved him toward the front door.

"Where are we going?"

"Back to Safir's to beg for her spare bedroom."

"You think they will come back?" Efrat asked as he stumbled beside him with weak legs.

"No, but somebody will be coming back here, and I don't want to be the one paying the bill when they arrive."

"Good point." With some effort, Efrat made it off the stoop with Ethan, and he found a steady rhythm so that he was almost walking like a normal person—a normal drunk person, but still... "That was amazing," Efrat vaunted. "I mean not what I did, but the experience. I've never felt so connected to my power before. It actually felt like I was meant to be this way. For a second, I thought..." Efrat trailed off, not wanting to tell Ethan about the aggrandizing thoughts that were running through his mind as he was building his power for the first time.

Ethan glanced over at him; his brow dipped. "You thought what?"

Efrat chuckled and shook his head. "Oh, nothing. I'm just reveling in my own resume. What were you laughing about earlier?"

Ethan smiled but kept his eyes on the road ahead. "I was just sitting there congratulating myself for bringing you along. I knew you would come in handy."

Efrat considered Ethan's words carefully, but he didn't find any room to be amused by Ethan's wise choice. As trivial as it was now, it didn't sound like Ethan had brought Efrat along to keep him company, help him, or even protect him. It sounded like Ethan had packed a bag before leaving the prison, and Efrat was just another piece of cargo. A tool with which to carry out his plan. A beast that he could unleash when the collectors arrived to take him back.

Efrat had just become the very thing he had fought long and hard to avoid.

He was a weapon.

31

E THAN HAMMERED ON SAFIR'S door, and after a moment she opened it and smiled at him. "Back again already?" She opened the door for Ethan to come in. Efrat came around the corner and pushed past both of them to get inside. "Oh, both of you."

Ethan noted the disappointment in her voice and shrugged. "We had a little run-in with the collectors."

Efrat turned on the faucet in Safir's kitchen and stuck his head under the stream to get a drink. He groaned with the delight of quenching his thirst.

"What's wrong with him?" Safir asked.

"He finally got to use his power sans shackles." Ethan stepped inside and shut the door.

Efrat pulled his face from under the faucet and looked at Safir. "Why am I so thirsty?"

She frowned at him. "What happened?"

"I cooked a couple of collectors," Efrat reported with far less enthusiasm than Ethan expected.

"Cooked?" Safir asked.

Efrat raised his hand, making several pops of electricity that looked and sounded more like fireworks than his usual static. "Fried to a crisp."

Safir covered her mouth and looked between them. "Is that what I smell?"

"It's barbecue, baby!" Efrat shouted and then abruptly went back to drinking from the faucet. Ethan didn't even want to know why Efrat had downshifted into an asshole the moment he stepped through the door.

"Listen, Saf." Ethan touched her arm, drawing her attention back to him. "We kind of destroyed our apartment building, and I can't afford another deposit this soon. You mind if we crash here until I can get some money together?"

Safir's eyes lit with interest, and she glanced at her living room. "I only have two beds," she said coyly.

Ethan smiled at her. "That's okay," he whispered back to her. Ethan tracked her tongue as she licked her lips. He shouldn't have been playing with her emotions like this. Not when he knew he had no intention of accepting her invitations. But it was nice to watch her try. "Efrat actually still sleeps on the floor, so I can take the bed in the spare room."

A light went out in Safir's eyes as she realized Ethan had no intention of sharing her bed. "Oh." She frowned. "What do you mean he still sleeps on the floor?"

Efrat pulled away from the water, licking his lips. He gave Safir an embarrassed glance before landing a glare on

Ethan. "I like the floor," he defended. "Real men sleep on the floor." Efrat nicked Ethan's shoulder with his as he left the kitchenette. It only made him smile since he couldn't push it very far.

"Real men and monks," Ethan mumbled.

Efrat plopped himself down in the bowl chair and started playing a dangerous game of cat's cradle.

Ethan rubbed the bridge of his nose and leaned in to speak with Safir. "I hate to do this, but would you mind giving us a moment?" Safir looked at him, nearly in awe of his gall to invite himself in only to kick her out. "If I don't talk to him, he's just going to be an ass all night."

Safir rolled her eyes and grabbed her keys off the counter. "I need to pick up a few things, anyway. Just an FYI, there's a fire extinguisher under the sink."

"Hey," Efrat hollered over to her. "If you're going out would you get me some food? I'm starving."

Safir looked at Ethan as if she were about to strangle them both. He grimaced and pulled out his wallet. "I can give you some money."

"I thought you didn't have any."

"Very little, but it's all yours." Ethan offered her the last two twenty-dollar bills in his pocket and looked at her with pleading, pathetic eyes.

Safir waved his offer away . "I got it. What do you want?" she called to Efrat.

"Anything," he called back. "Not barbecue!" he amended as she was closing the door.

Ethan stood in the entryway, wanting and wishing he didn't have to approach Efrat like he was a sullen teenager and a wild animal at the same time. Once he was prepared, he moved into the living room and sat down in the chair across from him.

Efrat nodded at the remote control on the coffee table. "You wanna flip that on for me?"

Ethan looked down at the device and contemplated the request. "Why don't you just turn it on yourself?"

Efrat looked at him as if he had grown a second head. "Because I'll fry it."

Ethan shifted to lean over his knees. "I doubt that. Whatever Cleos did to you—it's working. You have control. Enough control to handle objects temporarily. You're just refusing to use it."

Efrat held his eyes on the dark television screen even though it wouldn't turn on anytime soon. "No sense in getting used to it."

"No sense in letting it go to waste either."

"You wouldn't understand."

Ethan sighed and shook his head. "God, I hate talking to you when you're like this."

"Like what?"

"How did you go from being on top of the world to under a rock so bloody fast?"

"Because I just realized the only reason, I'm here is to keep the collectors out of your hair!" Efrat yelled at him.

Ethan sat back in his chair. "That's it? You're mad because I'm taking advantage of you?"

"No." Efrat tried to sit forward in the chair, but it took a great deal of effort, so he just left the chair altogether and moved to the bar where he could sit on a stool. "I'm not mad that you're using me. Everybody uses me. I'm not even mad that you probably have no consideration for me beyond my usefulness."

Ethan resisted the urge to roll his eyes at Efrat's accusation of their lacking friendship. It was true; friend was not the right word for their relationship. If anything, they were more like brothers, bickering and fighting at every turn, but Ethan was not without some heart for the man.

"I'm mad because..." Efrat pinned him with a hard gaze that was more disappointment than anger. "I just realized that you have no intention of returning to the prison. You never did. This was your plan all along. That's why I'm here. I'm the key to your freedom."

Ethan stared at him, unable to deny the accusation.

The silence stretched out between them and finally Ethan spoke. "I can't go back. You know why."

Efrat's gaze shifted to the floor, and he nodded. "Yeah, I know why."

Ethan stood and moved to the door of the spare bedroom. He peeked inside at the sparse furnishing and hardwood floor. "We should probably consider tethering your hands so you don't burn the wood. I think she already regrets meeting us."

"Me anyway." Efrat moved into the kitchenette and opened the fridge by himself. He even pulled out a beer and popped it open without incident. Ethan wasn't sure if he had momentarily forgotten the risk or if he was just making an effort for his sake. "She seems to like you just fine." Efrat perked his brow at Ethan and took a swig of the beer.

Ethan snorted and nodded. "She only likes me for my magic."

"Mm-hmm," Efrat mumbled over his swallow. "I think she likes other parts of you too."

"Well, it's flattering, but..." Ethan trailed off. "A beer sounds good." He headed to the fridge and pulled a bottle out for himself. He drank a bit before heading into the living room to turn on the television. Years without the entertainment had made it seem like an event to him instead of background noise.

"I wouldn't judge you, you know?" Efrat said.

Ethan glanced at him. He was sitting on a bar stool again, watching him. "Judge me for what?"

"Safir." Ethan turned and stared at him. "She's a beautiful woman, and she's obviously into you. Any man in your position would have already taken a shot at her."

Ethan frowned and cleared his throat. "Any man in my position?"

Efrat took a drink before answering. "I'm not saying you should because of what happened. I'm just saying maybe this is one of those times where enough shit has gone down that it doesn't matter." Ethan tried to process his rationalization for adultery. "I'm just saying I'm not going to be the guy that calls you out on it. If you want to keep Cori in the back of your mind and put Safir in the front, then—"

"Cori has never been in the *back* of my mind. I think about her every minute of the day."

Efrat scoffed and looked around the flat. "Not every minute you don't." Efrat glared at him, practically daring him to deny that he was a hot-blooded heterosexual male.

"Fine. My thoughts have strayed, and yes, those extramarital thoughts have included Safir."

Efrat raised his beer to him. "Congratulations, you're human."

"Oh, thank you for the reminder. That's very generous of you. Is there a reason you are bringing this up? Why are you suddenly encouraging me to sleep around?"

"Because you're the do-right guy, and I know you won't make the wrong choice unless you can convince yourself it's the right choice."

"Well, thank you for the permission to cheat on my wife."

"I think we just established that you have no intention of returning to her, so what difference does it make?

Whether you call it cheating or moving on, it's bound to happen sooner or later. It's not like Cori will wait forever."

"Oh, I see where this is going. Tell me something. What happens if I do sleep with Safir?"

"Well, after she's done crying from the pain of your massive—"

"What does that mean for you?" Ethan snapped.

"Me?" Efrat asked. "I get the pleasure of listening to the two of you through the walls."

Ethan stood and moved closer to him. He took on his usual military wide-leg stance, which amused Efrat greatly. "If I sleep with Safir, I suppose that gives you permission to sleep with Cori. You can relay the tales of my philandering and be there to console her."

"I didn't mean it like that, you jackass!"

"I assume that you've thought about it, though. The abatement of your powers must have opened your eyes to new possibilities or old fantasies. I noticed that you said *I* had no intention of going back to the prison, not we."

Efrat's jaw tensed, but he smiled through it like this was just a fun game they were playing. "If my powers really are under control, then I don't have to go back to the prison. I can go anywhere and have my pick of women."

"But you don't want just anyone, do you? You want her because she's your Mount Everest."

Efrat's invulnerable façade slipped as the shock of Ethan's knowledge registered. Then he laughed and shook his head. "You just love to rub it in, don't you? You have no idea what it was like for me not being able to touch anyone."

"Oh, this again."

"Yeah, this again. You're so lucky Cleos didn't do this to me years ago."

"Is that so?"

"That is so."

"And why is that?"

"Because if I could have had her, I would have fucked her every chance I got."

Ethan let out a breath between his teeth that sounded like a hiss. His fingers were itching to curl into a fist and punch Efrat just for his verbal trespasses. "Just like that. No regard for her marriage vows or our family?"

"No!" Efrat spat. "I wouldn't have thought of that for a single moment, and do you want to know why!"

"Why!"

"Because I was in too much pain to think about anybody but myself! I would have given anything to make that pain disappear for even a few minutes!" Ethan's desire to punch Efrat was put on hold as he processed what he was saying. "That's why I said you should go after Safir," Efrat yelled at him, scolding him. "I can't even imagine how much pain you are in, and if you want to take a break from that, then go ahead. I'm not going to judge you. And I'm not going to tattle on you."

Ethan considered his words, and he understood why Efrat would associate sex with pain relief. His life exterior to human contact had made him long for it all the more. However, Ethan's lack of human contact was his own doing. He could still touch his wife. He just didn't want to.

"Your encouragement is appreciated, but unnecessary. And it doesn't matter what you would do to Cori if you were given the chance, because it will never happen." Efrat snorted. "Unless we're talking about something else. I was assuming that her consent was a qualification for this imagined affair."

"Fuck you!" Efrat stood and shoved his finger at Ethan. "You know I'm not that guy!"

"Then you'll never have her, I guarantee it."

Efrat bit his lip and shook his head. "Oh, don't make me say it."

Ethan gave him a mockingly apologetic shrug. "I think you're gonna have to say it."

"Okay, fine, she trusts me more than you." Ethan's head dipped low as he breathed in the air necessary to keep himself calm. "Who did she tell about her rings? She confides in me, not you."

Ethan raised his head to the sky and groaned. "Oh, Efrat, you're misconstruing her motives."

"Am I?"

Ethan lowered a piteous gaze to Efrat. He was no longer angry with him. At this moment, he could only feel sorry for his delusions. "Do you know why Cori tells you things she doesn't tell me or Danato?" Ethan stepped up toe to toe with Efrat. "Because you don't matter." Efrat's brow dipped slightly. "I know it's hard to understand. I used to be you when Danato was the only man she cared about impressing. And when we first got married, it would drive me nuts that she would talk to Cleos and not me, but over the years I figured it out. She doesn't want to disappoint the men in her life.

"You see, Efrat, when Danato gives her an order, she follows it out of an obligation to him and the prison. When I ask her to do something, she does it because she loves me. But you..." Ethan raised his hand and gently tapped Efrat's chest. "You have no hold over her heart. She doesn't have to follow your orders. She doesn't have to live with you if she betrays you. You're not her confident, Efrat. You're just her sounding board. And if she really gave a shit about you or what you thought of her, she would stop telling you things just like the rest of us."

Efrat took his evaluation of Cori's behavior in stride, even though Ethan could tell that he had legitimately hurt him. Somewhere in the back of his mind, Efrat probably really thought he had a chance with Cori, but that wasn't the case. She was using him, just like everyone else had been.

32

CORI HEARD A KNOCK on the office door and turned her attention to Belus as he entered the room. She wondered why he had bothered to announce himself, but perhaps he thought she and Danato were in an intense discussion. If a duty roster full of structural maintenance requests could be considered intense—then Cori had officially reached a level of hell that was apparently reserved for murderers and deceivers.

Belus waved a piece of paper at Danato. "Just got a message in on the taps."

Danato reached over his desk and scanned the wide rule paper with scribbled writing. He frowned and looked at Belus for confirmation. "Is this accurate?"

"Boys translated it twice."

"What is it?" Cori asked.

Danato glanced at her warily. "It's nothing," he said as if his sweetest tone could cover his lie.

"Let her see it," Belus said. Danato turned a foul gaze on him.

Cori appreciated that her long-time mentor was on her side; however, it was less encouraging when his words sounded like a double-dog dare instead of a petition to keep her informed. Since the incident with the genie, she had fallen several levels in his respect. Although she didn't regret her independent actions one bit, she wasn't looking forward to climbing her way back into his good graces. The truth was, his attitude and avoidance were making it impossible for her to want to start the climb. For now, she was just lingering at the bottom of the mountain, hoping not to get stepped on.

"You can't hide this from her," Belus insisted when Danato didn't readily agree.

"Fine." Danato handed her the paper.

She translated the chicken scratch carefully.

Attempts to retrieve the escapees have failed. Two collectors dead. Two severely burned. Suspected cause: elemental power. Petition for cleaner has been submitted as per protocol.

Cori read through the paper twice before looking at Danato. "Efrat killed a collector?"

"Yes." Danato took the paper back from her and stowed it in his top drawer.

"That's surprising."

"Yes, well, he always was an underrepresented threat in your eyes."

Cori frowned at the slight dig at her judgment. Since she was usually on the receiving end of Efrat's attacks, she didn't consider herself to be underestimating his abilities.

Besides that, she hadn't meant to imply that he couldn't kill a collector, just that she didn't think he would.

"I was afraid this would happen," Danato grumbled as he leaned back in his chair.

"Afraid of what?" she asked.

Danato looked at Belus, and as if there was an unspoken conversation between them, his second in command turned back to the door. Cori thought he was just shutting it, but Belus left the room entirely. Leaving Danato to drop the bad news that was written all over his face. "When I found out Ethan had left with Efrat, I was baffled. They aren't exactly the best of buds on a good day."

Cori nodded. Efrat's departure had also surprised her. She understood why Ethan had left—even if she was still struggling with not hating him for it, she at least understood his motivation to be away from his murderous wife. Efrat, on the other hand...

She honestly wasn't sure what offended her so much about his departure. She was certain that his leaving was just another peg to add to her abandonment issues, but it was a little more than that. It was as if Efrat had chosen Ethan over her. All the time and effort she had spent freeing him, acclimating him, and even comforting him had only resulted in him jumping ship the moment things got really difficult.

It was true her offense far exceeded any crime Efrat had ever committed. But still...

In a way, Cori felt he owed her. If not for his moral support, he at least owed her the support she needed to keep this prison running. With both Efrat and Ethan gone, she was stuck manning the ship with Riley. It was getting easier now that they had come to terms with each other's personalities. However, she was still having difficulty with some aspects of the dual abandonment—including a long bout of depression that she was currently burying behind her busy duties.

Despite almost never being alone, she always felt lonely. Even the people that she had a fairly good rapport with were avoiding her these days. She had reached a new depth in everyone's eyes. She was no longer just some irritating woman barking orders like she owned the place. Now she was the woman who had defied a genie, killed her own son, and made Gypsy go insane. The last part, of course, was not her fault—at least she didn't think it was. However, the woman's psychotic break coinciding with the former events had left the blame to slop over onto her. Cori was now a great big question to everyone.

What would she do next?

"I suspected Ethan had taken Efrat along as a bodyguard of sorts," Danato continued. "The only man capable of fighting off a collector is Efrat—that I know of, anyway." His brow furrowed. "I never thought that he could kill one though. They are not easily hurt."

"Not much can compete against a lightning bolt," Cori said.

Danato grimaced. "That's true."

"Will they send more collectors?"

"No. We have a limited supply of them, especially in the states. Even if they sent them back, I doubt they would do as they are told. They are mostly animals, but when they meet a foe of equal strength, they tend to relent. Survival instincts, but also a respect for hierarchy."

"So what? We just wait for Ethan to come back on his own then?"

Danato looked down at his desk. His head shook, but he stopped. "Sweetheart." His voice was soft again. It no longer lulled her like it used to. It sent shivers down her spine. It was a forewarning of bad news for her now. "I don't think Ethan ever intended to come back here. I think that's why he took Efrat."

Cori scoffed. "Danato," she said in a scolding tone. "He has to come back here. He has to—you know he has to. If he doesn't come back..." She trailed off as she imagined him going through the rest of his life without knowing that his son was alive. "You have to get him back here. Send him a message."

"It's not like I have an address, Cori."

"Then tattoo it on a fucking collector and send it out to find him."

Danato stared at her, not speaking—not giving her the answer she wanted. After a moment, he shifted out of his chair and moved around to sit in the chair beside her. "There's something else you should be aware of."

"What now?" She couldn't help but reject his compassionate approach. The nicer he was, the more she knew his words would hurt her.

"It's the protocol for a cleaner to be sent after the collectors fail." Cori didn't ask the obvious question. "It's only happened a few times on my watch, so I don't know how it works exactly, but they will send one."

"What's a cleaner?" She finally gave in to her curious nature.

"The collectors are sent to retrieve escapees. The cleaner is sent to eliminate them."

Cori narrowed her eyes at Danato. "You sent a hitman after Ethan."

"Not technically; it's automatic when the collectors are unsuccessful."

"You knew this was a possibility, and you still sent the collectors."

"I didn't think Efrat would be an issue for them. They hunt in packs. Even Efrat only has two hands," Danato rationalized.

Cori's objections froze on her lips, and she shrugged away her worries. "It doesn't matter. Efrat will obviously just kill whoever they send next."

Danato shook his head. "I don't think that will be the case. The cleaner has never failed." Cori frowned at his inability to leave her with one shred of hope. If this was his way of preparing her for Ethan's death, then he was doing a horrible job. "The thing is, sweetheart—"

Cori jumped up, ready to walk out rather than listen to him placate her. He grabbed her arm and yanked her back. He pulled too hard, and her tailbone hit the desk. She winced but tried not to let on how much it hurt. She was certain that he hadn't meant to be so forceful, and she didn't want to make him feel bad for his error in judgment.

"I need you to hear this," he insisted, keeping a grip on her arm. "It's a lot easier to kill someone than it is to capture them. It takes far less effort. You need to prepare yourself for the worst-case scenario."

Her eyes flickered over him. He seemed to watch her, waiting for her to react to the statement. As the tears welled in her eyes, he seemed to brighten. He seemed relieved that she was finally accepting the inevitable.

Before the floodgates opened, he pulled her into his arms and crushed her against him. The warmth of his embrace melted her heart, and she wept. There were so many things to weep for, but she didn't pick one over the other. She just let herself cry. Let herself have this moment to begin yet another mourning process.

It was probably for the best that she felt this pain early. By the time the next taps came in, she could brace herself for the inevitable bad news. Maybe if she drained her grief early, then the pain wouldn't crush her.

Danato hushed her and rubbed her back soothingly. After a long cry, she tried to pull away, but he held her tight. He leaned into her ear and whispered. "I'm here for you, sweetheart." The cool air of his breath against her ear sent a chill through her. He kissed her cheek and added, "For anything you need." He lowered his aim and put a delicate kiss on her neck. A prickling heat took the place of her earlier chill, and she pushed out of his grip.

He released her and gave her a sullen look typical of a funeral. She gave him a tepid smile. "Thank you," she said and made a very slow exit. She paused at the door and looked back at him. She was certain that he hadn't intended to make her feel uncomfortable. Danato was an infrequent teddy bear, but he was prone to sentiments and coddling when she really needed it. She had always enjoyed that side of him—the fatherly side of him. Today, however, it didn't feel right. It felt like he was using her grief to get close to her. To get close to her as a man.

"Everything alright?" he asked, no doubt noting the odd look of introspection on her face.

"No," she admitted. "I don't think it is." She walked away without further explanation.

33

"**W**HAT THE FUCK AM I looking at?" Heaton pushed the words through his gritted teeth. Unfortunately, Mace and Callin were looking at the tethered corpse with the same confusion and concern. The body count was now eight. Fortunately, Nevia didn't have access to the information he had, or the body count might have been higher.

They were nearly halfway through the address book and no closer to finding Nevia. Apart from discovering three transmorphs, which they were forced to dispatch despite the status of the humans they held, they hadn't uprooted enough information to satisfy their questions about the transmorph plots.

Though Nevia had left eight human corpses and the remnants of five transmorphs in her wake of carnage, this one was different. Much like the first murdered human, this one was also eviscerated. Yet, not violently.

Judging by the decomposition, the body lying on the long dining room table was more than a few days past its expiration date. The y-incision in his chest and the spread ribs reminded Heaton of the beginning of an autopsy. The organs were not ripped but rather cut from the body. Each of them was laid out on the table as if to be weighed and cataloged by a pathologist.

As far as he could tell, everything was accounted for. Heart, lungs, stomach, intestines, liver, kidneys, pancreas, and the bits and pieces he couldn't distinguish through the decay. At least she wasn't eating the organs. But why—God almighty, why—would she perform this ritual? This was not how feral animals behave. If he were willing to lie to himself, he might consider that this was proof she wasn't feral. But of course, that just left her open to the title of maniac.

"She killed the human first," Mace announced. Heaton and Callin looked at him, not entirely willing to take his prediction as fact without further explanation. "He's got a deep cut here." He pointed to the slit in the gray tissue around the neck. "Arterial spray." He pointed to the ceiling, where the brownish spots clearly didn't belong. "And a big ole fucking puddle right here." Heaton noticed that the blood was mostly pooled on the other side of the table.

"What does that mean?" Heaton asked, not sure that he wanted the answer.

"It means she's merciful... at least."

Heaton was certain this was another of those rare times when Mace was trying to be conciliatory. He may have been a complete ass most of the time, but despite that or because of it, he recognized the pain in others very easily.

"She didn't rip the transmorph to shreds like the others." Callin pointed to the nearly invisible, but intact sheath of the transmorph surrounding the body. It looked more like a sloughed snakeskin than a dangerous entity now. "She was looking for something," Callin said as he examined the body cavity. "Turn him over."

Heaton and Mace exchanged a look but didn't bother arguing the instruction. He was certain that the only reason Callin wasn't doing the deed himself was to preserve his clothing and avoid the smell on his hands. Mace lifted as Heaton pulled, and they rolled the body without disrupting the arm tissue.

"There." Callin pointed to the back of the corpse.

Heaton couldn't see what the other two were looking at, so he made sure the body was secure before moving around to their side. The man's back had also been cut, his spine exposed. Sadly, Heaton still didn't see the point of this. "She removed the cartilage spine."

"Yes, it's right here." Callin pointed to a plastic-looking framework he knew would fit like a glove against the corpse's spine. It was surprising how quickly these creatures were able to superimpose themselves on the body of a target. It was in cases like these that even X-rays were useless to identify the predator. Even MRIs could give questionable results.

"She took something else out." Callin pointed to the incision that ran up the neck and well into the hairline.

Mace reached forward and lifted the scalp to examine the opening. The chunk of tissue ripped off in his hand. He glanced at Heaton as if to apologize, but went ahead and removed another piece to get a clear view of the skull.

Heaton couldn't be sure what he was seeing since the body was in the dregs of putrification, but it looked as if there were rivulets on the skull, where the skin had become detached—prior to death.

"I'll ask again. What the fuck am I looking at?"

"I think she found a weakness in them. Whatever she did—it killed this transmorph without having to rip it to shreds."

Heaton stared at him blankly. In all the years that he had been killing these things, there had never been a weakness. Early detection was pure luck and circumstantial. There was rarely anything that could be done to save the victims when the behavior changes became too obvious to ignore. In truth, he didn't give a shit about how this transmorph was killed, but merely why it had been killed this way when all the others had not.

"This doesn't add up." He moved away from the body, giving himself room to pace as needed. "How does Jordan suddenly go from evisceration to dissection? What changed?"

"Someone is instructing her in the art of science," Mace answered, once again surprising Heaton since he had considered his rant to be rhetorical.

"Why do you say that?" Callin asked.

"Your girl wears lady boots, right? The ones with the pointy toes?"

Heaton shrugged. If it didn't have wheels or a dick, he didn't pay much attention to the details. "Yeah, sure."

"Then who's wearing the size eleven combat boots?" Mace queried. He didn't point out the obvious this time, since it shouldn't have been necessary.

Heaton looked down at the floor again. The big red puddle had long since congealed, as had the footprints that tracked away from it. There was a mess of unrecognizable patterns around the body, but further out the steps were clearer. In one direction were small prints of heeled boots, and in the other were larger gridded boot prints.

"Looks like your girl has a new partner," Mace said, more characteristically like an ass.

34

CORI HELD OPEN THE door to the stables as Riley carried Puff outside. There had been some argument on his side to name the whelp Torch, but Cori insisted that a cutesy name would be a better choice when it came time to introduce him to Danato.

As it turned out, it made no difference. Apart from his initial irritation with her secretive nature, Danato had not been angry about the whelp. She assumed that Penelope's protective nature had stifled any lethal actions he might have taken against the creature. However, he hadn't even bothered to interrogate Levi about the potential ramifications of adding a dragon to a previously fixed population. He apparently had bigger problems to deal with.

"I think he's gained weight overnight," Riley said as he struggled with the load in his arms. She was surprised that his dragon juice muscles weren't enough to keep the little guy in check, but he was a rather rolly-polly baby. Not to mention that Puff was taking advantage of his proximity to lick Riley's face. "Uck, stop it, Puff," he grumbled, trying to keep his lips clear of the lapping tongue.

"You could just walk him over," Cori suggested.

"No, I've tried that. He keeps trying to go over to Rodan's cage. That blasted beast tried to eat him the first time he saw him. I thought that would be enough of a lesson for him, but he is determined to get over there." Despite Riley's insistence that he would not help her with the whelp, he had become the animal's primary feeder. Cori knew it had more to do with his relationship with her than anything. She hated to admit it, but they were growing on each other. She once considered him to be a selfish asshole, but on closer inspection, he was turning out to be rather nice and helpful.

"Why would he be interested in Rodan to begin with?" Cori asked.

"I don't know. Maybe the heat attracts him. I've just started filing all this shit under magic."

Penelope mooed when they arrived in the hangar. She instinctively rolled onto her side, revealing her plump teats. Even though Puff had not been birthed from any of the dragons, Penelope had been able to provide him with the nourishment he needed. Which was good, since an extra eight gallons of milk a week was not likely to be covered in the budget.

Puff squirmed in Riley's arms, demanding to be let down. The instant he released him, the baby dragon tripped over his own feet trying to get to his supper. His final leap to his pseudo-mother resulted in a faceplant into her belly.

Cori and Riley laughed at the dragon's efforts to establish contact with the teat. He let out a frustrated squeal as the pressure of his own feet against her stomach made the nipple shift away from his mouth. Once he was locked on and found a massaging rhythm with his paws to push more milk out, he began to purr. It was a soft sound not unlike a cat.

"I don't understand why Puff isn't eating her," Riley said.

"What?" Cori frowned at him.

"Well, you know they usually—never mind." Riley shook his head and motioned for her to step outside with him. Since it usually took a good half hour to satisfy Puff's hunger, they had time to enjoy the frigid evening air while they waited.

Cori leaned against the building and closed her eyes. She was tired as usual, though there was no reason for it. Her time inside the bubble left her plenty of time to sleep, but it wasn't the same as the sleep she got in her real home—in her real bed. Inside the bubble, she no longer had dreamless sleep. Her evenings were filled with confusing, almost nightmarish scenarios. An apocalyptic-themed imagery that haunted her well into her day.

On the rare occasions that she fell asleep in the *real* world, she had the opposite problem. While she was free of nightmares, she had torrid sex dreams—always with the same starring character.

Ethan.

Not that she minded having an occasional evening tryst—especially ones of such a satisfying nature, but theoretically she was not supposed to be having dreams at all. The house was supposed to steal them to keep the dreamfeeders at bay. Perhaps the house knew that these were not harmful dreams. Or perhaps they were. Ethan was gone and probably never coming back. Continuing to lust after him in her dreams was only going to prevent her from moving on. She had already rebutted a few advances out of respect for Ethan, but how much longer would she or could she deny she was a flesh and blood woman with needs?

Despite barely just reaching a level of friendship with Riley, she was sensing a shift toward romance in some of their conversations. It was only natural. She was spending so much of her time with him, and they were getting to know each other—getting comfortable with each other. Lately, however, the level of comfort had brought on some discomfort. It was getting harder to fill the awkward silences that usually precipitated a first kiss. Every day, she reminded herself of how many days had actually passed, but it never felt that way. Even if Ethan returned now, she wasn't entirely sure she would take him back.

She had spent many months blaming herself for everything that had happened. The lives that she destroyed had weighed on her heavily, but now... She no longer cared what Ethan thought about her choices. She did, however, care a great deal about *his* choices.

He ran. The man with the strength of a dragon, the fortitude of a lion, and an elephant's worth of patience, had left her behind to deal with the fallout of denying a genie his prize. Even just thinking about his abandonment made her want to wrap her hands around his throat as he had hers. That had to be a sure sign that she had fallen out of love with her husband. And yet, she was still dreaming of him.

"Did I tell you I finally hooked up with that nurse who was giving me googly eyes?" Riley blurted out to fill the silence.

Cori hadn't really been paying attention to the silence this time. She turned her gaze to him and took in his nervous body language. He wasn't looking at her. He was staring out into the night sky over the wall. She could see him swallow when she looked at him, and the tip of his foot was unnecessarily digging a rut in the ground.

She assumed his blunt revelation was designed to gauge her reaction. Had she even an inkling of what she wanted; she might have been jealous. As it stood now, she was a woman standing at a buffet, deciding what to eat. If one dish or another vanished, it wouldn't matter, because she hadn't yet committed to a flavor, anyway.

If there was anything to be envious of, it was Riley's mental clarity. He was ready to move on. The woman he loved had been gone many years and had a family elsewhere. She didn't even have the memories of their relationship, which was the truest torture for Riley. He had been forgotten.

Cori gave him a lazy smile that did nothing to brighten her dismal eyes. "Is that the one with the curly hair or the one with the bob?" she asked—remembering that Riley had expressed interest in more than one woman during their last conversation.

"Curly hair."

"Mmm." Cori nodded. "She's cute."

"She's nice too. You would like her."

"You know I don't get too chummy with the nursing staff."

"I'll admit it's a challenge to the heart, but the alternative is pining over someone I may never have." Riley finally turned to look at her. He was no longer nervous and held her gaze tightly. "And I'm worth more than a maybe."

Cori sensed that this was his way of letting her know he wouldn't be waiting any longer for her to decide what she wanted to eat. She would be stuck with whatever crap was left on that buffet or go hungry. And though she was hungry, her appetite paled in comparison to the guilt that overwhelmed her when she considered taking a meal from another man.

She nodded. "Yes, you are worth more than that."

"And so are you," he added, before looking away. "You're still young, Cori. You're... attractive. You don't have to be alone."

She took a slow breath. This conversation felt like an intervention. Everyone had been quietly concerned about her current lifestyle—moving in and out of the bubble—jumping rope with two timelines. Belus was right that they didn't understand the long-term effects of this, but she had little choice now. The decisions she had made in her past were finally catching up with her. She didn't want to admit it, but she had no endgame. She had no way of balancing the chaotic worlds she had divided herself between. And sooner or later, it wouldn't be her choice anymore.

"I'm not really waiting for him, you know," she said. Riley didn't respond. "I'm just mourning him. I knew he wasn't happy here anymore—even before... But I never suspected he would actually leave."

Riley turned to look at her. This wasn't the first time they had conversed about Ethan. In fact, Cori had been inordinately honest with him about her relationship troubles. She suspected it was his inability to defend Ethan that made her open up. She wanted to talk to someone who couldn't sympathize with him over her. Not that Riley didn't call her out on her culpability, but it was not to serve Ethan, just to play devil's advocate.

She was certain he was about to play that part again when a loud squawking hiccup alerted them to the trouble in the hangar.

"Oh, shit, he drank too fast again," Riley grumbled and headed back in to burp the baby. He would likely not be back soon since there was a great deal of cleanup involved with a pent-up dragon burp. Cori laughed at the groans of disgust that followed shortly after a resounding belch.

She was about to head in to help him when she noticed Rodan sitting quietly in his cage. He had not rattled his bars once since their arrival. Nor had he called over to beg for a virgin to eat.

Cori meandered over to the edge of the perimeter and rapped her fist on the tungsten cage. It didn't make much of a noise—certainly not enough to wake a sleeping mountain. She grabbed the entrance gate and gave it a heavy shake. This version of a dinner bell should have at least unearthed his glowing eyes, but his brows did not lift.

"Hey, sleepyhead. Why aren't you asking me for a sacrifice?"

Cori waited for the rocky mound before her to crack and shift, but it didn't. As she watched her breath fog against the cool air, she realized there was no steam coming off Rodan. Even if he had developed a hard shell, he still would have had enough heat in his core to smoke like a luau oven.

"Rodan?" She reached her hand through the bars but didn't feel any heat coming from him. "Rodan?" She called a little louder and slipped through the wide-spaced bars.

Cori approached the monster carefully, hoping their history was enough to keep her safe even if her lack of virginity wasn't. She pressed her hand against his lowest boulders searching for heat, but the stone was ice cold. "Rodan!" She climbed onto the boulders, searching for any sign of life. A piece of rock fell in her grip and crumbled as it hit the bottom of the cage.

"No. No. No." Cori jammed her hand into the deepest crevice she could find.

"Cori, what are you doing?" Riley ran up to the cage and tried to squirm between the bars as she had.

"He's..." Cori paused as she tried to determine if the warmth at her fingertips was only her imagination. It wasn't much. Only in the difference between cool and tepid.

"Cori, what the—"

"Shh!" Cori leaned her head against what was effectively the creature's chest and listened for the thrum of flowing lava. "He's not dead, but he is in severe stasis." Riley squeezed himself into the cage just as Cori jumped off the rock monster and slipped out of it.

"Cori!" Riley yelled through gritted teeth. She came back to the bars and helped pull him through. "For the last time—"

"Rodan is dying. I need heat. I'm going to the weapons closet. You can help, or you can go, but..." Cori stared at the rock monster. A thousand thoughts crossed her mind, but only one was strong enough to stick.

Riley narrowed his eyes at her. "But what?"

Cori hated saying the next words, but she once again felt that there was something going on that she didn't fully understand, and until she did... "Don't tell anyone."

Riley shook his head. "What's going on?"

"I don't know, but I think someone is murdering our inmates. And my only witness is about to die."

35

Cori and Riley aimed the two now infrequently used elemental weapons at the mound of rocks inside the cage. Set to the flamethrower, they blasted the exterior rocks with a heavy spray of liquid heat.

Cori immediately distanced her face from the intense heat. "Holy crap, I forgot how dangerous these things are," she called over the roar of fire.

"When did you have an opportunity to use one of these?" Riley called back.

"Ah…" Cori smiled, enjoying the piecemeal history she got to share with Riley. "Just a minor altercation with the elementals during my early days."

"Minor? Since when is anything involving the elementals minor?"

"The prison was in lockdown; the guards were subdued. It was just Cleos, and I left to save the day."

"Cleos?" Riley scoffed. "What on earth did he have to contribute?"

"Well, not much on the physical front. It was mostly just moral support and advice. The real heroes were Rodan, Onna, and…" As Cori trailed off, her weapon slumped, and she started burning the grass before she released the trigger.

"What is it?" Riley asked, ever concerned about the plots forming in her head.

She stared at him wide-eyed. "They're killing everyone who was part of the rescue," she murmured.

"What? Why?"

Cori looked at the boulder pile, searching for signs of life. Rodan was ultimately an earth elemental. Though he didn't wield magic, his existence alone qualified him as a magical being. The flamethrowers had barely charred Rodan's outer layer. This man-made fire would do nothing to heat his interior. "Why indeed?" Cori mumbled, still trying to figure out why these particular prisoners were being targeted. Certainly, there were more dangerous enemies within these walls. Was it because they would help her? Was this about her? Was she the next victim?

"This was probably just an accident." Riley propped his hands on his hips and looked at Rodan. "You know how lazy the guards have gotten lately. They probably just over-watered him, thinking they could save time."

Cori stared at Rodan's vacant rock exterior trying to suppress her misfiring instincts. There was no proof that any of them had been murdered. "The guards have gotten very lax since Ethan left," she agreed with Riley's logic. She had hoped that Duke would have helped get them in line, but it seemed more and more of them just didn't get the work done, which left her tremendously busy. Too busy to notice when things weren't quite right.

"Plus, I've heard some talk about budget cuts. Maybe Danato had to make some hard decisions." Riley shrugged. "Maybe he was reluctant to tell you about Rodan since you have a history with him."

Cori nodded, but this time she wasn't in agreement. Rodan's body couldn't be moved from this cage. Letting him expire wouldn't be an unnoticed action. Danato would have warned her before she came upon him in this state. He would have wanted her to understand the issues surrounding his decision. At least she hoped he would have.

"Are you okay? You look a little ill. Do you need to sit down?"

Cori shook her head. "No, I'm just..." She turned to see the concern on Riley's face. She wanted to tell him she was not okay. There was a niggling feeling in the back of her mind that something wasn't right. For the last year, she had been making concerted efforts to be more open. She shared her concerns with her superiors and didn't hide her plots to fix problems that might otherwise be handled better as a team.

"Just what?" Riley reached out and touched her arm.

She glanced down at his contact, and he retracted. "I'm going to be so late." Cori glanced at her watch. "This clearly isn't working." She clicked the safety on the weapon and let it slump down against her thigh. "Danato is gonna want a report. Belus will have the paperwork for me. Shit."

"Do you want me to tell Danato?" Riley lowered his weapon as well.

"No," she sighed. "But would you head into the bubble and check on things for me?"

"Sure, but..." Riley's smile dimmed, and he narrowed his eyes at her. He stepped closer to her, but didn't touch her. "I feel like leaving is the wrong thing to do. Are you sure you're okay?"

"Should I make it an order?"

Riley frowned and stared her down.

"I'm fine, Riley. I'm just tired of losing people. Even if it is just a rock monster. You know?"

"Yeah, I get it." He reached for the strap on her shoulder, and she let him take the weapon. "I'll see you in a few days then." He pointed his finger at her, demanding she keep her real-world business to a minimum than asking.

Cori nodded and watched him head inside through the back door. Once he was gone, she jumped into a sprint toward the hangar where Puff was still feeding. She ran inside and yanked him off his surrogate mother. He let out a mournful growl as he licked at the air between his mouth and Penelope's teat.

"I thought you just wanted to get to his warmth," Cori grunted as she struggled to pull the hefty baby away from his dinner. "But he wasn't warm, was he? That's why you wanted to get to him. Right?" Cori turned her attention to Puff, and he looked up at her as if his dismally slow cognition was struggling to understand her. He groaned and licked his lips. "Can you save Rodan?" she asked, hoping that she wasn't just imagining this creature's intelligence.

Puff squirmed in her grip, and she released him to walk on his own. Instead of going back to feeding, he marched toward the door. Cori nearly rejoiced until he turned the wrong way. "No, Puff, Rodan." She ran after him and found him relieving himself on the side of the building. "Well, can't argue with that." She monitored the area as the dragon had a lengthy evacuation. After which, he sniffed a tuft of grass that had broken through the snow.

"Who am I kidding?" Cori said to herself. "You barely have enough fire to light a candle."

The dragon looked up at her with interest.

"What? Do you understand fire?" she was only asking to mock her own stupidity, but the dragon snorted and wiggled his nose at her. She shook her head and pointed at Rodan. "Fire."

Puff looked at her finger and then the blob of rock it was directing him toward. As if remembering his interest in Rodan, he bellowed and ran at a surprisingly fast gallop toward the cage. Cori caught up to him just as he pressed his chunky paws against the gate demanding entrance.

Cori complied by turning the winch and raising the door just enough for Puff to squeeze under. The whelp paced in front of Rodan as if searching for a way to get to the top of this mountain. He eventually let out a loud cry followed by an explosive burp that filled the cage with a wave of heat and light. Cori jumped clear of the scorching heat.

"Yes, good boy!"

Puff continued to burp, but with each expulsion his flame cloud lessened into a finely aimed burst. Cori could see that the dragon was aiming for the rock monster's heart. Though their flamethrowers couldn't make a dent in him, she could see there was a red ember starting to burn somewhere deep inside of him, making his rifts glow.

Puff let out one final exhalation of fire that she had to step even further away from. When the heat cleared and she was able to emerge from behind her shielding arms, she could see that Rodan's molten core was melting and spreading through his limbs. As the lifeblood of his mobility returned, so did the steaming and crackling. When the heat hit his face, his eyes began to glow. At first, it was just red embers, but soon after they turned bright gold as they swirled with livid intent.

Cori called Puff back out of the cage and lowered the door just as a low rumble emerged from the rock man. His joints popped and screeched as he rose to full height. She rushed to a safe distance just as he let out a roar that could have passed for thunder.

"Rodan!" Cori yelled over his grinding movements.

"Murderers!" His nearly incomprehensible voice yelled. As unhappy as Cori was to have murderers in their midst, she was elated that her instincts had not betrayed her.

"Not me, Rodan. I saved you."

Rodan shifted his gaze to her and the little dragon at her side. The poor guy had developed a bad case of hiccups and couldn't help but release little puffs of smoke with every convulsion.

"Rodan." Cori cautiously approached the cage again. "I need to know who did this to you. Who tried to murder you?"

Rodan's eyes dimmed back to bright red, and he sat on his hind boulders again. "He did." He pointed vaguely to the northern courtyard.

Cori already suspected what he was pointing at, but she needed confirmation. She needed to be sure. "Who, Rodan?"

"The small one," he answered.

"Belus," she whispered.

Cori felt a pang thread through her heart as an image flashed through her and before her. She remembered how it felt to have Belus's blood on her hands. It wasn't the first or last blood she had on her palms.

Cori shook away the unwelcome images of a bloody pencil shiv and Belus's incidental gunshot wound. She reminded herself that her memories were a part of who she was, and they had no control over her.

She was in control.

Cori walked toward the northeast edge of the building and peered over at the structure that she had suspected Rodan was pointing to. Belus's house.

There should have been questions mounting in her mind. Doubt should have been twisting her mind in circles. However, for once in her life, she was oddly calm. The truth was there, right in front of her. It had been for some time. She just needed to open her eyes to find it.

36

C ORI WAS NOT IN the habit of breaking and entering, especially when it came to spying on people she considered friends. However, this was an unprecedented circumstance. She had let too many oddities pass right under her nose over the last two months. Had her fluctuating timeline not distracted her, she might have put the pieces together sooner, but sadly it wasn't until she found a third potential victim that she saw the pattern. Someone was trying to kill off the elementals who had helped her during the prison break so many years ago.

The question of *why* had been circling in her brain like a vulture. The hungry maw of curiosity received a full-course meal when the question of *who* had finally been answered. A meal she could well have gone without. Having her friend and mentor named as the enemy did not sit well with her. However, it was his motivation that was still to be discovered.

Perhaps it was because she had already lost so many others, and her mind was desperate to rationalize everything that was happening. She wanted to believe budget cuts were responsible for these mandatory secret executions. The targeted victims were merely coincidentally her former comrades in arms. Regardless of his reasons, there was no more denying it.

Something wasn't right.

As she stood in Belus's foyer, she considered the last time she had been there. The conversation she had had with him. The decision that was before her. Save the world or save her son. It would have been a philosophical debate if not for the real hearts involved. Somehow, there was no longer room for logic or rationalizations when it came to her own flesh and blood.

All that was left at the end of that day was broken things. The empty boy in her arms. The vacant stares from her disappointed friends. And the missing air from her lungs as her beloved sought retribution for her sins.

She could see it clearly now. What she had looked like that day? A murderess. A villain so dark that even the hero had permission to stain his hands with her blood. It would have been positively Shakespearean had she died. Unfortunately, there was no rest for her. She was still suffering the consequences of her betrayal.

Now yet again, she was making choices that were leading her down a path that she might not be able to return from. She couldn't reveal her secrets to anyone because her trust in those around her was disintegrating by the day... by the minute.

Cori had tried to forget the earworms the Belus transmorph placed in her mind. She hadn't wanted to consider what it would mean if he were telling the truth—that a traitor was among them. And yet there she was, standing in Belus's house, trying to decide where to find the manuals that he had supposedly written.

She had previously searched the prison office and Danato's home office, but she had found nothing. If such a manual existed, it would be here. Somewhere he could monitor it.

Cori did a quick check to ensure Belus was gone and started searching his office with a fine-tooth comb. She removed every book from his shelves to check its true contents. She leafed through every file. She searched the drawers and even checked for false bottoms. To her surprise, one drawer had a false bottom. Beneath was a small gun with extra bullets, but no manual.

As a last resort, she checked the bathroom and the bedroom. But found nothing.

Desperation frayed the edges of her hope, and she checked the main room, checking under every cushion and in every crevice. She moved to the kitchen, opening every cupboard and every drawer. She found pots and pans, spatulas, and thermometers. She found his steak brand among the utensils and chuckled at the fact that she was now branded with his ridiculous little B.

She turned and stared at the island before her. The custom-crafted counter was just a little shorter than the average kitchen. The microwave, which traditionally sat above the stove, resided under on the island counter for easier reach. Beside it sat a fine collection of recipe books—French, Indian, and Mediterranean fare among the titles. A red binder with no label was an outlier on the shelf.

Cori pulled the binder out and opened it. At first, she thought it was nothing because of the handwritten script, but then she began to read. "Upper Management Risk Aversion Protocols" was the title. Beneath it, she saw a table of contents.

Her mouth dropped open as she saw a series of worst-case scenarios listed. Things she had never even considered, like a werewolf escaping his confinement during a full moon or a multi-perpetrator vampiric attack. There was even a section labeled Cleos—no specifics, just his name. As curious as she was to find out what Belus had written to prepare for him, she was more interested in the one labeled "transmorph invasion."

Cori flipped to the section and began reading through some data that she didn't entirely understand. Under the title of "Determinants" were several long paragraphs explaining why an invasion would likely go undetected. Ultimately, the transmorphs were always more vulnerable in the early stages of encapsulation, so a quiet attack was always best for them.

Belus noted a list of people or creatures that were not vulnerable to psychic influence and would likely be killed in the event of an attack. Cori's breath hitched when she saw Belus had put his name at the top of the list. Beneath his, he wrote Cleos, Medusa, and several other mind manipulators from the seducers' level.

Following this, Belus listed the natural elementals in the prison and the risk they posed to the transmorphs. He went on to explain that anyone with a branched earth power would be at risk. Cori didn't like this line of thinking—she had assumed that this was a focused attack on her rescue partners. She hadn't even considered there might be additional accidental deaths among the elemental population.

Still, in her mind, this was all just theoretical. Or it was until she reached the identification paragraph. Positive identification had always been difficult with transmorphs, even with x-rays. However, CT scans and MRI machines were better at distinguishing the duplication of tissues well into the middle stages of inhabitation. Belus posited in his manual that medical devices of this sort would likely be destroyed or damaged during the early stages of an invasion.

Cori shook her head, not wanting to recall the knowledge that she had about the medical facility's recent request for parts to repair their machines. Parts that were, for some reason, always back-ordered.

This wasn't happening.

This couldn't be happening.

As much as Cori's mind refused to acknowledge what might be occurring, her body shifted into autopilot. She ripped the pages from Belus's book and placed the binder back on the shelf. She stuffed the pages into her pocket and left the house.

37

T HE LAST OF THE long winter bit at her face and hands as she made her way to the prison's side entrance. She meandered down the hall to the elevators and stepped into the one waiting for her. She no longer questioned the convenience of being tied to the entity. In moments like this, she welcomed the unspoken camaraderie.

As the doors to the elevator closed, she felt the air around her shift, and something was in her mouth—choking her. Her arms flailed, but there was nothing she could do to stop the pressure on her face. The bars of a cell pressed against her back—forcing her to stay still as she was imbibed.

"Cori!" someone yelled at her.

Cori flailed at the newcomer, defending herself against a different threat.

"Open your eyes!"

She hadn't remembered closing her eyes. Nor did she remember falling to the floor of the elevator. She looked around, seeing no sign of the vile creature she had felt pressing against her skin only seconds ago. She was alone inside the elevator, cowering in a fetal position. Chuck was standing in the door's path, looking down at her with immeasurable concern.

"I heard you screaming from inside." He motioned to the double doors that led to the bubble. "Are you alright?"

Cori was fine. She wasn't in any danger. She had just experienced another hallucination—another memory.

Except... this was not a memory she should possess. Cleos had eaten away the excess memories from her time inside the transmorph. How could she remember something she had no memory of?

"Cori," Chuck whispered, sincerely worried. "Should I call Danato?" He reached for his radio, but Cori raised her hand to stall him.

"No, I'm sorry. I didn't mean to scare you. It was just a nightmare. I actually fell asleep on the way up. Can you believe that?" She hoped he would. "I haven't been sleeping well lately, and the dreamfeeders wasted no time. They know all my buttons." She stood and moved to the door. Chuck still seemed torn, as if he were witnessing her self-destruction and should intervene to help. He may have been partially right to do so.

As far as she was concerned about the risks of a transmorph invasion, this was a more pressing issue. Was her declining mental health just stress, as the doctor suggested? Was it a ramification of living inside the bubble, as Belus had said? Or was it something else? Or rather, someone else?

"Do you know if Cleos is upstairs?" she asked.

Distracted by the question, Chuck looked down as if he might have a clipboard to tell him as much. "I think so."

"Okay, thanks. I'll be back in a little bit." Rather than continue to placate him with assurances, she pushed the button for the top floor. His brow furrowed, but he stepped clear of the doors as they closed.

When Cori reached the top floor, the elevator wouldn't open. She pushed the door open button, but they refused to budge. She couldn't know for certain if the entity was acting on her behalf or because she sensed her dread, but either way, she needed to see Cleos. If her mind was coming undone, he was her best option to stitch it back up again. That was assuming he wasn't a transmorph already.

The doors finally opened, and she jumped out before the entity changed her mind. She entered the newly renovated top floor and called out for him, but there was no answer.

She shifted across the lobby to see down the lanes of glass enclosures and exhibits. With no sign of Cleos, she headed to the next aisle, which was devoted to larger artifacts, furnishings, and wall hangings. She weaved through a maze of tall vases and small statues. As she passed a section of mirrors, she made a concerted effort not to gaze at her reflection. Which was difficult, since she sensed abnormal movement in her periphery.

She stepped through the passageway into the next section. The lighting here was dimmer, the air cooler, and the objects were decidedly older. Much like the relic books she had discovered the other day, Cori realized these artifacts were new to the prison. This collection was something Cleos had brought in.

Unable to stifle her curiosity for these displays, she openly examined the stone tablets, tomes, and partial pillars on passing. As expected, they were all covered in languages she couldn't read. However, they were also spattered with blood. At least she assumed it was blood. It was the most logical conclusion given the propensity of past civilizations to use blood magic to direct their religious activities.

What was human history if not a series of bloodlettings at the hands of people who claimed to be pious?

As Cori continued through the section, she metaphorically transported across continents and through time. She caught sight of a totem pole and remembered the legends of skin-walkers told by Native Americans. Was it the werewolves that spawned these stories? Or was it the transmorphs? Maybe both.

Cori moved into the next section, which was dark, except for a few top windows that filtered in just enough light to keep from tripping. The remnants of construction materials filled the space instead of artifacts.

The renovation was either incomplete or completed unsatisfactorily.

Cori slowed to a stop before the broken drywall, not entirely sure what she was looking at. The walls in this section were new and prepped for a layer of blindingly white paint. However, they had been damaged in multiple areas. Chunks of drywall and dust were all over. Cori moved over to another aisle and found the same dismal destruction of perfectly good walls.

Why had they bothered to place these walls only to demo them shortly after? And why hadn't they cleaned up the mess?

Something wasn't right about this, and it wasn't just the lack of maid service.

Cori's mind demanded in no uncertain terms that she leave. Like imaginary claws sparking one's flight up a set of basement stairs, her amygdala was drumming with the beat of her heart.

Leave this place. Her mind demanded so clearly Cori thought she might be hallucinating again.

Unfortunately, she wasn't very good at following orders or doing the right thing, so she ignored that screaming whisper inside her head.

She moved to the next increment on the wall. The space between the studs. She kicked it, denting the drywall. She kicked it again, breaking through it. She pulled the debris clear and peered through the opening. The dim lighting made it hard to see, but there was some kind of insulation inside.

She pulled a few more pieces free to widen the opening. Still baffled by what she saw, she reached inside—palpating the stiff contents. It was not the kind of insulation she was familiar with.

She turned and scanned the room for something that could break the drywall up faster than her bare hands. As she searched, a crack sounded behind her. She turned to discover the wall bending outward, exploding under the pressure of something within.

She backed away, but a hand reached out and grabbed her wrist. She tried to wrench free, but the grip was ironclad. The face of her captor revealed itself as the drywall burst open and birthed the misshapen features of a transmorph.

Finally, understanding the gravity of the situation, Cori screamed. The hand that gripped her was now pulling her in like a fish on a hook. She struggled, but the creature was strong.

Before she could get enough purchase to rebound off the wall studs, the parasite lassoed her waist. Its inhuman hug pressed against her back. The oozing embrace of the creature surrounded her ribs.

Cori continued to scream and struggle, hoping against hope that this was another hallucination, but she knew it wasn't. Her damned curiosity had put her right in the path of the enemy.

No.

The path of her enemies!

Belus's manual was right. This *was* an invasion. And it wasn't just the start of it. They had been here all along. Hidden in the fucking walls like roaches and rats.

As the transmorph seeped into her mouth and blocked her vision, she had only one thought.

Who would be left to save them?

FELICIA JEDLICKA

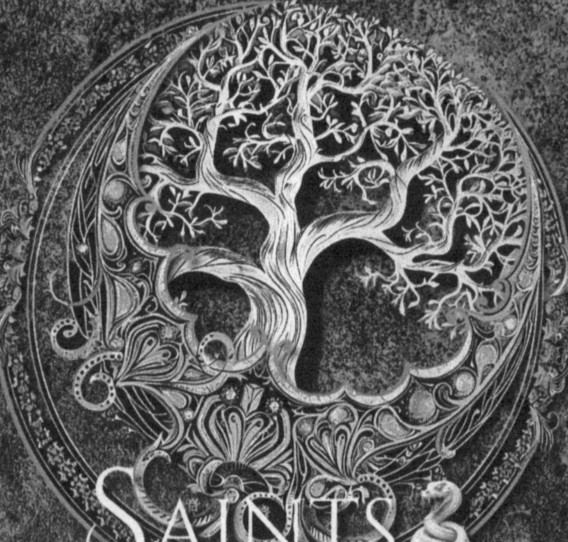

SAINTS & SERPENTS

Book 14

THE WARDEN

SAINTS & SERPENTS

The dangers of the prison are a happy memory compared to the treachery the warden's renegade employees are encountering in the "real world." New enemies and questionable allies are coming out of the shadows. Like sharks, they smell the blood in the water. The upheaval in the once sovereign authority of supernatural law has left a power vacuum, and each of them wants to be the one to fill the vacancy.

Heaton is only beginning to understand the war he's walked into. Nevia's murder spree may be justified, but her actions point to a deeper injustice. As Heaton searches for the root of the transmorph uprising, he encounters a dark horse—a woman of unknown origin and dangerous power. Calling herself his nemesis, she's about to alter the course of his life forever.

Ethan has his own dark horse to contend with—or maybe she's more of a pink one. Although his new foe looks to be sugar and spice, she is anything but nice. Hungry for his mage power, this diminutive little witch will stop at nothing to bind him to her coven.

With no white knight in sight and nooses securely wrapped around her loved ones' necks, Cori continues to play the role of the good little worker bee. Tensions rise as her fellow actors forget their lines and go off script. Act I is nearly over, and the curtain's about to rise on something far more dangerous. Unless Cori can find a way to stop the show, Act II might be her final performance.

Thank you so much for reading. I hope you enjoyed the ride and if you aren't getting off here, I encourage you to sign up for my newsletter so I can return your generosity with new release updates and special offers.

Sign-Up

You can also find me on Facebook or visit my website. Keep reading!

Website

Facebook

Author

FELICIA JEDLICKA writes immersive fantasy and science fiction that blends strange worlds with deeply human characters. Known for crafting character-driven stories with escalating stakes, Felicia weaves complex relationships, moral dilemmas, and epic confrontations into every book.

Whether it's a book about a top-secret prison, witches performing exorcisms, or the unraveling of galactic alliances, Felicia's work centers on the people at the heart of the chaos. Her prose is straightforward and infused with a sharp, elegant wit that pushes her story forward without stealing the stage.

When not writing, she can usually be found playing video games with her husband, cooking delicious meals from her garden, or hanging with her girls at her weekly girls' night.